HE TU...
AS HE ...

Zack clos... ...them in two easy
strides. Soon her naked breasts nestled against the
material of his shirt.

Danielle felt desire engulf her, but some instinct
made her place her hands on his chest and push him
away.

"Zack," she whispered, "we can't continue this."

A tan square-tipped forefinger came to rest against
her lips. "Shh." A crooked grin, partly happy, partly
filled with pain, tugged at the corners of his mouth.
"Danielle." The sound of her name rolled off his lips
like a caress. "I want you. Do you understand?"

"Oh, Zack," she murmured, her eyes glistening with
unshed tears. "If only it was as simple as that.
Whatever happened, wanting each other was never a
problem for us."

ABOUT THE AUTHOR

Eleanor Woods is well-known to romance fiction fans as the author of thirty-four contemporary novels about love. The proud mother of two, Eleanor is an inspired homemaker who is not only a gourmet cook but an expert gardener as well. She and her husband, Don, travel extensively on the dog show circuit and they have collected antiques from all over the United States. *Second Time Lucky*, Eleanor's first Superromance, is set in the author's home state, and it features the graceful plantation homes she loves.

Eleanor Woods
SECOND TIME LUCKY

Harlequin Books

TORONTO • NEW YORK • LONDON
AMSTERDAM • PARIS • SYDNEY • HAMBURG
STOCKHOLM • ATHENS • TOKYO • MILAN

Published May 1988

First printing March 1988

ISBN 0-373-70307-4

Printed in U.S.A.

To Nancy,
the kind of editor writers dream of,
and to Don,
the kind of husband who makes writing romances
so easy.

PROLOGUE

ZACK CARLSLEY FELT the gut-tightening sensation of fear in the pit of his stomach. There was no one overtly threatening him with bodily harm...no guns pointed at his head, and certainly no one attempting to destroy his business or wrest away his home. No, he thought, it was none of those things. The enemy slowly closing in on him was an incredibly beautiful woman. A woman from his past, a woman named Danielle. Rather, he assumed her to be a woman by now. At least chronologically she would be. Emotionally, well, he thought grimly as certain incidents from the past went through his mind, that was another story.

His tall, solitary figure was only barely distinguishable in the moon-dappled shadows beneath the spreading Spanish-moss-draped limbs of one of several huge oak trees dotting the grounds of Oaklaine. That particular tree shaded the bedrooms and bath side of the attached guest house. Some of the lower limbs of the tree actually dipped and curved in spots to such an extent that they touched the ground. In those varied positions, some of the limbs had shot out new tendrils of growth and, over the years, had become root bound. It was against one such limb, which nature had curved and dipped into a perfect U-shape, that the man was leaning.

The quickly moving clouds kept the brilliance of the moon involved in a constant game of hide-and-seek. Had there been enough constant illumination one would have seen the lines of a square-chinned, strong-featured face. Dark hair—the ends having a tendency to curl when the hair was just a shade too long—grew thick and flat against his head, the ends barely brushing the top of his shirt collar. Full brows, as dark as the hair on his head, crowned eyes as black as twin chips of ebony. His nose was straight and prominent. His mouth looked surprisingly sensual in a face so unyielding and harsh. Strong white teeth flashed as he drew back his lips and exhaled roughly. The light tan shirt, stretched smooth and flat across broad shoulders, was pulled taut by the simple exercise of inhaling and exhaling.

When he'd known Danielle, she'd been half-child, half-woman. But either way, she'd had the ability to reduce his thoughts to muddled nothingness, and his body to a fever pitch of passion that rocked his mind.

He ran a hand roughly over his face in an attempt to break the spell that even thinking of her seemed to cast over him. Danielle had been different from any other woman in his life. Different and the most lethal.

It had been her devil-may-care attitude, her seemingly endless search for something entertaining that had amused him.

Chalie, his kid sister, and Danielle had grown up following him. He'd hauled each of them out of the creek, picked them up from wrecks on tricycles, later bicycles, taught them to drive, suffered through their calf-eyed moments of declaring themselves in love with whatever pimply faced youth they'd happened to be smitten with at the time . . . the list went on and on.

Years passed. Zack went away to college, became an officer in the Marines and did his time in Nam. Once back home, in addition to keeping a sharp eye on the management of the family plantation, Rosewynn, he'd lost little time starting up his own business. He'd become involved in leveling old structures by use of carefully placed explosives. His fame had spread, and in precious little time he'd found his expertise in demand all over the world.

While he'd been so incredibly busy, something had been developing right under his nose. Little Danielle Lorman of Oaklaine, the neighboring plantation, had become a young woman, and a very beautiful one at that.

Zack had been floored!

He'd fought the god-awful desire he found himself beset with for a girl young enough to be his ... *No!* He corrected himself sharply as he stared moodily at the darkened house. *She damned well wasn't old enough to be my daughter, but there sure as hell had been times when I'd felt that way.*

After the marriage, the same zest for living Zack had found so amusing during his rushed courtship of Danielle became the bone of contention between them that eventually resulted in their divorce. He'd wanted a woman with whom to share his accomplishments, to listen to his plans for expansion within his company and for the future of Rosewynn. Danielle hadn't been interested in those sorts of things. She refused to settle down, and he refused to indulge her by compromise. And so, the battle of their strong wills was what brought about the ruination of their marriage.

Time after time since their divorce he'd gone back over those months with Danielle. Probing, sifting, raking through the ashes of a burned-out love, searching for any one particular reason that caused their breakup. But each time he thought he'd come up with *the* reason, he found five others that were contradictory. The search became futile, and he'd eventually abandoned it.

When he heard that Danielle had married Theo Kendricks, Zack had been on a job in San Francisco. He remembered locking himself in a hotel room, where he made one hell of an effort to consume the state's entire supply of bourbon. After four or five days of self-imposed punishment, his men braved the brunt of his anger and forced him out of his drunken stupor and back into the real world. A world where, when he closed his eyes at night, he saw Danielle in another man's arms, where he saw that man touch her...caress her...make love to her.

It was simply a matter of learning to cope, he kept reminding himself during those heart-aching days as he accepted Theo Kendricks in Danielle's life, simply a matter of coping.

And cope he did. By working till he was exhausted most nights, he was able to go to sleep the minute his head hit the pillow. He learned to tolerate those nights when sleep didn't come as quickly as he wanted it to. Danielle had left his life in the physical sense, but nothing on heaven or earth was able to remove her from his mind.

Over the years Zack was finally able to admit to himself, certainly to no one else, that jealousy had played an integral part in his being so obstinate. There were thirteen and one-half years difference in his and Danielle's ages. Thirteen years that hung over Zack's head like the sword of Damocles. Always there was the constant fear that she might meet someone younger, someone who enjoyed the same kind of life she did. From Chalie, he'd learned that Theo Kendricks, Danielle's second husband, had indeed only been three or four years older than she was. Nine months ago it was again Chalie who told Zack that Theo Kendricks had died in the crash of the private plane he'd been piloting. Danielle was a young, beautiful widow.

Now she was back. The phrase kept running through Zack's mind. *Danielle is back . . . Danielle is back . . .*

A shiver of apprehension ran through his huge frame. He ducked his head for a moment in profound bewilderment, his wide hands clenching into powerful fists as he sought to deal with the invisible monster of fear, of resentment, attacking him. Pain surged across the lines that crisscrossed the weathered planes of his face. He was thirty-nine years old—forty in five months—and he was practically falling apart at the thought of coming face-to-face with his ex-wife.

What would he say to her? How would he react? Would she be able to tell just by looking at him how devastated he'd been when she divorced him? Hadn't it been said time and time again that a person's eyes were supposed to be mirrors of his soul? Would she be able to look into his eyes and see remnants of the utter desolation that had been his constant companion in that first year, a desolation that slowly evolved into a dull ache that eventually became a permanent part of him?

And now, he wondered curiously, why the hell was he standing there like an idiot, watching her windows? It was a question for which he found no stock answer. There was no comforting retort that would assuage his bruised male ego. In a nutshell, he simply wasn't ready for the sort of upheaval in his life Danielle's presence was sure to bring. He didn't want her living in Natchez. He deeply resented the intrusion, and even though he was quite fond of children in general, he didn't want to have to acknowledge Danielle's daughter—the child Theo Kendricks had fathered.

Time had served, in a limited way, as a catharsis, and he didn't want the cleansing process halted by the same Danielle he'd been married to for almost a year, the same Danielle who had divorced him, the same Danielle who had taken his heart with her when she'd left him.

Zack knew in his soul he'd never forgiven her...never recovered from the loss of their love. He'd patched over the emptiness, he thought ruefully, layered the same patch with a what-the-hell attitude, and gone on his way. The inevitable process of days slowly evolving into months and months into years had eventually softened the anger and lessened the pain. But forgive? No! Never. There was no way he would ever forgive Danielle.

Suddenly his tall, powerful body was alert as the light in the bathroom of the guest house was turned off. A few minutes later the last bit of illumination was doused and the interior of the house was enveloped in darkness, leaving only the high-riding glow of the moon to wash the jewel-like beauty of Oaklaine in its cleansing luster.

She was in bed.

He unconsciously took a step forward, then abruptly halted. "Come on, Carlsley, get hold of yourself," he whispered. "Your ties with Danielle Kendricks are severed. She's a widow. She's a mother. She's also your neighbor and nothing more."

But Zack didn't want to surrender to the truth those words held. For in doing so, he'd release his final hold on his memories. Two vital and distinct sets of memories that, painful though they still were, held a curious fascination for him. On sleepless nights past, those same memories had fed the waning thrust of his anger. They'd brought smiles to his lips, and they'd penetrated the steel barrier surrounding his soul and knocked at the small, dark corner of his heart that still bore Danielle's name. They also stood to remind him that there was no place in his present or future for Danielle.

After continuing to stare at the guest house for several tense, unsettling moments, Zack turned and walked beyond the trees. There he gained a well-defined path that took him to a footbridge over the small creek separating Rosewynn from Oaklaine.

As he walked, everything around him—from the dew-kissed grass to the tall pines mixed in with the oaks laden with moss to the wild roses and occasional magnolia—seemed to be whispering one word: *Danielle . . . Danielle.* Zack briefly closed his eyes, feeling a mysterious kinship with the night and the forces pulling at him. Once the land over which he was walking had been a bloody battlefield between two opposing armies within one nation, and with differing ideologies. Now it quite likely would be turned into a battlefield of emotions, two people who felt they'd been wronged years ago still at war.

Tomorrow or the next day or the next, he most likely would find himself face-to-face with Danielle. With all that had happened to form their past, what effect would her presence lend toward shaping his future?

CHAPTER ONE

DANIELLE LORMAN CARLSLEY Kendricks was giving her temporary living quarters a thorough cleaning. When the clock in the living room struck one-thirty in the afternoon, she stopped scrubbing the old-fashioned bathtub resting on ornately clawed feet. It was, she decided, time for a well-deserved break. One slender hand slipped from the protection of a yellow rubber glove and caught the heavy curtain of her blond hair between thumb and forefinger. She lifted the silken mass off her neck, slowly turning her head from side to side in an effort to catch even a hint of the lazy breeze ambling throughout the guest house attached to the main house by a covered brick walkway.

Oaklaine.

In her mind's eye the name had always conjured up beautiful Southern belles in hooped skirts moving gracefully through the house and smiling cordially to the dashing young men who came to pay court. At one time Danielle knew such scenes had been common.

She remembered snuggling in her father's lap, and listening to him read from old plantation journals kept by his ancestors from the time Oaklaine first came into existence. One particular leather-bound volume related the tragic story of how all the Lorman men, with the exception of the youngest son, Joseph, had lost their lives in the Civil War. Thus the vast acreage that had surrounded the home during the South's zenith had been sold off during the Reconstruction, one parcel at a time, in order for the women and children to live. By the time her father, Tony Lorman, inherited the estate, there was nothing left but the house and grounds consisting of less than ten acres.

Danielle sighed, a faraway look in her blue eyes as she experienced a rush of sympathy for the generations of her people who'd lived here before her, people who had fought so fiercely to survive. Her features unconsciously assumed an expression of pride, while a sense of inner peace spread through her. Though certainly not in as dramatic a fashion, she, too, was continuing the tradition of a Lorman living at Oaklaine, and might possibly be adding her own triumphs and disappointments to another journal that would someday be read by another generation.

She thought of her own special times from childhood that had meant so much to her. The lazy summer afternoons when she and her best friend, Chalie, had escaped the watchful eyes of the housekeeper, Precious Love, and gone swimming in the small creek that flowed between Rosewynn, Chalie's home, and Oaklaine. They'd spent countless hours playing dress-up, giggling all the while. Then there'd been the Christmas holidays, Danielle's favorite, with garlands of evergreens, yards and yards of red velvet ribbon, baskets of pine cones and nuts, the glow of copper and silver, and finally—the tree itself. A blue spruce, a fir or a cedar... and always eight feet tall.

Danielle wanted her daughter to have those kinds of memories. But could she, a single mother, create an environment of love and gentleness for her own daugh-

ter at Oaklaine similar to the one her father had created
for her?

Her head dropped to her shoulder for a moment and
she stared upward. For the most part she'd had a happy
childhood. And though her mother, Claire, had died
when Danielle was only two years old, Danielle's father had been a kind, thoughtful person and he'd been
both parents to her. It was, perhaps, just such a realization that softened Tony's death four years ago due
to a fatal heart attack.

Lord! The years since she'd left Oaklaine had been
crammed with happy moments, and a multitude of
mistakes. She'd gone full circle, she quietly reflected,
watching the slowly revolving motion of the anti-
quated ceiling fan. Her first marriage to Zack Carlsley,
her best friend Chalie's older brother, had ended in a
bitter divorce. Her second marriage, to Theo Kendricks, had left her a widow.

Determined not to let thoughts of Zack or Theo ruin
what was a perfectly nice day, Danielle let her gaze
touch briefly on other details of the spacious bathroom
her father had had redecorated a few months before his
death.

How nice it must have been to have had the mone-
tary wherewithal with which to satisfy one's whims,
Danielle mused.

"Oh, well," she said, shrugging. She'd learned long
ago that wishing for something certainly didn't necessarily make it so. At any rate, what was it her dad used
to say? Something about the larger the bank balance,
the larger a person's problems...

A rough sigh escaped her slightly parted lips. If that
really were the case, then her life should resemble the
unblemished surface of a crystal-clear lake. Especially

in view of what she'd learned when she began the unpleasant task of settling her husband's estate.

Instead of the life-insurance policy she and Theo had discussed, Danielle learned, to her dismay, that he'd taken out a much smaller one. Consequently, some very serious bookkeeping had been the first order of business when she decided to leave Memphis and return to Natchez. Though certainly not a pauper, Danielle knew she'd be on a strict budget for several months.

Her reverie was broken by the sound of the back screen door closing. "Anybody home?" a familiar voice called.

"Follow the aroma of Lysol, Comet and Windex," Danielle yelled back, just as the tall, lissome figure of Chalie Carlsley appeared in the doorway.

"Wow! Truer words were never spoken," Chalie said, grinning, then wrinkled her nose. She walked over and sat down in a white wicker chair, her collar-length dark hair brushing her cheek as she moved her head. "You've got this place smelling like a darned hospital."

Danielle removed the other rubber glove, then sat back on her heels, her arms stretched behind her, her palms splayed against the floor. "Have you forgotten my renters from the fall?"

"Ah, yes." Chalie nodded. "Three little old ladies who wanted to 'walk where history had been made.'"

"Yes, well, most of their walks must have been through mud and sand." Danielle took a deep breath, then exhaled sharply. "Gems of kindness they may have been, but housekeepers they weren't."

"At least they weren't destructive."

"For which I'm eternally grateful."

"I'm free for the rest of the afternoon. Need an extra pair of hands?"

"Are you serious?"

"Never more so." Chalie chuckled, then pulled at the blue-jean cutoffs she was wearing. "I even wore clothes to fit the occasion."

"Then the answer is yes!"

"Somehow I expected you to say that." Chalie was quiet for a moment as she studied her friend fondly. "This is like old times, isn't it?"

Danielle nodded. "You know, I was just thinking about some of the things we used to do. Life was so uncomplicated back then."

"Do you really think it was? Or have we simply forgotten those moments that were so traumatic to us then?"

"Could be. Forgetting certainly isn't the case now, is it? For the last eighteen months or so, my life's been a vicious circle. There's no way I can forget what's happened, yet hardly a day goes by without me wishing I could."

Chalie stared at her friend, a look of sympathy in her warm brown eyes. "Just because you asked Theo for a divorce, Dani, doesn't mean you caused his death."

Danielle thoughtfully regarded Chalie. "I thought I was doing a rather nice job of hiding what's really on my mind. How did you guess?"

"Because I know you so well."

"So you do," Danielle murmured. "If Theo had been a wife beater or had some other really terrible faults, I could have hated him with a clear conscience. As it was, his only faults were being weak and being under the total domination of his mother. In the end, he was pathetic. And you're right, I do feel guilty—horribly so.

Since his death, I think I've finally accepted that he really did marry me in hopes I would be strong enough to deal with Lenore for him.''

"That wasn't totally illogical thinking for someone in Theo's position, love. On the other hand, it's the very fact that you did stand up to Lenore Kendricks that's caused her to dislike you so intensely."

"Care to share any other of your observations regarding the situation?" Danielle asked dryly. In fact, she was glad of the chance to talk out some of her frustrations. And who better to help her find peace of mind than Chalie? They'd spent the first twenty years of their lives sharing secrets and hurts and triumphs. Was life coming around full circle where their relationship was concerned?

"Really, there isn't that much to share," Chalie said thoughtfully. She slid further down in the chair, propped her elbows on the wide wicker arms, then brought her fingers together in a pyramid beneath her chin. "From what I saw during the times I visited you and Theo, it can't have been easy dealing with a mother-in-law as possessive as Lenore. I really don't envy you still having to contend with her because of Trish."

"Isn't it ironic?" Danielle remarked ruefully. "I find myself in the unique position of *allowing* my daughter to spend time with the same people who have threatened to bring a custody suit against me. They must think I'm incredibly naive or very stupid."

"It would be nice to assume they see you as being kind, which I happen to know you are. Unfortunately, we both know Lenore doesn't look at life that way, don't we?"

Danielle slowly nodded. "And that's sad. That's also what makes their threat of a custody suit so ridiculous."

"Surely by now they've given up on that idea. Besides, even a fool would know they couldn't possibly win such a case. Why...they'd be laughed out of court. There are also two other very important factors. You aren't unfit as a mother or person, and Trish certainly hasn't suffered emotionally from any action on your part."

"Precisely." Danielle smiled with suspect sweetness. "However, since the subject of Trish's custody was broached purely as a form of emotional blackmail to keep me from leaving Memphis in the first place, no one really knows what Lenore will do next. And this is America, honey. Every person has the right to his day in court. Be it suing someone else or being sued."

"And of course, win or lose, you will be forced to spend money you shouldn't be spending, creating a huge deficit in your already very limited funds. Right?" Chalie asked curiously.

"You win the gold star." The corners of Danielle's mouth became bracketed with annoyance. "And if I find myself in a financial bind, then my in-laws are counting on me buckling under, just as Theo always did, and rushing to them for help. They know perfectly well that I've put over half of the money from Theo's life insurance in trust for Trish's education. I've kept enough for us to live on till we're settled, and I have a job. What they don't know is that without having car payments or rent to pay, my expenses have been drastically reduced. Plus, there was enough money left in Dad's estate to pay the taxes and insurance on this place for a couple of years, as well as enough to take care of the remodeling I'm having done.''

"If you do need a lawyer, I'd suggest Harvey Graham. I know he represented Zack in your divorce, but he is a super lawyer. I'm sure Dane would handle it for you, but his speciality is corporate law.''

"By the way, how is Dane?" Danielle asked. She liked Dane Ewing. He and Chalie had been in love for ages. "How long do you plan on making that man wait, Chalie?''

"I wish I knew." Chalie replied in a flat emotionless tone, considering how gently she'd spoken to Danielle only moments ago.

"Not being able to have children is not the end of the world, Chalie," Danielle told her. "I think you're underestimating Dane when you refuse to give him the chance to show you how much he cares.''

"He might feel that way at first, but what about later?" Chalie countered. It was a question that had become an absolute nightmare in her life.

"Did it make my marriage to Theo any better?" Danielle asked her. "I gave him a beautiful little girl. He barely knew Trish. Her relationship with him stemmed more from my making him part of her life than from any real effort on his part. Did fathering Trish make Theo a father?''

"Apparently not.''

"You know not," Danielle said softly. "Stop going from doctor to doctor, Chalie, and concentrate on Dane. You can always adopt a baby.''

Chalie got to her feet, her expression troubled. "Let's drop it for the moment. Okay?''

"Sure," Danielle nodded. In truth, she was ready to scream with frustration at her friend's balking.

Couldn't Chalie see that the kind of love she and Dane shared wasn't something to be treated so shabbily? Didn't she know that real love between a man and a woman was something to be cherished? It had to be nurtured...cared for, or it would die, Danielle wanted to shout.

Chalie walked over to the plastic tub beside Danielle that held all sorts of cleaning supplies and an assortment of rags. "May I assume this job is being done according to the edicts of Precious Love?"

"You may." Danielle grinned. "Is there any other way?"

"Certainly not when we were growing up. That dear soul kept as close to us as our shadows, didn't she?"

"Yes," Danielle agreed. "Frankly, Oaklaine doesn't seem the same without her. I'd give anything if Trish could have the privilege of growing up with Precious Love in her life."

"That doesn't seem likely, does it? I mean...you've mentioned several times how busy she seems to be living in Florida with her sister."

"Oh, she is busy...and happy. And you're right. The chances of her ever coming back to Oaklaine are slim to nil. But—" Danielle shrugged "—one can dream."

"Indeed one can." After gathering up what she needed in the way of cleaning materials, Chalie glanced at Danielle. "By the way, you do remember me telling you that I have a fantastic four-year-old program? Let Trish attend sometime. It'll help her learn to get along with other children, and give you a break as well."

"I haven't forgotten. I'm sure she'll love it."

"Are you giving her the front bedroom?"

"Probably."

"When will she be getting here?"

"On Saturday. I could have made it sooner, but frankly, I didn't have the heart. Even though the Kendrickses and I aren't on the best of terms, they do love Trish. And they needed this time with her."

"You're a kinder person than I would be under similar circumstances," Chalie remarked. She started to walk away, then paused. She looked at Danielle. "I'm glad you decided to come back. I've missed you."

Danielle stared at her friend, her lips curving into a tremulous smile. "Thanks. I'm sure, though, there are one or two who won't share your enthusiasm."

"It would be silly for me to pretend ignorance, so I won't. In time, you and Zack will have to work out your own terms of peace. I also won't try to play the great mediator, either."

"Thank you," Danielle said softly. "I must admit that the thought of eventually coming face-to-face with him has given me some bad moments. I haven't seen Zack since the day I stopped by Harvey Graham's office and signed the divorce papers. However, I hope others will feel the same way as you, and not make a big production of my living at Oaklaine again."

"Come, come, Dani," Chalie quipped mischievously. "Where's your sense of fair play? The gossips have to have something to occupy their time. Besides, being talked about is the price one pays when one leads such an *interesting* life." She took a graceful sidestep and dodged the cleaning rag Danielle threw at her. "Don't get ugly, Dani, you need my weak mind and strong back."

Danielle's "Ha!" joined Chalie's ring of laughter, bringing life to a house that had known happiness in the past, and had stood empty for too long. It was close to midnight by the time the cleaning and the flow of conversation came to a halt. A tired but pleased Danielle stood on the veranda of Oaklaine and watched the tail-lights of Chalie's car disappear around a curve in the driveway as she drove the mile or less to Rosewynn. After she'd gone, Danielle could hardly wait to get into the sparkling tub she'd scrubbed so thoroughly earlier in the day.

In minutes, she was undressed and easing into the softly scented water. As she sank into the porcelain bath, faint groans of pleasure rushed past her lips. Danielle felt her tired, aching muscles responding to the soothing warmth enveloping them. She leaned her head back against the high rim of the tub and closed her eyes.

Dear Lord! She was exhausted. Yet along with that exhaustion was an enormous sense of pride in what she'd accomplished within the past six months. In the face of adversity, not the least of which had been the death of her husband, Theo, she'd been steadfast.

Poor Theo. Poor weak, cowardly Theo. He'd burned the candle at both ends, and considered it the only way to go. At first his zest for life had been what appealed to Danielle. She was young, pretty and recovering emotionally from what she labeled at the time, "a bad experience." She'd just divorced Zack.

Theo's belief that the nights were made for partying appeared to be exactly what Danielle needed to help her forget a face with features carved from granite and cold, dark eyes that could stare into the very soul of a person. She remembered the excitement radiating from Theo when he walked into the law office in Memphis, where she was a legal secretary. He was a local attorney, and wanted to discuss a particular case with her boss.

That same excitement held true during their eleven-month courtship and on through the first eighteen months of their marriage. The problems within their relationship only began to surface when Danielle learned she was pregnant.

Theo had tried to share her happiness over the news that they were to be parents, she would give him that. His parents had been ecstatic to learn they were to be grandparents, with Lenore doing her usual fussing over Theo. The older woman's smothering attention to her son annoyed Danielle even then, but she'd held her tongue. She simply marked it up to the mother and son being close.

Danielle reached for the soap and facecloth, causing the water to lap against her creamy throat. Her eyes stared into space as she relived those moments when she'd seen her marriage falling apart, but she'd been helpless to prevent it.

After Trish's birth, Danielle had made a feeble attempt to rejoin the circle of friends that was such an integral part of Theo's life. But after the third or fourth time, when she found herself wondering what on earth she was doing with a group of people whose company she no longer enjoyed, she decided it was time to talk with Theo.

"What do you mean, you think I should stay home more in the evenings?" he had asked, stunned. "Are you implying I should give up my friends?" He'd showered and was dressing to go out. Danielle was giving Trish her six o'clock bottle. The prospect of another evening alone wasn't something she was looking forward to. "Why on earth would I want to stay home in the evenings?"

Danielle felt like throwing a brick at his thick head. "One would hope the company of your wife and daughter would be enjoyable," she snapped.

"Ah, come on, Dani," he'd wheedled. "I function under a very stressful job ten, twelve hours a day, sometimes longer. I need my friends. We play a few cards...we talk. I need their spontaneity. They help me to relax. Can't you understand that?"

"Frankly, no. You're twenty-nine years old now, Theo, and you're *still* going out to play, and you're *still* asking your mother's permission. Only difference is, when you were five and six, you went out in the morning. Now you go out in the evening."

Apparently Theo, angered by the on-target accusation regarding his life-style, confided in his mother. The next day Lenore Kendricks paid her daughter-in-law a visit. She was quick to point out that Theo did not need a shrew for a wife. He was a very *sensitive* man, and should be treated with understanding.

From there the marriage began a definite downward trend. In spite of having encouraged her son to get married and settle down, Lenore simply couldn't tolerate another woman in his life. And though Danielle knew Theo wanted to break away from his mother's domination, she watched helplessly as more and more he buckled under to the pressure Lenore applied. Unconsciously, he'd wanted Danielle to fight his battles for him. She'd wanted him to be man enough to make the break for himself. The happy moments of their marriage became fewer and fewer, till there was nothing left, nothing but the shell, the pretense, and finally death.

With a rough sigh of frustration rushing past her lips, Danielle finished her bath, then got into her pajamas. She hadn't fully understood Theo's problems when they were married. There was no reason to think that, because he was dead, she would suddenly be blessed with total insight into his personality. Just as she would never be sure why or how he really died.

That disturbing thought stayed with her long after she'd turned off the light and waited for sleep to claim her and release her from the guilt that rode her conscience.

CHALIE CLOSED THE FRONT DOOR behind her just as her brother appeared in the doorway of the library at Rosewynn.

"This is a nice surprise," she said, smiling. "I thought you'd planned on staying at your apartment in New Orleans tonight."

"I had," Zack said. "But I decided I'd better get back and make sure that new fencing up on Cutter Road was taken care of."

They walked into the library and over to the desk where Zack had been working when he heard Chalie come in. He glanced down at her less than spick-and-span outfit.

"You and Dane been to a costume party?" he asked as he resumed his seat.

Chalie wrinkled her nose at him as she perched on one corner of the desk and clasped one up-drawn knee with both hands. "Nothing so frivolous, I assure you, brother dear. I've been washing walls and windows and floors and doing all manner of housewifely chores."

"At midnight?" Zack asked, his dark brows comically arched, his expression letting her know he didn't believe a word she was saying.

"I've been helping Dani," Chalie returned in the same pleasant tone of voice. "She and Trish will be using the guest quarters till Mr. Smith finishes the papering and painting in the main house. I had some free time this afternoon, so I offered to help her. It really did seem like old times."

"There's no chance of her changing her mind about living at Oaklaine?" Zack asked, his expression becoming tense, his features pinched.

"She's staying, Zack," Chalie said softly, her heart going out to her brother. She could feel his pain, and it broke her heart. That same bleak light had been in his dark eyes ever since he'd heard that Danielle was coming home to stay. "Maybe I shouldn't say this," she began in an attempt to comfort him, "but Dani is just as apprehensive about coming face-to-face with you as you are about her."

"Don't start trying to play cupid, Chalie," Zack said harshly. "Danielle's probably feeling guilty as hell because she knows she destroyed our marriage. She refused to accept the role of a wife and mother. Her father spoiled her, Precious Love spoiled her and even I spoiled her." He ran a hand around the back of his neck. "Everybody who knew her tended to let her have her own way. She was like sunshine. When she entered a room, she brought a special glow with her."

"Did she really change that much, Zack, after your marriage?"

"You were here," Zack told her, an unpleasant scowl controlling his features. "Even with Rosewynn being big as a barn, you and Birdie couldn't help but hear us argue. Our marriage was merely a brief lull in Danielle's social life."

"Zack," Chalie murmured in a near whisper, "you loved her so much you wanted to lock her away from the world. She couldn't live that way."

Zack stared angrily at Chalie for several long moments. But slowly she saw the anger change to that familiar bleakness in his eyes. She wanted to go to him and comfort him, but she knew he wouldn't welcome such a show. On any other subject in the world, they were extremely close. But where Danielle was concerned, Zack wouldn't allow anyone to intrude.

"I almost hate her." He stared into space for a moment longer. "Actually that's not the truth," he said tightly. "I *do* hate her."

IT WAS MID-MORNING of the next day before Danielle worked her way through the steadily growing pile of odds and ends she'd carted up to the attic to be stored away. Numerous grunts of exertion and an occasional *ouch* or *damn* could be heard in the musty confines as she worked at trying to find adequate space for everything she wanted to keep.

Finally, with things more or less in place, she glanced curiously at the corner where her own special childhood treasures were stored.

"What the heck," she said aloud, shrugging after only a moment's hesitation. "A few minutes won't hurt."

Thusly armed with purely illogical justification, she padded over and tugged the first box from the dust-laden corner. One fantastic find led to another and another, till she'd reacquainted herself with most of the familiar mementoes from her childhood that had been carefully packed away for her by her father and Precious Love.

She looked at her watch and, seeing that she needed to get to the hardware store and several other stops before noon, Danielle began the arduous task of returning the boxes to the same spot they'd occupied in the attic for practically her entire life.

It was while she was attempting to push the first box into the corner that she became aware of something barring its way. She pulled the box out again and looked closely into the gloomy space.

A small book appeared to have fallen from the shelf above and each time she pushed the box forward, the book kept it from slipping into place.

"Now I really will need to shower before I run those errands." Danielle groaned, then crawled into the narrow space. She reached forward, grasped the book and backed out, noticing as she did that she'd found what looked to be an old diary. *This might prove to be interesting reading,* she mused as she tucked it in the waistband of her slacks, then quickly completed her task and left the attic.

When she reached the kitchen and she'd washed her hands at the sink and dried them, Danielle grabbed a paper towel and wiped the dust from the small leatherbound book. *Regina Claire Lorman* was written in very small but elegant script across the front.

Her mother. It was her mother's diary. A curious blending of inquisitiveness about the woman she'd never really known, but who had given birth to her, and the warmth of love for that same woman slowly eased over her. Forgetting that she needed to go to town to buy new hinges for the kitchen cupboards and insecticide for snails and weed killer for the lawn, Danielle began gently leafing through the pages. The edge of each one had been turned a yellowish tan by the passage of time.

From moment to moment her lips curled in gentle amusement while she read the daily accounts of her mother's life before Danielle had even been born. There were references to Birdie Carlsley, Zack and Chalie's mother, who was also Danielle's godmother. The Hamptons were mentioned, and other close friends, the Langs and the Carrolls. The account of Zack slipping off in the family car and wrecking it drew a soft chuckle from Danielle. She'd heard that story a number of times and always found it difficult thinking of Zack—even as a teenager—not being in total control. And then...as the pages were turned, another name began cropping up. A name with which Danielle was unfamiliar.

Elizabeth Cox.

Danielle frowned. Elizabeth Cox? She read on, becoming totally enthralled when she found that her father and Elizabeth were distant cousins. The daily accounts became even more intriguing, with Claire Lorman's neat handwriting revealing that the mysterious Elizabeth was pregnant, and was going away.

After that juicy tidbit of old gossip, Danielle grinned and flipped through the pages...reading one paragraph, scanning another. Only a few remained when her eye caught Elizabeth's name again.

Danielle read, read again, then reread the incredible story unfolding on the last five pages of the diary.

Dear God!

Her face turned dangerously pale, and her heart began beating wildly.

March 3, 1960

Our lovely baby daughter has been with us now for three days and nights. She's two months old and has such a lovely little face, a tiny cherub's face. Already Tony and I love her. We've waited so long for a child of our own. It's difficult to believe anyone can truly understand the depth of our happiness.

The only dark cloud on the horizon is knowing the very precious gift Elizabeth is giving up. When I took little Danielle from her the other day, I couldn't help but cry. Even though I desperately wanted the baby, I felt so sorry for Elizabeth. She will never know the joy of feeling those tiny, precious arms around her neck, or experience the happiness of slipping into the nursery late at night and watching her daughter sleep. That seems so sad to me. I'm sure it must have been a difficult decision for her to make. I also have very mixed emotions about her being so emphatic that Danielle never learn the identity of her natural mother.

But I suppose if the tie is to be broken, then it should be done cleanly, with all parties being protected. However, with us having been away from Natchez for a year in order for Tony to complete the study he's doing for the Department of Agriculture, I seriously doubt anyone will ever question that Danielle isn't our own. Only my very close friend Birdie knows the true story. She has a lovely new baby daughter of her own, Chalie. Birdie was thrilled when I asked her to be little Danielle's godmother, as I am little Chalie's. Thinking of our daughters growing up together brings tears to my eyes.

Tony has insisted on allowing Elizabeth six months in which to make certain of her decision. On one hand I could certainly understand her reasons if she wanted Dani back. On the other, I think it would absolutely kill me to lose her. It's a request of which I can't even ask God's help. How can I say 'Please allow me to keep Dani' if Elizabeth decides she wants her back? In this particular instance, the painfully slow passing of time is the final arbiter . . . that's the only way it can be.

Danielle slowly raised stunned eyes and looked unseeingly around the kitchen. She didn't want to believe what she'd read in Claire Lorman's diary, but no matter how hard she wished it so, there was nothing she could do that would erase the words from the weathered pages.

Hardly aware of moving, she walked over and pulled out a chair from the table and sat down, still clutching the diary in one hand.

She was adopted.

Tony and Claire really hadn't been her—parents, she thought. No! They had been her parents, in every sense of the word, she remembered longingly. The love and security Tony Lorman gave her all those years hadn't vanished just because she'd suddenly found out he wasn't her biological father. Neither had the memory of Claire, the loving woman she'd always considered her mother, the same woman who'd written those beautiful words about her in that diary. After all that had passed, how was it possible to think those two people hadn't loved her?

In her heart Danielle knew the answer to the question, but the shock of finding she was adopted was profound. She was also left with the discomfiting knowledge that—unless she had died—somewhere there was a woman named Elizabeth . . . a woman who was her biological mother.

CHAPTER TWO

DANIELLE STEPPED THROUGH the front door of the main house and closed it behind her. As she turned to walk across the veranda that ran along the front and both sides of the house, she saw a car come to a sudden halt. It stopped in the circular area at the edge of the long brick walk that stretched from the wide cypress steps leading up to the veranda to the parking area. Two couples got out of the car, looking around them with obvious excitement.

Oh, please, Danielle silently implored, *please let me get rid of them quickly.*

Ordinarily, she enjoyed answering the questions asked by tourists who came year-round to see Oaklaine and the numerous other antebellum homes in and around Natchez. But this hadn't been an ordinary day for her, and she certainly wasn't in the mood to play hostess.

"Good morning," a tall, slender man said, smiling. He and Danielle met at the centuries-old wrought-iron gate, which had the same design as the fencing bordering the grounds in front. He glanced at a brochure he was holding, then looked at Danielle. "Oaklaine," he murmured in a gentle voice. "Was it really built in the early eighteen hundreds?" By then the others were standing beside him.

"Oh, yes." Danielle nodded, smiling in spite of her own private upheaval. She turned and looked at the white facade, with the long green shutters flanking each of the floor-to-ceiling windows. "And believe it or not, there have been surprisingly few repairs to the basic structure—"

"It says here—" the man again indicated the brochure "—that the home is still occupied by direct descendants of Samuel Lorman, the man who originally owned Oaklaine, and personally oversaw the actual construction."

"That's correct," Danielle smiled shyly, a little bit embarrassed at the openly curious looks that revelation brought from the group. "My name is Danielle Lorman Kendricks. The first Samuel was my great-grandfather. The number of *greats* are confusing."

"How romantic," one of the women said softly.

"Is the guest house mentioned in the brochure a later addition?" her husband asked.

"Yes, it is." Danielle nodded. "It's a combination of the old kitchen and a huge storage area. Although the particular Lorman responsible for the addition saw to it that most of the lumber used in the remodeling was taken from two small buildings that had been built the same time as the house. The wood is cypress, oak and heart of pine."

"Is it too early in the day for a tour?" one of the women asked.

"I'm so sorry," Danielle replied, and really meant it. They seemed like very nice people. "I'm afraid the house isn't on the tour list. All the homes built before a certain date are listed, of course. I believe you'll find an asterisk by the ones you may go through."

"When will this one be open?" another of the group asked.

"I'm not sure. I've only recently returned to Oaklaine, and right now we're about to begin painting and repapering some of the rooms."

"May we look around the grounds?"

"Please do." She nodded toward a clump of cedars edging the west side of the front lawn. "Beyond those trees, you'll find the original carriage house, several pieces of livery, and odds and ends of old tools."

"We noticed when we turned off the highway that you and Rosewynn share a common road. Are the two families related?" the other man asked.

"Just good friends. The two houses were built at the same time by two bachelor friends, Zachary Carlsley and Samuel Lorman."

"What's Rosewynn like?"

"Oh, it's lovely, and much larger. Unlike Oaklaine, after the Civil War, Rosewynn managed to hold on to most of its land. It's still very much a working plantation."

"What does that mean?" she was asked.

"A working plantation is nothing more than a farm. Of course, different geographic locations determine the kinds of crops that are grown, and now the most sophisticated equipment is used in planting and harvesting. At Rosewynn they tend to concentrate on cotton, soybeans and corn. If cattle are involved, then of course they must think of food sources for the herd. Rosewynn is famous for its prime beef and the bulls raised there."

"You say Oaklaine lost most of its land after the Civil War?"

"Yes, we did. Other than the flowers, about the only thing there's room for here is a small vegetable garden. But then—" she grinned "—since I'm not a farmer, I really can't complain."

The visitors asked a few more questions, then—much to Danielle's delight—took her at her word and meandered off toward the carriage house. In minutes Danielle was in her blue Datsun and on her way to town.

As she drove along, her thoughts were taken over with the diary she'd found. Her mind became inundated with images of what she imagined the elusive Elizabeth to look like. Would she be tall? Would she be pretty? Was she in good health? Why had she decided to give up her baby?

So many questions . . . questions to which she had no answers. In a weird sort of way, Danielle found herself faced with the same sense of despair regarding Elizabeth that she now associated with Theo and the last months of her marriage.

Theo also had found being a parent more than he could cope with. It wasn't that he hadn't loved Trish, Danielle reminded herself, it was a simple case of him having such deep emotional problems involving his relationship with his own parents, he simply wasn't capable of coping with the added responsibility of raising a child of his own.

Yet when Danielle asked for a divorce shortly before Trisha's third birthday, he begged her for another chance, promising he would honestly try to be a better husband and father. His parents had been furious when they heard what she'd done, reminding her that a child needed both parents, not just one. Even then there had been overtones of a custody struggle if the divorce did become a reality. The remaining months of the marriage had served to solidify, in Danielle's mind, that two adults simply living in the same house had nothing to do with a happy marriage.

She'd already made up her mind to leave Theo, and had even told him of her decision, when the plane crash occurred that took his life. And, as Chalie had pointed out yesterday, Danielle still bore the guilt of wondering if her announcement had triggered some unknown reaction that caused Theo to take his own life.

And what about Elizabeth? Had she chosen a life without the socially censured attachment of an illegitimate child some twenty-six years ago? Danielle wondered. Thoughts of the woman who was her natural mother kept picking and pulling at her peace of mind. Theo's actions had been motivated by an unwitting selfishness that had to end in physical or emotional destruction. Danielle believed that knowing Elizabeth would provide a key to a wealth of happiness for both of them.

THE CLERK IN THE COMBINATION feed and hardware store nodded toward the can of snail pellets Danielle was considering. "I'd say that's the best cure for snails on the market, ma'am."

"Are you sure?" Danielle asked somewhat skeptically. "I seem to have inherited more than my share of the pesky things."

"Positive." the young man smiled. "My mother swears by it. But if it happens not to work for you, then by all means return it. We'll be happy to refund your money."

Danielle placed the container on the counter and smiled at him. "Can't argue with that, can I?"

At that moment an older man slipped behind the counter. He carried a ticket book in one hand and went straight to the adding machine. Danielle caught only a glimpse of his face, but she immediately recognized him as Asa Johnson. His daughter Melissa had been a classmate of hers. She seemed also to remember hearing Chalie say something about the Johnsons having bought the hardware store. Was Melissa still living in Natchez? she wondered.

"I'll see to it that the load of fencing gets out to your place by three o'clock, Zack," Asa remarked over his shoulder. "Will that be all right?"

Danielle felt her scalp tightening. *Zack!* A shiver of fear and dread rushed over her. She had it, or was supposed to have had it, on excellent authority that Zack was in Mexico blowing up buildings. How on earth was it possible for Asa Johnson to be talking to him about fencing?

"Three o'clock will be fine, Asa. Just be sure to remind the driver to drop half the load at the barn on Cutter Road. Harry will tell him where he wants the rest delivered."

Harry. Cutter Road.

Danielle felt her chest constricting painfully, squeezing against her heart, yet not having the slightest effect on its suddenly erratic beating. She knew quite well that Harry Akins worked for Zack, and that Cutter Road ran through the north section of Zack's property. And if those two points alone weren't enough to validate her fear, Danielle hadn't had the slightest difficulty distinguishing the deep voice of her ex-husband.

"How's Miss Birdie?" the clerk asked.

Zack heard the question and answered it, but from the moment he'd come out of the back of the store,

where the feed was kept, and into the front section, his
attention had been focused on a slender woman standing with her back to him. Her honey-colored hair was
caught and held at the nape by a narrow green ribbon.
The weight of the hair was resting against a khaki
blouse tucked inside the waistband of white slacks.

A gut-sharp kick of resentment consumed Zack.

He knew every line, every angle, every soft feminine
curve of that female body beneath the tailored blouse
and slacks. He knew everything about the woman, and
he sure as hell didn't look forward to running into her
each time he had business at the hardware store...or
any other place, for that matter.

Suddenly the only sound to be heard in the store was
the click, click of the old-fashioned adding machine as
Asa Johnson studiously tallied Zack's bill.

From the instant she heard his name, Danielle knew
Zack had spotted her. Her body became rigid, the fine
hairs on the back of her neck standing on end. She felt
the boring points of his eyes through the material of her
blouse, leaving her skin hot and uncomfortable.

"Will there be anything else, ma'am?" the clerk
asked Danielle.

For a brief moment, Danielle simply stared at him as
if she hadn't the faintest idea what he was talking about.
That momentary loss of composure brought the faint
pink of embarrassment to her face. "Er...no. No, thank
you. I think that will be all." Darn it! Her voice was
shaky, and her hands were trembling when she took her
wallet from her purse to pay for her purchases. If the
gods were feeling generous, they just might allow her to
escape without a confrontation with Zack.

Asa Johnson swung around, his homely face breaking into a smile as he walked forward, his hand ex-

tended. "Well, I'll be!" he exclaimed. "Thought that voice sounded familiar. Danielle Lorman...I mean Carlsley...I mean..." Suddenly the light in his eyes became one of profound embarrassment as it dawned on him that he was caught smack between Mr. and the former Mrs. Zachary Carlsley!

At some point in her future, Danielle was quite sure she would look back on the incident in the hardware store and find it amusing. At the moment, however, she didn't see anything at all funny about it. "Mr. Johnson." She smiled, even though she felt like running for the safety of her car. She also offered her hand. "It's nice to see you. How is Melissa?"

"Fine, fine. She's a nurse, working in New Orleans," Asa Johnson said hurriedly, then for once in his life, found himself speechless. Zack Carlsley was a valued customer and a friend. He'd known Danielle all her life, and thought well of her. This surely was one fine mess!

"That's nice," Danielle remarked and nodded calmly. She took a deep breath. There was no way in heaven she could avoid it. She had felt Zack's presence as acutely as a ticking time bomb. Unless she wanted to act like a total idiot in front of Asa Johnson and his clerk, she had no choice but to speak to him and get it over with. She turned, her arms clutching the bag containing the items she'd purchased, her features set in an unreadable mask.

"Hello, Zack."

As if following the lead of some unseen master, brown eyes became locked with blue ones in a duel of emotions. Looking...appraising...remembering. Remembering love, remembering pain, renewing old resentments and gathering emotional ammunition for future encounters that were sure to come. Expressions became fixed as each sought to demonstrate indifference to the other. They were unwitting actors, portraying roles thrust upon them years ago.

Arrowed fingers of lazy afternoon sun slanting through the wide display window at the front of the store turned honey-colored hair into a tangle of burnished gold. At least that's how it seemed to Zack.

"Danielle." The sound of her name on his lips felt stiff, awkward. One part of him wanted to ignore her, to finish his business and rush from the store. Another part of him drank in the sight of her like an excessively dry sponge soaking up moisture. But neither of those frames of mind tempered the resentment in his heart. At that precise moment Zack was positive he hated her. "How are you?"

"Fine." She nodded briefly. Still stiff-necked as ever, Danielle thought as she stared at his stern features. She saw the same seriousness that had made him a virtual stranger after they married. Danielle often compared the feeling between them during their courtship and marriage with water rushing from a faucet, then slowly diminishing to no more than a mere trickle. That initial rush of wedded bliss in the first weeks of marriage had suffered the same steady ebbing, until there was nothing left but the hurting words, or so it seemed at the time to the very immature Danielle. "I thought you were out of the country blowing up things."

"Sorry to disappoint you. I have been, for the last three weeks. I got back a couple of days ago."

As he watched the play of emotions on her face, Zack found himself momentarily forgetting that the innocent-looking beauty standing before him had broken his heart, remembering instead what it was like to bury his face in the silken fragrance of her hair. For some reason, its sheen and silkiness had always intrigued him. Hate, desire, resentment . . . they were all swirling, indistinguishable, in his heart.

That's real good, Zack, real good. The woman did every damned thing to you but grind you into the ground. Now you stand here wanting to run your stupid fingers through her hair. Smart, buddy, real smart.

"Chalie's been a big help to me." *It's incredible,* Danielle thought as she continued to stare at Zack, who was casually dressed in faded denims, a plaid shirt and dusty worn boots. Zack looked as though he hadn't changed at all, and that irked her. It also made her wonder why she cared how he looked. Other than the light sprinkling of silver in the raven sideburns, he was simply as devastating as she remembered...and she had tried hard to forget. So hard, in fact, that Theo's facade of lightheartedness had blinded her to the troubled man she'd married on the rebound.

"It's good practice for her when she and Dane get married," Zack remarked without a hint of feeling in his voice. There was an air of mystery about her, he decided as his gaze went over each feature, every line of her body. He silently cursed Theo Kendricks and the intervening years for having been responsible for adding that mysterious dimension of parenthood to her life, and he silently cursed Danielle for having taken that privilege from him. By the very depth of his love for her at the time, the challenge of fathering her child should have been his and his alone.

Six years. Lord, it didn't seem possible, Danielle mused, that it had been that long since they'd seen each other. Six years ago she'd sworn to hate Zack till the day she died. Judging from the stormy look in his eyes, it looked as if he'd made the same vow. "Practice or no, when Chalie marries, I'm sure she'll make an excellent wife." She cast a brief smile Asa Johnson's way. "See you later," she said simply. She looked at her ex-husband. "Zack."

She turned and walked toward the front exit, her shoulders squared, her head held high. It didn't take a genius to figure out that Zack Carlsley had about as much love for her as she did for him.

For the first time, she doubted the wisdom of returning to Oaklaine. Yet at this point in her life, she really didn't have a whole lot of options open to her. Her childhood home offered her the solace and comfort she needed in order to recover from an extremely trying time. It would also provide Trish with an easy, gentle background against which to make a new life. The child wasn't deeply disturbed over her father's death, but at times, Danielle found herself answering questions that made her heart ache for her daughter.

Just as she turned to push her body against the door, a long, plaid-covered arm snaked out and performed that small courtesy for her. A long arm that, by its very closeness, sent a confusing chill through her body.

"Thank you," Danielle murmured without even looking up as she stepped onto the sidewalk. There was no point in looking up, for she would have known who made the helpful gesture even without seeing the color of the shirt.

She shifted the paper bag to her left arm, then rummaged with her right hand in the depths of her purse for her sunglasses. As she put them on, she was thankful for the protection the dark glasses offered her against Zack's probing gaze.

"I must confess, the idea of meeting you in Johnson's hardware store hadn't occurred to me." Even to his own ears, the words sounded harsh, Zack thought. But he seemed as incapable of toning down the manner of his speech as he was of stifling the core of discontent burning deep in his soul.

The remark brought Danielle's head up. "Fortunately there are no laws that say I must restrict my movements in order not to embarrass you by us not appearing in public together," Danielle said coolly. Was he under the misguided impression that he owned the whole darned town? Did he want her to ask his permission to move, to breathe?

"That's not what I meant, and you damn well know it," Zack retorted just as icily, the glow in his eyes warning her of his anger. He felt defenseless against her beauty, defenseless against the feelings he'd once held for her. She'd hurt him, and he wanted to hurt her back. But somehow he wasn't finding that an easy thing to do, and it angered him. "The Danielle I used to know wouldn't have been caught dead in a hardware store."

"The Danielle you used to know had no reason to go to a hardware store," she snapped. "Is that a crime?"

"Why did you really come back here?"

There was nothing gentle or soft about the way he couched that question, and Zack felt a little more in command of the situation.

His query was blunt, bordering on rudeness, and Danielle felt a moment of acute loneliness while she tried to come up with an answer. Why was she allowing Zack's ugly mood to get to her? she wondered.

"I needed a break," she said candidly, holding his direct stare without the slightest difficulty. "I also wanted my daughter to, if possible, grow up at Oaklaine. My childhood was a very happy one, and I'd like Trish to have some of those same memories when she's grown.''

A deep scowl settled over Zack's features. "Considering the hurry you were in to leave these parts when you divorced me, I'm surprised you'd return with the idea of settling down, much less want to raise your child here."

"You know something?" Danielle asked resignedly. "The tone of this conversation is remarkably like others we had when we were married. We didn't agree then, and it isn't likely we'll start doing so at this stage of the game. Excuse me, Zack, I have to get home." She started to step around him, but Zack's hand shot out and grasped her upper arm.

"I understand your in-laws will be bringing your daughter by on their way to New Orleans. When do you expect her?"

It was on the tip of Danielle's tongue to say something really sarcastic, but she didn't. He honestly did like children. When they were married, she'd refused even to talk about getting pregnant. Zack had become angry, and they'd had one of their biggest fights on the subject. Later, after Trish was born, Danielle thought of those moments, moments when she'd foolishly gone against his wishes more to get back at him for his possessiveness than because she disagreed with him. Not having children had seemed like such a necessary stand to take then, a way of letting her staid husband know that even if he kept her away from the world forever, she wasn't about to let him turn her into what *he* thought *she* should be as a wife. Now she realized how foolish they'd both been. But she seriously doubted Zack ever saw any of his own mistakes.

"Tomorrow. Frankly, I'm surprised I've been able to hold out the entire week. Trish and I have never been apart. Zack," she rushed on before she lost her nerve, "with you at Rosewynn and me at Oaklaine, I know it's going to be the talk of the town for a while. I'm sorry it has to be that way, but as I said earlier, I wanted to raise my daughter here. I hope you'll understand."

Zack watched her with that considering gaze that was so disconcerting. "I don't give a damn about gossip, Danielle, and I can remember a time when you didn't care, either." He lifted one wide shoulder in an indifferent shrug. "If you want to live at Oaklaine or Timbuktu, then by all means do so. It doesn't matter to me one way or the other. I suspect we can manage to occasionally meet without trying to insult each other."

This time it was Zack who turned and walked away, his expression brooding. So it wasn't just a brief stay, as he'd hoped when he first heard Chalie and Birdie, his mother, talking. Danielle was back for good—both she and her little girl. He got into his gray Mercedes, his lips compressed into a rigid line of disapproval as he started the engine and drove off.

Demons spawned from memories of the past plagued his thoughts, memories for which he'd found no cure. Memories that had haunted him for six long, miserable years.

Later in the afternoon, Danielle looked out over Rosewynn's east lawn. It was still one of the most beautiful views she'd ever seen. But she wasn't there to refresh her memory of that beauty. After finding the diary, she knew she had to talk with Birdie. As soon as she got home from the hardware store and her disturbing meeting with Zack, she'd called her godmother.

Marian Carlsley, known as Birdie to her friends and family, smiled at her former daughter-in-law as she handed Danielle a paper-thin, delicately patterned cup and saucer.

Birdie was of medium height and slender, a very attractive fifty-nine. Though her dark hair held its share of silver strands, the manner in which Mother Nature had added her special touch of gray was quite beautiful. "Even though most southerners consider coffee *the* drink, I still find a good cup of tea much more invigorating. Don't you, dear?"

"Oh, yes." Danielle nodded. Actually, since she seldom drank either coffee or tea she really didn't have an opinion. But she wasn't about to say so to Birdie. Disagreeing with Birdie usually brought on rather comical lectures that made little or no sense. "Most definitely tea."

"I was so delighted when you called and said you were coming over for a visit. I know you've only been back a week now, but I haven't seen near enough of you in the past few years. You must drop by more often," her godmother told her.

Danielle wondered if Birdie would be nearly as pleased when she learned the real reason for her visit. "With Mr. Smith finally starting to work in the front parlor tomorrow, you'll have to come over and lend us your professional opinion. Even though you aren't as active with your decorating shop as you used to be, you still have a very sharp eye for color and balance."

The compliment pleased Birdie so much she positively beamed with pleasure. "What a nice thing for you to say. I'd be delighted to help any way I can," the older woman promised, smiling. "You're such a sweet child. And even though you're a grown woman, you're still my godchild. Years ago when I agreed to take on that responsibility, I made a commitment for life," she said proudly.

"And one you've kept extremely well," Danielle said warmly. "You've been like a second mother to me, Birdie. Mothering comes as naturally to you as breathing. I hope I can do half as well with Trish as you've done by Chalie and Zack."

"Oh...I don't know about that, dear. Chalie is going through a bad patch right now with Dane, and I can't seem to help her. He's pushing her to set a date for their wedding, and she's being as stubborn as a Missouri mule. I'm hoping you'll be able to talk some sense into her. And these days, Zack storms around the place like an ill-tempered beast. For the life of me, I can't imagine what's gotten into either of them."

"Perhaps it's spring fever," Danielle said gently, not bothering to point out that both of them had a pretty good idea what was bothering Zack.

"But it's the beginning of fall," Birdie corrected her.

"So it is," Danielle murmured. She leaned back in the comfortable chair and raised the cup to her lips. The tea slipped easily down her throat, it's warmth pleasant. Funny, but any time she saw tea or heard any reference made to the beverage, she thought of Birdie. "Did Chalie tell you that she spent hours and hours yesterday helping me?"

"Yes." Birdie nodded. "And I was pleased. You two have always been so close."

"Just as you and my mother were."

"Oh, my, yes," Birdie assured her, rallying to the subject with enthusiasm, just as Danielle knew she would. Birdie launched into the familiar story of why the families were close with such enjoyment that Danielle didn't have the heart to stop her. And even if she had tried, it wouldn't have done any good. Birdie loved to tell her stories. "And surely you haven't forgotten how the first Samuel Lorman had sworn to remain a bachelor till he died. That was only a few weeks before he met Amelia Hampton of Savannah, who was visiting relatives in the area. Well, my dear, story has it that the young and beautiful Amelia knocked the dashing Samuel for a loop. He fairly worshipped her. In quick succession they married and had two children. But why on earth am I repeating all this?" She frowned. "You know your family's history."

Danielle sighed. "I thought I did, Aunt Birdie."

"*Aunt* Birdie?" She smiled softly. "I can always tell when you have something serious on your mind, Dani. I become Aunt Birdie and you begin chewing at your bottom lip. It's the same with Zack and Chalie. In any emergency, I become Mother."

"Sorry." Danielle grinned. "Force of habit, I suppose." She was silent for a moment. "I guess I may as well begin," she finally said as she set her cup and saucer on a round, glass-covered wicker table. She bent down and removed the small, faded diary from her purse beside her chair. "I discovered something that's really knocked me for a loop almost as much as Amelia did Samuel. Bear with me, Aunt Birdie, while I read you a few pages from mother's diary."

As she began to read, it was as if the entire house became silent, listening to the sound of Danielle's voice and the story being revealed. When she finished, she closed the diary, then looked expectantly at Birdie as each of them grappled with her thoughts.

"Oh, dear," Birdie finally murmured, her composure clearly shaken. "I honestly never dreamed I'd find myself in this situation. I'm pitifully unprepared and I haven't the faintest idea where to start. Where on earth did you find that?'' she asked curiously, nodding toward the diary.

"In the attic. All this week I've been carting stuff up there. This morning I decided I'd better make myself find a place for it all. So while pushing boxes back into place I found the diary, wedged into a corner. It had fallen from the shelf above where some of Mother's things are kept.''

"Oh, Dani. What can I say, my dear?''

"Just tell me what happened, Aunt Birdie,'' Danielle said softly but firmly. "I'm over the worst of the shock now, but I'm a long way from being satisfied. If my natural mother is still alive, then I think I would like to find her.''

"Oh, dear,'' Birdie repeated. It was an expression family and friends knew could mean anything from extreme happiness to total despair. "I really do think Zack should be in on this discussion. Yes, indeed,'' she said firmly, "Zack should definitely be here.''

"Zack?'' Danielle asked, puzzled. "Why?''

"Because, my dear, he's your husband. The two of you should share something as traumatic as this. You need a man to help you make the right decision.''

"Aunt Birdie,'' Danielle began gently, "you know quite well Zack and I are no longer married. I really don't care to involve him in my personal business.''

"Nonsense,'' the older woman stated firmly. "As you well know, young lady, I do not recognize divorce. Of course, in the case of you and Mr. Kendricks—'' she spoke of Theo as though he'd been ninety instead of a young man "—I was forced to make an exception. But, mind you, only after little Trish was born. Now that the hand of providence has had its way, I'm hopeful you and Zack can rebuild your lives together.''

Danielle was well aware of the problems Birdie had been having recently. An extreme reaction to an anesthetic several months ago while having surgery at times made it difficult for her to remember things and make important decisions. She'd been forced to give up her business, and that had set her back. But even though she felt sorry for Birdie, Danielle still couldn't pretend everything was fine between her and Zack.

''I think Zack and I can be friends of a sort, Aunt Birdie, but that's as far as it goes. Now, why don't you tell me what you can remember about Elizabeth?''

''Elizabeth was a beauty,'' Birdie began in a slow, thoughtful voice as she focused on a series of events from the past, a part of the past she thought was long dead and buried. ''She was a third cousin to Tony, you know, so don't go thinking there's no Lorman blood in your veins. There is. You have her coloring and her hair, but you're built along more petite lines. She was tall and slender... like a model.'' Birdie paused. ''Seems like I heard someone say she did become a model, but I'm not sure about that. Your father was James Enoch. He was an engineer. I remember him as being a very gracious man, and handsome as well. He and Elizabeth shared a relationship that could be described as war and peace. After one particularly bitter quarrel, he left the area. Some say he went from here to work on a dam in California, but I was never sure. At any rate, a couple of years after you were born, Elizabeth wrote Claire that James was dead.''

''Then he didn't know about me?''

''I'm fairly certain he didn't. Even at eighteen, Elizabeth was a very stubborn young woman. Once she made a decision, she stuck with it. So when she told James Enoch she never wanted to see him again, she meant it. Elizabeth was...she was very determined, Danielle.''

"Do you know if she's still alive?" Danielle asked.

"I honestly don't know, dear," Birdie murmured. "Until you were around eighteen months old, Claire always sent Elizabeth pictures of you. Then Elizabeth wrote and asked Claire not to send any more snapshots. Later we heard that she'd married a man of considerable wealth.''

"Where did she go when she left here?"

"New Orleans.''

"She's lived within a hundred miles of me for most of my life and I was totally unaware of her existence," Danielle mused. "How odd.''

"Not really," Birdie told her. "Now that you know the story, it seems odd. But before this morning, you never had reason to doubt you were Claire and Tony's natural child. Remember this, honey, there's more to being a mother than giving birth. You were everything to your parents. Surely you aren't feeling unwanted.''

"Oh no, no, nothing like that," Danielle assured her. "In spite of Mother dying when I was so young, Dad always made me feel extra special. I tried never to let him know how much I missed having a mother. At first I didn't let him know because I was afraid it would hurt him. Later on, I was afraid he'd rush out and marry the first woman he saw.''

"Poor Tony.'' Birdie smiled sadly. "He was such a gentle person...and he loved Claire so very much. But enough of that," she said and threw up her hands in a fluttery little motion that was typically Birdie. "What are you going to do with this information?''

"What do you suggest?"

"Forget about it," Birdie said firmly.

"I seriously doubt I can do that."

"Why not, for pete's sake?"

"Maybe it's not too late to get to know the woman who gave me life, Aunt Birdie. And from what I read of my mother's diary, she certainly didn't hold any grudges against Elizabeth. Why should I?"

"Oh, dear." Birdie glanced nervously around. "I do wish Zack were here. Surely he could talk some sense into you. You mustn't even think of trying to get to know Elizabeth, Dani."

"But what you aren't considering, Birdie, is that she could be a very lonely woman by now. Except for Trish, I am alone. Why shouldn't we get to know each other? There are so many things we could do together. Little mundane things a mother and daughter do, things like meeting each other for lunch, being together for the holidays, visiting back and forth, shopping together, laughing together. Aunt Birdie, I've never had anyone to share those moments with. I'm certainly not saying I was deprived of love. I wasn't. On the other hand, can you possibly understand what it would mean to be able to say to my friends, 'I think I'll go visit my mother this weekend,' or, 'Sorry, but I won't be joining you. My mother will be visiting me this weekend.' Those are simple words that so many take for granted, but they're quite special to me. Please try to understand."

"I'm sorry," Birdie whispered, her eyes brilliant with tears. "I honestly never knew it meant so much to you. I just naturally assumed you were content with the attention Tony gave you, along with the spurts and starts of affection from Precious Love and me."

Danielle got to her feet and quickly covered the distance between Birdie and herself. She sank to her knees beside the older woman's chair and tightly clasped one veined, fluttery hand between her two steady ones. "Aunt Birdie, you always went out of your way to see that I was included in every possible event." She smiled gently. "You added something extra to the word 'godmother,' and I've never forgotten that. I loved you then, and I love you now. Why, I was with you so much, half the people in Natchez always thought I belonged to you. You and Precious Love never let me feel unwanted or uncared for. But in spite of our relationship, I still missed not having a mother. Perhaps it's a void that can never be filled. Who knows? Though if there's a halfway chance that it can be, then I have to try. One thing I have learned during the last few years, Aunt Birdie, is that we all make mistakes. Well, if this is one of mine, then so be it . . . but at least let me have the privilege of making it."

"Surely you aren't thinking of doing something immediately, are you?"

"No, no," Danielle soothed her, feeling terribly guilty for upsetting the older woman. "And please don't let this worry you. I'll keep you fully apprised of everything that takes place. What with trying to oversee the painting and papering at Oaklaine, I have more than enough to keep me occupied for days to come. I wouldn't dare think of taking off without letting you know. Okay?"

Birdie sighed, her attractive face creased with worry. "Not really, but I don't suppose there's a thing I can do to stop you, is there? Be careful, Danielle. Sometimes the things we think we want most turn out to be the very things we should never have asked for."

Danielle leaned forward and kissed one pink cheek, then stood. "I'll be fine. Please don't worry."

"What's this about worry?" Zack's deep voice asked as he came through the door and out onto the veranda. Sweat covered his forehead, and damp patches could be seen beneath his arms and bordering his waist.

Danielle stared at him over his mother's head, noting that he wore the same form-fitting faded jeans and plaid shirt he'd had on in the hardware store. Her gaze dropped to the sleeves of the shirt, rolled back to reveal tanned, muscular forearms covered with the thick dusky shadow of dark hair.

The words sexy and explosive kept running through her mind. *Don't be stupid or foolish. Remember who he is,* she scolded herself.

"I really think you should talk with Zack about it, Dani," Birdie murmured conspiratorially, drawing even further curious attention from Zack.

He advanced onto the veranda, regarding both women suspiciously. "What's going on?" He looked from Danielle to his mother, then back to Danielle. "Is there some kind of trouble?"

"Nothing at all." Danielle smiled in spite of her momentary irritation with Birdie. "I'm thinking of beginning work on my family tree, and I needed to ask your mother some questions. I have to go." She bent and retrieved her purse, stepped around a still-frowning Zack to kiss Birdie's cheek, then headed toward the steps. "Thanks for answering all my questions, Birdie," she said as she left. "Stop by Oaklaine when you get a chance. By the way, the wallpaper you helped me choose is just perfect."

She'd barely cleared the steps when Zack turned to his mother. "What the hell's going on, Birdie?"

"Oh, dear." His mother fidgeted, her fingers tapping nervously against the arm of the chair. "Oh, dear."

Zack gritted his teeth in frustration. *Oh, dear* be damned! "Calm down, Birdie, and tell me what's going on," he commanded, in a far gentler tone than he was feeling. "Is Danielle having some kind of personal problems that she needs our help with?" Zack had heard Chalie mention the Kendrickses from time to time and he was aware of their dislike for Danielle. Were they causing her trouble now? he wondered.

"Apparently she doesn't think so, Zachary," Birdie replied grimly, "but I certainly do. Sit down," she told her giant of a son. "I really hate to go against Dani's wishes, but after all, you are her husband. All right," she quickly amended as she encountered his icy stare, "her ex-husband. Nevertheless, you should be with her during this time."

Zack became very tense. A curious weakness washed over his entire being, leaving him feeling cold and clammy. "You should be with her during this time." Those few words ricocheted off the walls of his mind like savage bullets numbing his brain with their force. Danielle was ill. His face paled beneath his tan. "What's wrong with her, Mother?"

"Mother?" Birdie frowned. "First Danielle calls me aunt, now you call me mother. And nothing's physically wrong with her, Zachary. However, it could be emotionally painful for her if she continues to insist on finding her real mother."

"Her what?" he asked incredulously, then sat back, shocked, and listened to Birdie's explanation. When she was finished, Zack slowly shook his head.

"That is incredible," he muttered. "No wonder she appeared so uptight this morning when I ran into her at the hardware store." He was silent for a moment, feeling a curious letdown. He'd wanted to be the reason for Danielle's uneasiness, and that realization was about the most ridiculous one he'd had in his life. "This is weird. With Claire dying so young, you'd think Tony would have made sure Danielle knew the story."

"I seriously doubt that it ever occurred to him. To Tony, Danielle was *his* child. I'm sure that over the years he completely put Elizabeth out of his mind."

"A very generous and loving gesture toward Danielle, but about as practical as selling deep freezes to Eskimos. Now he's dead, and Danielle is alone except for a tiny daughter. What a hell of a time to learn that she's adopted. Though not a grim and frightening revelation, I imagine it had to be something of a shock."

"Of course it was a shock," Birdie agreed. "At the moment I'm sure she's feeling hurt, betrayed, disappointed . . . I didn't agree with keeping her in the dark regarding her birth, but it wasn't my decision to make. Now that she does know, however, I'm glad I'm here to help soften the blow. Where are you going?" she asked Zack, who had gotten to his feet rather abruptly and was beginning to walk away.

"Out," he said over his shoulder.

"Out where?" His mother eyed him skeptically.

"I'm going to finish helping Harry with those calves. After that, I'll put your mind at ease by dropping in at Oaklaine. If Danielle needs me, I'll help her, Birdie. But only because she's Chalie's friend, and your goddaughter. No other reason."

CHAPTER THREE

DANIELLE PLOPPED THE paint roller with its long extension handle into the rectangular pan, moved it back and forth a few times to generously coat it with paint, then swung it around to the back wall of the shed and began rolling it up and down. Since heights invariably made her dizzy, she ignored the stepladder and remained on the ground. And even though her method of working caused her to strain unmercifully in order to reach as high as possible, she had decided it was far better to suffer from a stiff neck than a broken one.

Her head was resting on her shoulder and her eyes were squinted to avoid the fine mist of paint that whipped out from the roller each time it turned.

Suddenly a big white blob landed on the tip of her nose.

"Damnation!"

"Having problems?" a deep, smug voice asked.

Startled, Danielle swung around, the softer part of the roller catching her visitor square on the side of his very dark head.

"Danielle!" Zack yelled angrily, throwing up one arm in a protective gesture. "Watch that damned thing," he ordered as he did a quick sidestep in order to dodge the errant roller a second time while Danielle tried equally hard to control it.

"Go to the devil, Zack Carlsley!" she fired right back. One corner of her bottom lip was caught between her teeth while she struggled to control the paint-smeared missile. Suddenly her foot became entangled with an exposed root. She staggered backward, knowing there was no way on earth she could keep from falling. She closed her eyes when she heard the sickening, squishy thud of her behind connecting with the paint pan.

Zack, who had backed well out of range of the extended handle, braced fists on hips and stared at her in disbelief. He saw an angry, absolutely beautiful woman, staring murderously at him through several long tendrils of golden hair while seated in a paint pan. How was it possible for one small woman to do so much damage with such a piddling amount of paint and one roller? "Having your usual good time, I see," he quipped, struggling to keep from laughing at the absolutely furious individual several safe feet in front of him.

"Get off my property before I fill your detestable behind with birdshot," she threatened in a low, savage voice. It was one thing to make mistakes, but something else again to do so in the presence of one's enemy. Come to think of it, though, she realized as she was glaring at him, she had managed one fairly good stroke with the roller right on the side of his head!

"Ah, I'm not sure my heart can withstand the warmth your words invoke," he said mockingly. "Why are you painting? Rather, why are you trying to paint?"

"Why not?" she snapped as she struggled to her feet. "It didn't seem to me to be a very complicated procedure. Especially once I found out how much Mr. Smith charges per hour. Unlike you, I have no building to rush out and dynamite in order to make mucho dough. And just for your information, I *will* get the hang of painting. Even if it kills me," she added with considerably less fire in her voice.

"Well, from the looks of your labor so far," Zack dared to point out, "I'd say there's a fifty-fifty chance of that happening."

"Naturally you'd say that," Danielle replied, her eyes blazing. "Though I would like to remind you that if you hadn't come sneaking around like a damned ghost, I wouldn't have messed up."

God, she was so beautiful, Zack thought as he watched her. Beautiful but unpredictable. "Still blaming other people for your mistakes, hmm?"

"What's that crack supposed to mean?" Danielle demanded angrily.

"Actually, there was no hidden meaning," he smoothly replied, pointedly ignoring her anger. "I seem to remember you always managing to find blame with me for whatever inconvenience happened to you, big or small."

Danielle unscrewed the extension from the roller, then dropped both pieces onto an old drop cloth. She unthinkingly brushed a hand over the front of her shirt, succeeding only in making its paint-smeared condition worse. The rather soggy condition of the seat of her jeans caused her to move as though one leg was stiff, adding to her misery. "Frankly, Zack, I'm not in the least interested in discussing those few months we were married. As far as I'm concerned, they were nothing but one huge mistake."

"For once I agree with you. However, I didn't come over here to—"

His words were cut off by the sound of car doors slamming and a small excited voice calling, "Mommy! Mommy!"

"Oh, my Lord!"

"Your little girl?" Zack asked, his dark brows arched as he pondered her less than enthusiastic outburst. "I thought you were anxious for her to get home."

"I am," Danielle wailed. "It's my in-laws I'm not looking forward to seeing, especially my mother-in-law. She never misses a chance to make me feel inadequate as a mother—even as a human being. For her to catch me looking like I've been whitewashed is the last straw."

Zack strode forward. When he reached Danielle, he bent down and grabbed a corner of the drop cloth and rubbed the majority of the paint from her behind. Once that was done, he made a big, irritating deal out of looking her over, front and rear. "Well," he said as he shrugged, a terrible glint of mischief in his brown eyes. "I must admit that at this precise moment, you don't exactly look like the mother of a four-year-old. And your jeans are definitely ruined. On the other hand," he continued, observing the murderous clouds building in her blue gaze, "it's what's in the heart that counts. Or so they say." He tacked on the last four words in a soft, under-the-breath kind of tone that had Danielle barely able to control the urge to kill.

"Please disappear. All I need to make this a total catastrophe is for Lenore to find my ex-husband hanging around." She quickly wiped her hands on the drop cloth, then began hurrying toward the corner of the guest house.

"Sorry," Zack said pleasantly, "no can do. I want to meet Trish. You and I both know there's nothing between us but a lot of bad memories. If your in-laws have trouble accepting that, then that's their problem.''

"And lest we forget, the great Zack Carlsley doesn't compromise for anyone, does he?'' Danielle murmured just as the Kendrickses and Trish rounded the corner. ''Very well, do as you please. Just try not to antagonize Lenore,'' she warned him. ''Trish!'' she cried out to a little girl with blue eyes and a blond ponytail who was dressed in pink shorts and top. The child was running eagerly ahead of her grandparents.

''Mommy!'' Trish cried happily when she spied her mother. She immediately turned and started toward Danielle. When she was within a few feet, her expression turned to surprise. ''Mommy,'' she finally said, ''you look funny.''

In spite of the paint, Danielle bent and kissed her daughter on the cheek. ''This will have to do for now, but I get lots and lots of hugs later, young lady.'' She grinned, then made as if to smear her hands on the child's face. Trish, taking to the game with childish delight, darted out of reach.

''Be careful, Trish, that you don't fall and hurt yourself,'' Lenore Kendricks told her granddaughter sternly as she joined the threesome.

Danielle looked at the perfectly controlled features of her mother-in-law. Didn't the darn woman ever smile? Not once in the years they'd known each other had Danielle seen Lenore looking really relaxed. She'd spoiled Theo and she would have done the same with Trish if Danielle hadn't stopped her.

''Hello, Lenore.'' Danielle turned to her father-in-law and nodded. ''Simon. I trust you had a nice trip?''

''It was very pleasant.'' Lenore surprised her by responding politely. ''I'm afraid we're a day early, but

Simon got a call from an old friend who, along with his wife, will also be attending the convention. He suggested the four of us get together a couple of days early."

"How nice," Danielle said, smiling. Was it possible that the visit was going to be an enjoyable one? she wondered. Suddenly becoming aware that both Simon and Lenore were openly staring at Zack, Danielle had no recourse but to introduce him.

"Zack Carlsley?" Simon repeated as the two men shook hands. He frowned. "Carlsley...Carlsley. Why, you must be—I mean—" he stammered, embarrassed.

"I'm Danielle's ex-husband. Is that what you're getting at?" Zack asked directly.

Lenore glanced from Zack to Danielle, her expression guarded. "I wasn't aware the two of you had become such close friends again."

Danielle looked helplessly at Zack, beginning to feel a resurgence of the tension brought about by the elder Kendricks and their usual open hostility toward her.

"It would be difficult for us to be enemies, considering we share a common entrance to our respective homes. Not to mention how close the places actually are to each other," Zack said easily.

"You mean you own that lovely place we caught a glimpse of through the trees when we made that first turn?" Simon asked.

"Rosewynn . . . yes." Zack nodded toward the twin chimneys on the south side of his home, which were barely visible through the trees. "I also own several hundred adjoining acres. Danielle's and my ancestors, the men who built the two houses, were friends. Thus the close proximity of the homesteads and the resulting friendship that has existed between the Carlsleys and the Lormans for generations."

Danielle linked her fingers behind her back to keep from reaching out and strangling her darling ex-husband. Proximity and homestead indeed! He sounded precisely like a very pompous ass!

"I should think a divorce would go a long way toward breaking off any friendship, regardless of how many generations there are behind it," Lenore remarked.

Zack started to speak, but an excited outburst from four-year-old Trish caused all the adults to turn around quickly. Instead of finding the child hurt or frightened, they saw her patting the head of a gentle, tail-wagging golden retriever, who was showing its approval of the child by licking her animated face.

"Look, Mommy," Trish called out. "We've got a dog," she said as she pointed toward the retriever.

"I see." Danielle smiled, then walked away from the group to be with her daughter. "This dog's named Dolly. Isn't she pretty? She belongs to that man over there with your grandparents. His name is Zack."

"Really? Can Dolly live with us?" she asked.

"I don't think so, honey, but I'm sure she'll visit us often." Danielle took a small hand in her warm one. "Would you like to help me fix coffee for our guests?"

Trish nodded, then began to skip beside her mother. "Can I have some coffee to drink?" the child pleaded as she began her usual wheedling. She loved coffee, and never lost a chance to get a taste.

"Since I haven't seen you in a whole week—" Danielle grinned "—I suppose I could bend the rules a bit. Let's ask the others in." She walked to where Zack and the Kendrickses were talking. "Do you have time for a cup of coffee?" she asked Lenore Kendricks.

"Coffee sounds nice." Lenore nodded and actually smiled. "If it's possible, Danielle, I'd also like to see the main house. Mr. Carlsley here has been telling us that you've chosen to live in the guest house. Is there some problem?"

Danielle heard the hopeful tone in Lenore's voice, and for a moment felt really sorry for the woman. The Kendrickses desperately wanted her and Trish back in Memphis, but it simply couldn't be, for Danielle wouldn't risk them turning Trish into a miniature of Theo. "No problem—" Danielle shrugged "—other than I thought it more practical. The main house needs some painting and repapering inside. And since the guest house has been redecorated, it made more sense to live there till the work on the main house, which begins tomorrow, is completed. When that's done, Trish and I will move there."

She looked at Zack's impassive features. The familiar expression was a sure sign, if she remembered correctly, that he was in a grand snit. "Can you join us for coffee?" She was hoping he would refuse and leave. Thus far, the events of the day had left her feeling slightly punchy. Having to referee the hostile remarks crisscrossing between Zack and her in-laws was the last straw. It had been hate between the three at first sight.

Zack was surprised to find that he didn't like the idea of leaving Danielle alone with the unpleasant Kendrickses. And though it really was none of his business who she had in her home, he'd never met two more sour-faced individuals in his entire life. They appeared hell-bent on getting a fight going before they left. For a moment he was tempted to accept the invitation to stay for coffee, if for no other reason than to see Lenore Kendrick puff up like an inflated bag.

"As much as I hate to leave such charming company," he said, staring straight into Danielle's eyes as he spoke, "I must." Only she could discern the less than pleased gleam in his own eyes. "I have a man coming to see me about buying one of my bulls."

So Zack said his goodbyes to the Kendrickses, then walked over to where Trish had gone back to the patient Dolly. Danielle watched him go down on his haunches beside her daughter, saw him say something to her and watched both of them laugh. A sharp pang of wistfulness shot through her as she observed the exchange. Well, at least he was still kind to children, that much was in his favor.

She turned to Lenore and Simon. "Shall we go inside?"

Once inside, Danielle hurried to the bathroom where she did a sketchy cleanup job. She quickly changed into another pair of jeans and shirt, but there was still paint in her hair, and various other places she didn't even want to think about.

The next hour went far more pleasantly than Danielle had dared hope. Conversation with her in-laws, while rather stiff at first, warmed up nicely. However, Lenore's sly little remarks regarding Zack and the proximity of their homes began to grate on Danielle. Zack was in the past; why couldn't the darn woman see that?

Not wanting to make a scene in front of Trish, Danielle went to the back door and gave a sharp whistle. In seconds, Dolly appeared, her lovely plumed tail swaying rapidly from side to side.

In nothing flat, Trish was settled in her new room with Dolly for company. Danielle watched for a moment, then sighed. If only her problems with the Kendrickses could be settled as easily.

"More coffee?" she asked pleasantly as she returned to the living room and to her seat on the sofa.

Simon declined with a slight shake of his head.

"No, thank you," Lenore said crisply. "Danielle, Simon and I've considered the situation from every angle and we really think this move you've made is wrong for Trish."

"Lenore, please, let's don't get into that discussion again."

"We have a responsibility to see to it that Theo's child is looked after properly," Lenore told her.

Danielle looked down at her hands, trying to understand, yet deeply resenting the rude implication. "I've told you dozens of times that I'm more than willing to allow Trish to spend time with you," she said evenly. "Isn't that enough?"

"No, it isn't," Simon spoke up. "And even though our lawyers have told us not to expect much, we feel a judge should settle the matter of where Trish lives."

"For Trish not to live with me would mean I was unfit." Danielle tried hard to hold on to her patience. "And since we all know that isn't so, then you have no case. All you'll be doing is forcing all of us to spend money needlessly."

"Precisely." Simon nodded. He rose to his feet, then offered his hand to his wife. "Think about it, Danielle. Our wealth is considerable. All of it will be Trish's one day. We're offering you the chance of not having to worry about finding a job or of having to manage on a budget. Think it over."

"I don't suppose it would do any good for us to ask you to return to Memphis with us, would it?" Lenore made one final plea.

"None whatsoever." Danielle's response was firm. In their feeble attempt to try to regain a part of Theo, they'd try to buy her. There was no possible way she could accept their offer. "Oaklaine is a wonderful place to raise Trish. I know we'll be happy here. Someday I hope you can accept that."

"Does Zack Carlsley have anything to do with that happiness?" Lenore asked stiffly.

"No, he doesn't," Danielle answered, forcing herself to remain clam. "I make no apology for the fact that I was once married to Zack or that he lives so close to me now. I'm not so insensitive that I don't understand your concern for your grandchild, but I hardly see how you can tie Zack in with my decision."

"Whatever we decide to do, I hope you understand we're only looking out for Theo's interest," Lenore pointed out.

Danielle's temper was fast getting out of hand. "Just as I hope you realize that Trish is *my* daughter, and *I* will have the final say in raising her."

Lenore turned to Simon. "I think it's time for us to leave." She looked at Danielle. "May we say goodbye to Trish?"

"Certainly. Her bedroom is right through there," Danielle said, indicating the short hall off the living room.

In keeping with Lenore's mood, the goodbye became a major production. Danielle gritted her teeth and clenched her fists till her fingers were sore in order to keep from screaming. In the end, it was Trish who brought the proceedings to a halt.

"Bye, Grandmother 'Nore. Bye, Gramps. I'm going out to play with Dolly," she said the moment Lenore released her for the second or third hug. She scampered from the bedroom, down the hall, through the kitchen and out the back door to the yard, the retriever right behind her.

Danielle made no comment as she followed the Kendrickses to the front door.

"You'll be hearing from us." Simon nodded with his old-world courtliness. He cupped his wife's elbow and escorted her to the car. Danielle watched till the black Lincoln was out of sight, then slumped wearily against the doorjamb.

She slowly shook her head. It was such a sad, unpleasant situation. Lenore and Simon were old and tired and pathetic. All the attention they'd showered on Theo was now leveled at Trish. If they did decide on it, how on earth was she ever going to be able to afford a custody battle? She had enough experience as a legal secretary to know that lawyers didn't come cheap. Through Simon's company, excellent legal advice was at their fingertips. While she, on the other hand... It didn't bear thinking about.

The sound of laughter and Dolly's excited bark coming from the direction of the shed where she'd been painting jolted Danielle out of her unpleasant reverie.

"The paint," she murmured as she darted out the door and began running toward the sounds. The moment she rounded the corner of the shed, she came to a sudden halt.

"Look, Mommy," Trish yelled, immediately spying her parent. "This is Satan. This is Uncle Zack's horse."

For the second time in less than five minutes, Danielle leaned against the solid support of wood. Zack was

walking patiently beside satiny black Satan, the stallion he'd had for years. He glanced at Danielle for a
moment, his dark eyes noting the harassed look on her
face and the tense, rigid set of her shoulders. He silently damned the Kendrickses, then turned back to
Trish. One large hand was placed behind her tiny bottom, while the other held the reins gathered against the
pommel of the saddle.

Zack's thoughts were reduced to a jumble of confusion. He found himself inevitably drawn to the child
chattering in his ear, the child Theo Kendricks had fathered. But Danielle is her mother, a tiny voice reminded him. Danielle. Zack had watched that same
Danielle grow up. Now, after all that had passed between them, he once again found himself in the unique
position of standing on the sidelines, where she and her
daughter were concerned, watching, waiting, ready to
help if they needed him. Was fate mocking him by
forcing him into the role of Danielle's protector?

There was a soft, blowing whicker from Satan—as if
he recognized Danielle and was saying hello. The sound
brought a brief smile to Danielle's lips. She'd always
been terrified of horses, especially the black stallion.
She had a sinking feeling Satan knew of her fears.

"My," Danielle said, smiling as she watched them
make another large circle on the grassy back lawn, "you
are a big girl. Hold on tight, sweetheart." She walked
over and began picking up the roller and paint pan.
She'd only been temporarily deterred from her project,
she thought with determination, certainly not stopped.
Tomorrow she would paint the shed.

While Danielle was washing out the roller and pan at
the outside faucet beside the shed, she felt something
brush against her leg. She glanced around to find Dolly

sitting beside her, her mouth open and her pink tongue lolling to one side.

"What's the matter?" Danielle chuckled. "Did your friend desert you for a horse?" Dolly's response was a short "Woof!" She wiggled all over. "Don't worry, I'm pretty confident she'll return to you as soon as her feet touch the ground."

"To my knowledge, Dolly hasn't learned to talk yet. However, anything is possible."

Danielle turned off the faucet and wiped her palms against her thighs in an attempt to dry them. She turned, her face a study of conflicting emotions. "Promise me one thing," she said as she met Zack's gaze.

"What's that?"

"If she does start talking, she's mine."

"Well," Zack said, glancing down at his latest conquest. "Considering the fact that Miss Dolly hasn't been seen at Rosewynn since this young lady arrived this afternoon, I've got a pretty good idea she's already yours."

"No, Zack." Danielle shook her head. "I refuse to let you do that. I haven't forgotten that the Rosewynn goldens have quite a reputation in the show ring. Confirmation-wise, Dolly looks to be an excellent specimen of the breed."

"Specimen?" Trish piped up, tired of being ignored but too tired to argue. Her head was resting on Zack's shoulder, and her eyes were beginning to droop, as he cradled her in his arms.

"Nothing for a termite to worry about." Zack chuckled after taking a quick look at the little girl. "I think she's about had it," he said in a gruff voice to Danielle.

"If you'll hand her to me, I'll take her inside and put her down for a quick nap. It's almost five o'clock, and it'll play havoc with her bedtime, but that can't be helped."

Zack turned away rather abruptly. "Never mind, I'll carry her."

Danielle offered no comment. Instead, she fell into step beside him and found her tongue glued to the roof of her mouth. She'd been courted by him, she'd married him, she'd argued with him and she'd divorced him. In the end it was as though they'd each resolved to hate the other. Now...what on earth was she supposed to say to him by way of polite conversation?

In the temporary bedroom she'd fixed for Trish, Danielle turned back the blue-and-white patchwork quilt that served as a coverlet on the single bed. She watched Zack gently remove tiny pink sneakers, then slip the child beneath the covers. Without hesitating, he bent and dropped a soft kiss on Trish's forehead. "Sleep well, princess," he whispered.

Before Danielle could move, he wheeled around and strode from the room. By the time she reached the kitchen, she saw him at the tree where he'd tied Satan's reins to a low limb. Zack swung into the saddle, and in seconds horse and rider were through the narrow gate and racing across the huge green meadow.

There was a curious sadness in Danielle's heart as she stood staring at the beginning of shadowy twilight. The day had been an absolute nightmare. She'd learned she was adopted, she'd had her first encounter in six years with her ex-husband, she'd had a really disturbing visit from her in-laws, who were still threatening to initiate a custody battle. *Truly,* she mused, *my cup runneth over!*

An hour later, a weary, perspiration-soaked Zack walked Satan into the stables at Rosewynn and handed the reins to Jerry Waites. "Thanks, Jerry. Be sure and cool him down slowly. We've been out quite a while."

"Don't worry, Mr. Carlsley, I'll take care of him."

And he would, Zack thought to himself. Satan would be cosseted and fussed over because he'd been ridden long and hard. *But what about me?* He posed the silent question. *What about me?*

It was a moot point, and he knew it. It had been a spontaneous thought and he hadn't fought it. Lately he'd had a lot of thoughts like that. Moments from the past popped into his head without the slightest provocation. Thoughts, for the most part, of Danielle. He quickly made his way to the house, entering through the kitchen.

"You are late, and I do not like to be kept waiting!" That blunt, terse statement was delivered by Rosie Warren, the short, plump woman who had been both housekeeper and cook at Rosewynn for over twenty-five years.

"If you don't get a civil tongue in your head, I'm going to fire you." Zack scowled, never slowing down on his way through the kitchen.

"Ha! There's about as much chance of that happening as me marrying Fred Dantin," Rosie came right back.

"Better watch old Fred, Rosie. He's liable to slip up on your blind side," Zack warned, without giving her a chance to have the last word.

He scaled the stairs quickly and once inside his bedroom, he began shrugging out of his clothes the minute the door was closed. He left a trail all the way to the adjoining bath, where he turned the shower on, adjusting the water till it was like needles of ice piercing his tanned skin. Perfectly honed muscles rippled as he flexed his shoulders beneath the spray in hopes of ridding his body of some of the tension dogging him.

Inside he was bleeding with pain. He was hurting, and he wanted to strike out at someone, anyone. He'd held Danielle's child in his arms. He'd felt her soft gentle breath against his neck. He'd known the whispery touch of her small arm on his shoulder. She'd looked up at him and smiled, and called him Uncle Zack.

Dammit! His large hands balled into hard fists. He closed his eyes, his lips drawn back to reveal strong, clenched teeth. Beautiful, golden-haired little Trish. So beautiful. So like another little girl he'd known at one time in his life. Trish should have been his child. His.

He'd never forgive Danielle for taking that privilege away from him. Never.

But then—how could he not forgive her, when deep in his heart he knew a part of him would always be claimed by her?

Zack shied away from the answer. There was that inevitable truth mixed in with his angry feelings, feelings he wasn't capable of sorting out at the moment. He'd felt betrayed by Danielle when she'd left him, and that feeling remained with him. In his opinion, she'd been childish and totally unreasonable. It would be nice to think she'd changed, that motherhood had matured her, but deep in his heart Zack recognized the thought for what it was, nothing more than that, just a thought.

His features were a pleasant mask during the time it took him to finish showering, dress and join Birdie and Chalie for dinner.

"Were you able to help Danielle arrive at a sensible decision?" Birdie asked as they began eating.

"If you're asking did I talk her out of looking for Elizabeth, then the answer is no," Zack replied shortly.

"But I thought you went over to Oaklaine for that express purpose," Birdie reminded him.

Zack shook his head. "I never implied that I was going to try to get her to forget about what she read in the diary. That was your idea, Birdie. I simply wanted her to know that she had my support, whatever she decided to do. Because she has no family, and because I was married to her at one time, I do feel a certain obligation to Danielle."

"An obligation I'm sure she would tell you to stick in your ear if she knew about it," Chalie said, grinning at her brother. "Surely you can't have forgotten how stubborn Dani is."

"Not at all. Though now that I've met her in-laws, I'm convinced she needs every ounce of stubbornness and anything else she can muster in order to cope with the sour-faced Kendricksses."

"The Kendricksses?" Chalie repeated. "When did you meet them?"

"This afternoon at Oaklaine. They brought Trish home a day early."

"Trish is home?" Chalie smiled. "That's great. Dani has been missing her like crazy."

"It's a damned shame their reunion had to be marred by Lenore Kendricks's sour mug." Zack scowled. "From the minute that woman set foot on the place, she began picking away at Danielle. Course—" he grinned at Chalie "—I must admit your friend wasn't at her best when her mother-in-law arrived."

"What do you mean?" Chalie asked. Zack brought them up-to-date with what had taken place at Oaklaine earlier, and was promptly stricken with a sense of déjà vu. There had been countless times in the past when he'd related some humorous incident Danielle and Chalie had been involved in.

"I can just see her sitting in that paint pan," Birdie said, then chuckled. "And you. No wonder you slipped upstairs without answering me this afternoon. Half your hair was white." She shook her head, her lingering smile fading to an expression of concern. "That dear child has a unique ability for getting into trouble." She pinned her son with a stern look. "That makes it doubly necessary for you to look after her, Zachary. She needs a firm hand to guide her."

"Just try using a firm hand, *Zachary*," Chalie murmured for her brother's ear alone, "and Dani will take more than a paint roller to you."

"What was that, dear?" Birdie asked innocently.

"Er, I was just telling Zachary that parenthood really agrees with Dani," Chalie quickly improvised.

Zack looked at his sister with a grin of amusement, then turned to his mother. "I remember well enough what Elizabeth Cox looked like, but other than her looks, I'm afraid I'm in the dark. What was she really like?"

Birdie slowly shook her head, her expression weary. "The first thought that comes to mind is her coldness. Perhaps calculating would be a better word. At any rate, she could never be described as the type of woman to put another's welfare before her own."

"Do you think she really loved James Enoch?" Chalie asked, intrigued on the one hand by the story, yet concerned for Danielle on the other.

"Frankly, I don't," Birdie said bluntly. "But you'd need to know something about Elizabeth's background to understand her. She was one of Tony's *poor* relatives. Not destitute, but, in her opinion, certainly not in the Oaklaine class. Somehow I always got the impression she was angry at life for not making her wealthy. It was as if she resented anyone who happened to have more than she did. Actually, she did quite well for herself. She had two years of college on an academic scholarship and probably could have managed to finish, but by then her eye was on a modeling career."

"You don't think she told James she was pregnant?" Zack asked.

"No, I don't. James was a charming man and seemed to be an honorable one, as well. I also think he loved Elizabeth. But his work took him all over the world, and Elizabeth wanted her own career. She wasn't about to let a baby or a man or anyone else deter her from her goals in life."

"She really doesn't sound like a pleasant person at all," Chalie said. "I hope, if Danielle is successful in finding her, she will have mellowed some so that their reunion will be a happy one."

"That's a nice thought," Birdie remarked, "but a highly unlikely one. Elizabeth isn't the sort of woman to change."

"What we all have to accept," Zack said, breaking into the conversation, "is that finding Elizabeth is very important to Danielle. Other than Trish, she really is alone. I imagine that can be very frightening if one dwells on it."

Zack pushed back his chair and rose to his formidable height. "Now, if you ladies will excuse me, I have some paperwork to do.'' He walked around to where his mother was seated, then bent down and kissed her cheek. "Don't worry, Birdie, I do plan on talking with Danielle about Elizabeth. Today simply didn't seem to be the right time.''

"Thank you, son. Don't work too late,'' she said to Zack's retreating back.

Three hours later, after going over numerous reports and estimates, Zack pushed back from the desk just as the door to the study opened and Chalie entered the room.

She walked over to the desk. "I've been thinking about Danielle,'' she told Zack.

"And?'' Zack asked, recognizing his sister's serious mood. He leaned back in the large chair, his hands crossed behind his head as he waited.

"Before she left Memphis, the Kendrickses threatened to take her to court to try to get custody of Trish.''

"You're kidding!''

"No. Danielle is worried that they might still try such a thing. They have no grounds, Zack, nothing at all. They know that, but it's a surefire way of getting back at Danielle. Any time a person's morals are questioned, there's always that tiny shadow of doubt left in some people's minds. Of course, she'll have to defend the suit, and that means spending money she shouldn't have to.''

"And of course, Danielle doesn't have money to fight unnecessary lawsuits, does she?''

"No. I suppose Dane *could* defend her, but that's not his field. Actually, I have a much better idea.''

Zack regarded his sister resignedly. "Let's hear it.'' First Birdie, now Chalie. They both seemed hell-bent on getting him involved in Danielle's business. Couldn't they see that he didn't want to be placed in that position any more than could possibly be helped? Couldn't they see that his being around Danielle was like having a knife plunged into an old wound?

"Something isn't right about Theo's death. Danielle is afraid she might be responsible."

"How?" Zack asked, immediately forgetting that only a moment ago he hadn't wanted to be involved any more than was absolutely necessary with Danielle's problems. "Theo died in a plane crash. How on earth can Danielle feel responsible for that?"

"She asked him for a divorce a few days before he crashed, and he was very upset. To her way of thinking, she can't help but wonder if that caused him to become so despondent as to want to kill himself. His law partner and the Kendrickses refused to let her go through his desk after he died, and there were several other puzzling little incidents. His parents more or less took over. At the time, Trish was sick, and Dani had her hands full. After things settled down—in a fashion— she finally realized the only thing she really wanted to do was to get away from Memphis."

"What are you asking me to do, Chalie?"

"Help Dani, Zack. You've met the Kendrickses. Lenore is only interested in revenge. An expensive court fight means nothing to her, but a prolonged legal battle could ruin Dani. She might wind up being forced to leave Oaklaine."

"I don't think either you or Birdie seem to be looking at this situation realistically. I'll offer to put her in touch with Harvey to help with Elizabeth, but she might not want my help with the Kendrickses."

"Unfortunately, she isn't in a position to be choosy. At least let her have a chance to refuse."

"I'll give it some thought," Zack promised. He rose to his feet. "Now that you've accomplished what you came in here to do, why don't you go to bed? I'm going for a walk."

"Sure," Chalie said smugly, not at all fooled by her brother's sudden desire for fresh air. In spite of his apparent indifference, she knew he was concerned.

Moments later, Zack let himself out of the house. Without consciously thinking about it, he found himself on the path that led to Oaklaine. When he reached the footbridge, he paused.

Should he go on? he asked himself.

The question might just as well have never been posed. For after that brief hesitation, he didn't stop till he reached the stand of oaks sheltering the house. He paused in the shadows, his narrowed gaze briefly encompassing the grounds.

He took a step forward, then froze. Someone was moving in the shadows to the right of the shed Danielle had tried to paint.

The safety of Danielle and Trish burst into his consciousness like an explosion. With no concern for himself, and moving with incredible speed for such a large man, Zack skirted the area till he was behind the intruder and slowly working his way toward the house. When he gained the protection of the shed, Zack slipped behind it, hugging the wall as closely as possible.

He heard the sound of twigs snapping as they were pressed against the ground beneath the hard soles of shoes. Zack took a deep breath, his body tensed.

The footsteps grew closer...closer. Suddenly Zack moved, his left arm snaking out with lightning speed and grasping the collar of the culprit. He transferred the weight of his body to the ball of his right foot and swiveled, his free arm raised, his hand balled into a tight, powerful fist.

"Zack! It's me," Danielle croaked, sounding for all the world like a very weak frog.

Like a mime holding his audience enthralled by his movements, Zack slowly lowered his arm, instinctively shifting the weight of his body to both feet. His breathing was rough and deep, the force fanning Danielle's cheek.

"Do you realize I could have broken your jaw, or worse, if I'd hit you?" he asked hoarsely. His hand at her collar opened and the tips of his fingers were suddenly against the soft skin of her nape. Zack felt tiny flames licking each part of him that was touching her.

Danielle was trembling from head to foot. She wasn't certain her knees were going to continue supporting her. She'd been frightened half out of her mind, and the shock of Zack's hand against her body wasn't helping in the least.

"What on earth are you doing here?"

"Birdie and Chalie were worried about you," Zack answered, hesitating only briefly.

The high-riding moon chose that moment to peep through the branches of the trees, casting a silken reflection over the two people standing on the velvet carpet of grass.

"It's been an unusual day," Danielle whispered, her eyes meeting Zack's. Though every other aspect of their married life had been pure hell, she still felt the strong sexual pull pulsing between them.

Please, she quietly prayed. A woman in her position was completely vulnerable to any show of sympathy or friendship. Please let Zack go away... let him leave before one of them said or did something they would be sorry for later. It would only lead to further resentment between them in the morning.

Zack's hand slipped to her shoulder, the gentle pressure bringing her to lean against his hard chest. His arms became a cradle of gentleness as he sheltered her against his heart. She was alone and frightened, and he was offering her a measure of comfort, nothing more. "Elizabeth?" he murmured against the silkiness of her hair, which smelled like wildflowers.

Danielle shivered. Heaven forgive her, but just for a moment, she needed the comfort he was offering, her battered nerves gratefully accepting his kindness. "So Birdie told you."

"About your real mother?"

"Yes," Danielle answered.

"She told me."

"I figured she might."

"Let's take one thing at a time, Danielle. Chalie filled me in on the Kendrickses and how they treated you after your husband died. What happened with them this afternoon after I left?"

"Actually, the visit wasn't too bad till right at the end. They're pathetic, yet what they want from me is very simple. Theo was their whole life, and now they want Trish. Some unpleasant words were exchanged between us. It looks as though the custody fight I thought I'd avoided will come to pass. They don't approve of me leaving Memphis."

"Don't worry about the custody suit. We'll have Harvey Graham start working on that right away. Okay?"

"I'm really not in a position to say no, am I?"

"Of course you are. I'm not pushing you or trying to take over, Danielle. But in this instance there's no really sensible reason to refuse. You're Birdie's godchild, and you were Chalie's best friend long before we married. For the sake of those relationships alone, I'm offering you my support."

"Thank you, Zack," Danielle whispered.

"You've gone through hell today, haven't you?"

"And back again."

A strong hand tucked itself beneath her chin, preventing her from looking away. "Did seeing me for the first time in years add to the overall trauma?" he asked, his own emotion unfathomable.

She couldn't decide if he was hoping his presence had disturbed her or if he was mocking her with the question. But either way, of their own volition her lips were slightly parted, and Zack knew he was going to kiss her. She was in his blood, and the only way to exorcise her ghost was to fight fire with fire.

"Oh, yes," Danielle admitted, becoming enchanted by the moonlight and the beautiful spell something or someone had cast over them. She was using him, but it wasn't intentional. They were alone; they were functioning as one; this was Zack. She prayed he would understand. And if he didn't kiss her, she was going to die.

Their lips touched—they drew back, then quickly touched again. Tentative, questing. Renewing remembered sensations and tastes. Breaths became mingled while tongues touched and dueled sparingly before engaging in a primitive ritual slightly less arousing than the ultimate sexual gratification between man and woman.

Danielle felt herself floating. She deliberately closed her mind to the source behind that flight into unreality. She needed this moment to help save her sanity, to help fight the fear inching its way throughout her body at the remote thought of losing her child.

Tomorrow.

Tomorrow would be soon enough for her to face the cruelty of that most annoying of all responses . . . common sense in the light of day.

CHAPTER FOUR

EVEN THOUGH BEING IN Zack's arms and having him kiss her merely intensified the fantastic high she was on, Danielle's senses were extended to such a state of awareness she knew the exact second he began to withdraw from her.

The action was hardly more than a hairbreadth of movement, but she felt it just the same. She slowly removed her hands from his shoulders, her gaze searching out his in the play of dappled moonlight. Years may have passed, she thought, but Zack was still a master at keeping his feelings to himself. His face was as unrevealing as stone.

"I'm sorry," Danielle said in a shaky voice barely above a whisper. "I really didn't mean to fall apart like that."

"It happens to the best of us," Zack assured her, keeping his tone deliberately casual as he widened the space between them by moving back a step.

Like Danielle, it was taking him a moment or two to get himself under control, but his pride prevented him from revealing that chink in his armor.

This was Danielle, a tiny voice of caution whispered, and Danielle could destroy him if he wasn't careful. She was still as potent as she'd been the first time they'd made love, and his body responded just as eagerly—as if the intervening years had never happened.

Somehow that fact surprised Zack. Or did it annoy him? He couldn't decide which. Had he wanted her to be so unappealing sexually as to leave him cold and unmoved? Would that have made him feel better?

"Well, at least Trish is back home. That helps a bunch," Danielle said lightly, breaking the tense silence. What was she supposed to say to him now?

She hesitated another moment, then slowly began walking toward the house, rather surprised, but pleased in an odd sort of way when Zack fell into step beside her.

She was nervous, Danielle admitted to herself. Ever since she'd returned to Oaklaine she'd had some anxious moments when she would think of running into Zack. Yet today, the circumstances had been so wild, she'd had very little time to think about her first meeting in years with her tall, rather intimidating ex-husband.

"It's a beautiful night, isn't it?" She knew the remark sounded corny, but it was the best she could do.

"Beautiful," Zack answered. She was trying with all her might to get a grip on reality, and somewhere in the very depths of his soul he found himself pulling for her. Even though he didn't trust her Zack appreciated a fighter. And at that precise moment, with all that was happening in her life, Danielle had to feel as if she was fighting for her very survival.

As she walked beside him, Danielle wanted desperately to pretend that she was unaffected by Zack's kiss, but that just wasn't the case. At the moment, even the simple act of breathing was difficult. And yet, she reasoned, this brief interlude with Zack was merely the continuation of an extremely intense day. In fact, the last fourteen hours had all the characteristics of a nightmare.

"Your daughter is a beautiful little girl," Zack told her. "I envy you."

Again Danielle's tongue felt glued to the roof of her mouth. How on earth was she to respond to a remark such as that? The memory of how she'd refused to have a baby when they were married had often flitted through her mind, leaving her with a vague sense of guilt. Zack had to be thinking of the same thing. In fact, the possibility of him and Trish being thrown together hadn't really occurred to her during the time she had taken making up her mind to return to Natchez. All her thoughts regarding Zack had revolved around how *she* would react. "I'll remind you of that remark the first time you see her being a typical brat," Danielle said, laughing.

They'd reached the back door. She looked up at him, reluctant to be alone, yet certainly not wanting him to think she was reading more into his kiss than a gesture of comfort. "Would you like to come in for a drink?"

"Need to talk?"

Danielle offered a halfhearted smile bordering on embarrassment. "Frankly...yes. I honestly think I'll explode if I don't."

Zack reached behind her and opened the door. "In that case, I'll listen," he said, his tone of voice far more pleasant than when she'd run into him at Asa Johnson's hardware store.

Several minutes later Danielle carried a steaming mug of coffee over to the round oak table where Zack was sitting. "Sorry, but instant is all I have at the moment. At least it's decaf. I have a grocery list a mile long to take care of tomorrow."

"This is fine." Zack nodded, waving away her apology with the casual sweep of one wide hand. "When I'm on a job, instant coffee is usually one of the staples. Even an old dyed-in-the-wool coffee drinker like me can't always tolerate what some people call coffee...especially in some foreign countries."

"I suppose not," Danielle dutifully murmured, then lapsed into silence. Perhaps it wasn't such a good idea asking him in, she thought. Other than the healthy dose of sexual awareness between them, they seemed to still be at an impasse when it came to understanding each other. What happened to the Zack she used to know? The patient Zack who'd been as much a part of her childhood as her father and Precious Love? The long-suffering Zack she'd developed a crush on when she'd been fifteen? How had they progressed to such a stage as to be as cool to each other as total strangers?

Zack, sensing her discomfort, found himself in the unique position of wanting to ease the tension he saw eating away at her. Yet the voice of common sense was warning him to steer clear of any personal involvement with Danielle. It was imperative that he remember exactly why he was sitting in her kitchen, having coffee at close to midnight. "Birdie gave me a rather sketchy account of what you found in your mother's diary," he began. "Want to fill me in?"

In answer to his question, words began to fall from Danielle's lips like water rushing over a broken dam. Her astonishment at learning she was adopted had left her with countless questions and fears, all of which she shared with her ex-husband. Nothing Zack or anybody else said or did could take away what she learned, but perhaps talking it out would help her come to grips with the situation a little better. Finally, after realizing that

Zack hadn't said a word for ages, Danielle's mouth curved into an embarrassed smile. "I'm sorry," she told him. "But you did ask."

"So I did," Zack said, grinning back at her. He leaned forward, his strong forearms resting on the edge of the table, his wide hands cradling the mug of coffee. "Are you sure you want to find Elizabeth, Danielle? You know, there are some women who don't want to be reunited with the children they gave up for adoption. Have you considered that Elizabeth might be one of those women?"

"Of course I have," she said tersely. "I have no intention of arriving at her door unannounced, if that's what you're thinking. If I can find her, and after we've spoken by phone, then I should think one or two discreet visits would certainly be needed for us to get to know each other before anyone else learns our story."

"What if there's another family?" Zack asked, his questions continuing to undermine her confidence. Listening to Danielle talk, he became determined to see that she let Harvey Graham handle the search for Elizabeth. The lawyer might even be able to talk her out of the idea. However, from the gleam in her eyes, Zack really didn't look for that to happen.

Danielle was silent for a moment. In her haste to become acquainted with the woman who had given birth to her, she'd forgotten about whether she'd now have brothers or sisters. There was a very strong possibility that if Elizabeth had married she would have had children. The cold hand of fear gripped Danielle's heart. If there was another family, would there still be room for her in Elizabeth's life? How would those children react to having an *outsider* stepping in and wanting to claim part of their mother's time and love?

Zack saw pain in her eyes. He reached across and caught her slim hand in his warm grasp. "Believe me, Danielle, I'm not trying to make this any harder. But it's something you must consider from every possible angle. By taking that first step toward locating Elizabeth, you could leave yourself and her open to a great deal of heartache."

Tears shone brilliantly in her eyes. "Don't you think I've looked at the situation from all possible angles?" she whispered, her voice not at all steady. "I've also thought about what I'd say if she were to tell me she doesn't want to see me." Danielle shook her head. "Believe me, Zack, since learning this morning that my mother might exist, Elizabeth has taken over a great deal of my thoughts."

"Well, now that Trish is with you, you'll have less time to dwell on the subject. Birdie told me you weren't going to begin your search immediately."

"I did tell her that," Danielle said, sighing. "More to pacify her than anything else. She seemed adamantly opposed to the idea."

"She's only thinking of you and Trish," Zack reminded her.

"Sometimes a person's concern can be a heavy burden," Danielle said softly. "I'll feel terribly guilty going against her wishes, but I have to."

"At least you've learned that caring and loving bring with them certain responsibility." Zack's words surprised her. Danielle stared at him, feeling the razor-sharp edge of rebuke in his voice.

"Does anyone ever do everything they're supposed to, Zack?" she asked him without thinking, refusing to look away from the piercing glint of his dark eyes. The conversation was taking on the undertones of another time and place, which was totally unrelated to Elizabeth.

"There are mistakes and then there are mistakes, Danielle," Zack remarked, watching her over the rim of his coffee cup. "Some can be forgiven, others can't."

"Never?"

Zack felt air forcing itself in and out of his lungs at regular intervals. He felt the tiny hairs on his neck begin to tingle, felt the cold rush of desolation stealing over his entire being as he looked deeply into the blue depths of her eyes. He saw a beautiful woman and, at the moment, a very vulnerable one. But he remembered another woman, the one who had walked away from their marriage without a backward glance. Would he ever be able to forgive her?

"Never, Zack?" Danielle persisted, stubbornly refusing to let the issue drop. She was well aware of the mistakes she'd made when she was married to him, but she wasn't about to let him take his insulting shots at her each time the mood struck him.

"I think we have enough to contend with at the moment without dredging up old differences, don't you? If you have no objection, then I'll set up an appointment for you with Harvey."

"At this point, I doubt I'd refuse the devil's help," Danielle answered. He'd really sidestepped the issue...this time, she thought. But there'd be other chances. She got to her feet. "Thanks for listening."

"Anytime," Zack said gruffly. "Good night." He stared at her for another second, then turned and walked out the door.

For several long and painful moments Danielle stood at the door and stared into space, her mind blank save for images of the different emotions she'd seen in

Zack's eyes. Because of his refusal to discuss certain aspects of the past, she couldn't help but believe he was still hurting...still bleeding from the pain she'd caused him years before.

For some reason Danielle wanted to be able to look back on her marriage to Zack without cringing when she thought of how poorly she'd filled her role as his wife.

But why—at this point in life—did that matter so much? What had her suddenly wanting Zack's forgiveness? She shook her head as the perplexing question kept going around and around in her head.

THE NEXT MORNING found Chalie sitting in an office, anxiously awaiting the appearance of a doctor. The minute she heard the door open behind her, she turned her head and looked at him, an expression of hope clearly visible in her eyes.

"Good morning, Chalie," George Webber said, smiling. He patted her shoulder, then walked around his patient and seated himself behind the desk. "I know you're anxious, so I'll give you the results of the test you had made. Chalie, I really wish I had better news for you, but I don't."

"There's no change?" Chalie asked in a low, husky voice.

"None at all," the doctor told her. "It's all here," he said, touching her file. "Nothing's changed since the last time I put you through that same battery of tests."

"I suppose I was hoping for a miracle."

"Don't feel bad about trying one last time," he said, trying to comfort her. "The clinic Dr. Tabor's associated with in Houston is tops in its field, just as he is. But when he tells you that you can't have children, then my advice to you is to believe him.''

"I really don't have much choice, do I?" she asked bitterly.

George Webber sighed as he heard the despair in Chalie's voice. In the past two years he'd watched her go from one specialist to another as she tried to find even a glimmer of hope that somewhere there might be something that could be done to enable her to have children. Unfortunately, her particular problem was a genetic one, and at the present time there was no surgical procedure to correct the condition. He wished there was. Chalie and Dane were friends of his, and George was very much afraid this latest news might hurt their relationship.

After a few more minutes of polite conversation, of which Chalie later remembered very little, she left the doctor's office. As she stepped out onto the street, a warm hand caught hers in a firm grip. Chalie looked up in surprise, straight into Dane's eyes.

"Bad news?" he asked, falling into step beside her.

"No worse than last time," she replied in a flat voice.

"It doesn't matter, honey."

"You say that now, Dane. But I think you've forgotten something. I happen to know how much you love children."

"Of course I do, so do most adults. But that doesn't mean my life will be without meaning if we don't have children of our own. Adoption is a fantastic way to become parents."

Chalie heard the words, but they held no comfort for her. In her heart she knew Dane was simply masking his own disappointment, trying to make her feel better. She wondered how long it was going to be before she released him from an engagement that was fast becoming a prison for him.

WHILE CHALIE WAS SEEING George Webber, Danielle began the morning by taking an eager Trish on an inspection of the many treasures Oaklaine held in store for little girls. They began with the two apple trees and the pear tree, and thoroughly explored the delights of the old carriage house. Next came the gazebo, which Trish excitedly proclaimed her playhouse. From there they went to the lower part of the back property, where several plump Rhode Island Red hens happily clucked and scratched among the oak leaves. Trish was barely able to contain her excitement. The lone rooster, however, eyed their approach to his domain with a certain malevolent gleam in his eye. Danielle, having already been involved in one skirmish with the mean-tempered bird, picked up a stick in readiness.

"Why do you have that stick in your hand, Mommy?" Trish asked.

"So I can whack the daylights out of that ornery old rooster if he tries to bother us."

"What's a rooster?"

"The boy chicken. That one over there." Danielle pointed to the golden-colored king of the chicken yard. "Those others are hens. They are the ones that lay the eggs."

"Eggs?" Trish's eyes rounded in astonishment. "Eggs like I eat at breakfast?"

"The very same kind of eggs." Danielle nodded. "You can come down with me in the afternoons to gather the eggs. Would you like that?"

"Yes." Trish nodded excitedly.

"There's one rule though that you must remember. You're never to come into the chicken yard alone. Understand?"

Trish nodded, although she looked confused. "Why? Does a monster live in there?"

"Only the rooster," her mother told her. "The other reason is I don't want the chickens to get out of their pen."

They watched the chickens a while longer, with Trish plying her mother with countless questions that only a four-year-old could come up with. As they turned and began walking back to the house, Danielle glanced toward Rosewynn land beyond the fence and saw several mares and a young colt grazing, their mahogany coats glistening like satin in the early morning sun.

She stopped, then squatted beside Trish. "Look over there, honey. There are some more of Uncle Zack's horses."

The minute Trish spied the animals, she raced to the fence. She pressed her face against the wire, the build-up of excitement—for once in her life—leaving her speechless.

Danielle chuckled as she watched the tiny wheels of her daughter's mind spinning away as she came up with at least ten questions at once. "That's a baby horse, Mommy. See it?"

"Yes." Danielle nodded. "Isn't it pretty? It's called a colt."

"A coat?" Trish frowned.

"Colt. A colt."

"Oh. Why?"

"I don't know."

"Oh. Is Satan a colt?"

"No, honey. Satan is a grown horse. He's a stallion."

"I don't see him."

"That's because Uncle Zack keeps him in a special pasture."

"I like Uncle Zack. Will he come to our house again?"

"I'm sure he will," Danielle said pleasantly. *He enjoys making snide remarks to your mother,* she wanted to say, but of course didn't.

"Is he going to be my new daddy?"

The question took Danielle completely by surprise. Was Trish really missing not having a father that much?

"Why don't we just let Uncle Zack be your special friend? Is that all right?"

"Okay."

Danielle drew a deep sigh of relief at the easy answer. Frankly, providing Trish with a father was something she hadn't given a great deal of thought to. In fact, she hadn't given it any thought.

Out of the corner of her eye, Danielle saw movement. She turned and looked to her right, then smiled. Dolly, the golden retriever, was making her way toward them, her pink tongue hanging out one side of her mouth, its color a striking contrast to the brushed gold of her lovely thick coat. "You have company, Trish."

The little girl looked up at her mother. "I do? Who?"

"Why don't you turn around and see for yourself?"

Trish did as she was told, then laughed happily when she saw the dog. "Dolly! It's Dolly, Mom."

Mom. Danielle mulled the word over. A few minutes ago she'd been Mommy. Now she was Mom. Changes . . . moving on . . . discarding the old, taking on the new.

Their lives were undergoing dramatic changes. Were those changes for the best? But as she stood back and watched the child and dog greet each other, a sense of well-being washed over Danielle. Returning to Natchez had been a difficult decision to make. She'd always heard it said that a person could never go back, that things were never as one remembered them. Well that saying had been proven a fallacy in her particular instance, because there couldn't possibly be a little girl any happier this morning than Trish.

Yes, she told herself, she'd made the right decision. She'd chosen to raise her child at Oaklaine, and she knew in her soul she'd chosen well.

After setting out some playtime boundaries for Trish and Dolly, Danielle headed back to the house, to check on Mr. Smith, the paperhanger-cum-painter, who had arrived at the crack of dawn. Seeing that he was indeed as good at his craft as she'd been told, she went to the kitchen. After getting out the new shelf paper, scissors and ruler, she turned on the radio to her favorite classical station, and started relining the cupboards. It would be easy to keep an eye on Trish through the window while taking care of a job that definitely wasn't her favorite.

During the course of the morning, an old friend, Cathleen Summers, dropped by to welcome Danielle home. When she left, she took Trish with her to play with her four-year-old, Susie. The next interruption came when Danielle looked up from measuring a piece of paper for a drawer and saw Chalie and Birdie coming through from the dining room.

"What a nice surprise," she said, smiling as she went over to kiss Birdie on the cheek. "I didn't hear the car, so you must have walked over."

"How could you hear anything with all the racket he's making?" Birdie remarked, nodding toward the bedrooms where Mr. Smith was working.

"Racket?" Danielle looked surprised. "I hadn't noticed."

"Mother has taken exception to the way your paper is being hung. She's having one of her difficult days," Chalie said quietly to Danielle. "She's been lecturing Mr. Smith for the past ten minutes. I'm surprised you didn't hear *her*."

Danielle quickly shut off the radio, then turned back to her guests. "I suppose that's why. But I was in there a while ago, Birdie, and I liked what he was doing. Several people recommended him to me." She didn't bother adding that Birdie had been one of those people.

"Humph!" Birdie Carlsley exclaimed. "That's why you're a legal secretary and I'm a decorator. I don't care one iota for the way he's turning your corners. Later on, the edges will curl."

"Mr. Smith seemed to know what he was talking about, Birdie," Chalie said in an attempt to soothe her annoyed parent. "Besides, Danielle has already contracted with him to do the job."

"That's true," Danielle said, jumping to the man's defense. Heavens! If she didn't keep Birdie away from Mr. Smith, she might be sleeping in the guest house forever. "Chalie, while I fix coff—er, tea, why don't you and Birdie wait for me on the patio? It's really nice under the oaks now that summer is almost gone."

"But I really do think I should get someone else to do your work for you, dear," Birdie said to Danielle, refusing to budge from her stand regarding Walter Smith's credibility as a paperhanger.

"How sweet of you to offer, Birdie, but for the moment I think I'll stick with Mr. Smith. Besides, as Chalie pointed out, I do have a contract with the man."

A few minutes later a relieved Danielle—relieved from the standpoint that she was glad to get Birdie a little farther away from Mr. Smith—joined Chalie and Birdie on the flagstone patio with a tea tray. She placed the tray in front of Birdie, then pulled out a chair and joined them at the glass-topped table.

"Where is little Trish?" Birdie asked, pouring the tea as regally as a queen. "Do you realize I haven't seen that child since she was a baby? Of course I've looked at the pictures Chalie has of her, but that isn't the same."

"I'm so sorry, Birdie. Cathleen Summers dropped by for a visit. She invited Trish over to play with her little girl. But don't worry. I'm sure you'll see plenty of Trish."

"I'm glad she's making friends," Chalie spoke up. "That'll make the move much easier for her, and help her adapt to her new home."

"Yes, it will." Birdie surprised Danielle and Chalie by agreeing. "I realize most people readily point out how easily children can adapt to unpleasant upheavals in their little lives, but I still think they're more vulnerable than we know."

"Your theory has become more popular in the last few years, Birdie," Danielle told her. "Children are very much affected by early events in their lives."

"Well, I don't think we need worry about Trish," Chalie said to Danielle. "You've done a marvelous job of helping her accept Theo's death and the move. I've had several children in my kindergarten from either broken homes or who have lost one or the other parent through death. Usually there is a period of several months where the child is withdrawn, sometimes even sullen and something of a problem child. It takes tremendous patience on everyone's part to get him back on track.''

"I'd like to take credit for Trish's behavior, but I'm afraid it's more a case of her and Theo not being very close.''

"What a shame," Birdie murmured. "But...in time you'll remarry and Trish will have a father.''

"Danielle might prefer raising her child as a single parent, Birdie," Chalie pointed out. "A woman doesn't have to be married to feel fulfilled, you know.''

"Nonsense," Birdie scoffed. "A loving marriage can bring untold happiness to a man and a woman.''

Danielle, who was listening to the exchange, knew she and Trish were the *supposed* subjects being discussed. However, she had a feeling that Chalie and Dane's problems were the subtext in Birdie's pronouncement.

During a lull in the conversation, Danielle had a chance to really study Chalie, and wondered at the tense set of her features. Was Birdie's condition getting on her friend's nerves? Danielle wondered.

"Playing hooky from kindergarten today?" Danielle asked. She knew Chalie loved the children, yet from her friend's expression, it was obvious something was wrong.

"Doctor's appointment," Chalie replied.

"Aren't you feeling well?"

"I'm okay," was the clipped reply, which elicited a measured look from Chalie's mother.

Birdie changed the subject by asking Danielle if she'd come to any decision regarding Elizabeth, which took the conversation in a different direction. When Danielle refused to back down from the idea of looking up her birth mother, Birdie decided it was time to go back to Rosewynn.

"But I thought Zack was to pick you up here," Chalie reminded her.

"He was, dear." Her mother nodded. "But I suddenly remembered something I must do." She gave Danielle a quick hug. "Take care of yourself, and bring little Trish over to see me."

"I will, Birdie." Danielle smiled, shrugging her shoulders as she and Chalie exchanged glances.

"I'll see you later," Chalie murmured. "I really would like to talk."

After they were gone, Danielle took the tray into the kitchen, then went in search of Mr. Smith.

"I'm sorry if Aunt Birdie said something she shouldn't," she told the older gentleman. "She really isn't in good health these days."

"Don't worry, Danielle. I've known Birdie Carlsley since first grade, and I know how her mind kind of comes and goes. She's had a tough time of it with all those operations. If it will make you feel any better, I reworked three rooms at Rosewynn last spring."

"What about Birdie?" a deep male voice asked from the doorway of the master bedroom.

Danielle swung around, her heart racing crazily when she saw Zack's huge frame filling the aperture. Startled blue eyes dovetailed with dark brown ones in a visual caress as potent as wide tanned hands whispering over bare skin. He was dressed in a dark suit, white shirt and conservatively striped tie.

Yesterday he'd reminded her of one of the old Marlboro commercials that used to run on television, the total cowboy, his features weather-beaten and rugged.

Today he was the epitome of the successful executive, his bearing tough and commanding.

Zack's gaze devoured the sight of her. He felt like a drowning man grasping at a rope. Danielle was wearing slacks again, and though she was facing him, he knew the shape of her body like he knew the back of his hand. He knew the way the material would be smooth across her hips, lightly conforming to the fullness of her buttocks and the slender length of her thighs. His gaze traveled upward to where pebble-hard nipples thrust impudently beneath the cotton material of her blouse.

He knew a moment of triumph. Their years apart hadn't changed the quickening shaft of her desire, and he knew she wanted him. A peculiar rush of relief—or was it happiness?—enveloped him.

Zack wondered if being in his arms last night had meant more to her than just a body offering comfort.

And that, he acknowledged, made him ten kinds of a fool for even thinking about whether or not his kiss had caused her unrest. But...crazy or not, he still wanted her. And Zack knew beyond a shadow of a doubt that he wouldn't be satisfied till he'd made love to her and exorcised her ghost from his heart and his mind forever.

CHAPTER FIVE

AWARE THAT THEY WERE supplying Walter Smith with entertainment to rival the most popular soap on television, Danielle managed to get Zack into the kitchen by telling him that she needed his advice.

"What's the problem?" he asked, the minute they were alone. He glanced around the kitchen, noticing the fresh coat of paint that had been added to the trim, and the sparkling condition of the floors and appliances.

He was surprised. The Danielle he used to know hadn't been interested in anything even slightly domestic, much less capable of almost single-handedly turning Oaklaine into a very attractive home for herself and her daughter. At least she was taking motherhood seriously.

"Mr. Smith was finding it very entertaining watching us," she told him. "Coffee?"

"Please." Zack nodded, a frown furrowing his brow. "What were we doing to entertain Walter Smith?" He leaned against the counter edge, his eyes following her as she moved around the kitchen. She seemed perfectly at ease in her surroundings. The old Danielle avoided the kitchen like a plague.

"Think, Zack," Danielle said. "We were married once, remember?"

The corners of Zack's mouth flexed resignedly. "I see your point. But you really shouldn't let it bother you."

"That's a little difficult, don't you think? I mean, yesterday poor Asa Johnson became so flustered when he found us both in his store, he almost choked. A few minutes ago Mr. Smith would have stood in one spot all day and watched us if we hadn't left the room. I hate to think what will happen if we ever show up at the same party."

She handed Zack the dark blue mug of steaming coffee, then quickly turned back to the chore of measuring papering for the drawer, hoping he hadn't seen how badly her hand was shaking.

"Oh, I'm sure we'll come up with something that will please everyone—one way or the other," he remarked.

Danielle inhaled deeply. What did Zack have that hadn't been there when they were married? she asked herself. When she was growing up he'd been Chalie's older brother—at one point her idol, sometimes a friend of the two girls and at other times their tormentor. During their brief courtship and only slightly longer marriage, he'd turned from a man who'd gently wooed her to a hard-nosed husband demanding more of her than she was able to give.

Outwardly there didn't seem to be any changes in him, other than a few lines in his face that weren't there before. But for some unfathomable reason, she was acting like a total fool over the man. A man *she* chose to divorce several years ago. It didn't make any sense at all. Yet, if Danielle planned on living at Oaklaine—and she did—then she had to come to grips with Zack. There was no way in the world they could live in such close proximity and not bump into each other rather frequently. Was she going to turn into a nervous wreck each time she saw him?

"Have you come to any kind of a decision regarding Elizabeth?" Zack asked. Privately, he was hoping she would say she'd decided to drop the entire matter, but he knew that wasn't likely to happen. He'd seen the excitement in Danielle's eyes last night when she'd told him she had to at least try to find Elizabeth Cox. He knew that particular look too well. Even though he was still leery of becoming involved with Danielle emotionally, he didn't want to see her become caught up in something that could hurt her.

"None, other than I *know* I'll find her. I'm holding off for a few days because I promised Birdie I would. However, that doesn't mean I can't begin making phone calls."

"What kind of phone calls?" Zack asked.

"Well..." Danielle began, then hesitated, meeting and holding his dark penetrating gaze uncertainly. Today was entirely different from last night. Being in Zack's arms and having him kiss her left her with reservations about being so open with him. In her opinion, he saw way too much. At any rate, she suddenly found herself shy of sharing her ideas with Zack, yet something inside her was hoping for his approval. "It seems to me that the most logical place to begin would be to ask for a copy of any marriage license issued to Elizabeth Cox. Your mother told me yesterday that she'd heard years ago that Elizabeth married a man from New Orleans."

Before Danielle could guess his intentions, Zack reached over and removed the ruler and scissors from her hands. He placed both articles on the counter, then caught her hand and pulled her around to face him. "I like to be able to look into a person's face when I'm talking to them...particularly a beautiful woman's face.

Competing with scissors and rulers and shelf paper is damaging as hell to a man's ego.''

A peculiar lightness fluttered through Danielle's heart as she stared into his eyes. He'd called her a beautiful woman. Zack had actually paid her a compliment. It had been years since she'd heard anything complimentary from him. ''I've heard the male ego is fragile as a woman's vanity,'' she remarked, grinning.

Zack shrugged his broad shoulders, his expression light and pleasant. For some crazy reason, he felt like jumping up and clicking his heels together. ''You probably heard correctly. Come with me.'' He turned, pulling her with him. ''I remember a perfectly comfortable patio out back. In fact, I distinctly remember getting in Tony's way and worrying the hell out of him when he was building it. Let's make ourselves comfortable while we discuss your plans for finding the missing Elizabeth. Okay?''

There was a lump of excitement as big as her fist lodged in Danielle's throat. ''I'm open for ideas,'' she finally managed to say, knowing that basking in Zack's favor could end at any second, but determined to enjoy it to the hilt while it lasted. ''I think I should warn you, though,'' she told him as they sat down at the glass-topped table, ''I *am* going to find her. So if you're bent on discouraging me, then there's no need for us to have this discussion.''

There was a glimmer of admiration in Zack's gaze as he thoughtfully regarded her. The way she gestured by lifting one shoulder to enforce an idea or point...the play of the early fall shadows against her hair...the way she caught the tip of her tongue between her lips when she was undecided about something...all those little mannerisms brought back memories to Zack that

merely reinforced his desire for her. There were brief
moments when he was able to put the bitterness of the
past out of his mind, and in those rare moments it was
Danielle he wanted in his arms, Danielle he wanted to
make love to. "Your way or not at all, hmm?"

"Not really," she said firmly as she sat back in her
chair. "Obviously I'm open to your suggestions or I
wouldn't be discussing the matter with you. But I want
it understood that the bottom line is . . . I'm not stopping till I find Elizabeth. So I'd appreciate advice on
how best to go about my search, not reasons I should
drop the whole idea." For some reason she felt she was
on trial where Zack was concerned. That fact made her
even more nervous and edgy, but she wasn't backing
down from her resolve to find her biological mother.

"The Danielle I used to know would have raced off
to find Elizabeth without listening to anyone's ideas or
suggestions."

"The Danielle you used to know did a lot of things
that didn't make sense, Zack," she murmured softly. "I
like to think time and circumstances have gone a long
way toward helping me grow up."

"Sometimes people have to prove themselves before
others will trust them again."

"Trust should be freely given, the same as love. There
shouldn't be conditions attached."

"I disagree," Zack said. "If one person's trust in
another has been damaged, then I'd say it's almost impossible for those two ever to share the same feelings
again. There'd always be that trace of uneasiness, no
matter what else they had."

Danielle leaned forward. The weight of her upper
body rested on her forearms, which were pressed flat
against the thick glass of the table, her palms cupping

her elbows. "You're really talking about me, aren't you, Zack?" she asked curiously. "I'm the someone you feel you can never trust again, aren't I?"

"Something like that," he replied in a low, gruff voice. He wasn't sure how the conversation had veered from searching for Elizabeth to their relationship. But it had, and perhaps it was for the best. Perhaps both of them needed to get the resentments, the frustrations, the heartache of the past, spread out before them.

Danielle dropped her gaze, finding the accusing gleam in his eyes an annoying reminder of things she'd rather forget. "Your performance in that marriage wasn't lily-white, you know."

"But I didn't quit," he quickly countered. "Not once did I ever suggest to you that we separate or get a divorce, Danielle. That was entirely your decision."

"One you'll obviously hold against me till I'm dead and buried," she snapped. "What a fantastic world it would be, Zack, if we were all as perfect as you think you are." Now she was being petty, she thought grimly as she dropped back in her chair, but she couldn't help herself. She resented like hell the fact that Zack had the nerve to sit there and tell her how much he still distrusted her, while her own actions toward him reminded her of a rejected puppy dog begging for just a moment of his master's attention. Just because she'd disappointed him didn't mean she planned on doing penance for the rest of her life.

"Why does it matter to you what I think of you?" he asked, knowing full well the question was a loaded one . . . and one she wasn't likely to answer.

"It doesn't," she replied lightly, just as the back door flew open and Trish erupted onto the scene.

"Uncle Zack!" she cried out happily, going straight into his opened arms. "Mommy said you would come see us again."

Zack made a comical face at his most devoted fan as he lifted her onto his lap. "Oh, she did, did she?"

"Yes," the little girl said and nodded. Trish began laughing—as he intended she do—at his comical expression. "You look silly. I saw your mama horse and the baby colt," she announced proudly, gleefully skipping from one subject to the other.

"I'm glad," Zack said, smiling.

Danielle watched and listened to the conversation, one part of her glad that Trish now had a definite male figure in her life. There was another part of her, though, that was more than a little put out that Zack had so completely captured her daughter's heart. It was the first time Trish had ever returned from an outing that she hadn't hugged Danielle first. Was Trish missing having a father more than Danielle realized?

Across her daughter's blond head, she met Zack's enigmatic gaze.

"Jealous?" he asked, mouthing the words.

"Certainly not," Danielle said aloud, her cheeks showing the slightest bit of pink at how perfectly he'd read her mind.

From the moment she arrived until Zack left, Trish sat in his lap. As he was about to walk away, he reached out and cupped his warm palm to Danielle's cheek. "Life can really throw us some curves, can't it, kid?"

Danielle felt the remark summed up their predicament perfectly. "Indeed."

"By the way, why don't you let Harvey take on the job of finding Elizabeth? Birdie and I feel a little support wouldn't hurt."

"If I go to Harvey with this tale about a mother I hope I have, the man will probably think you're lucky to have gotten rid of a female with so many problems."

"Harvey is very discreet," Zack remarked. "Any personal opinions he has, he'll keep to himself. Let me know what he says. Okay?"

"Sure." Danielle shrugged. She wasn't so sure she wanted Zack nosing around in all her business. Besides, being around him and knowing how he felt about her was nerve-racking.

Zack continued to hold his hand to her face, his eyes narrowed thoughtfully as he stared at her. "You're a petite, beautiful woman, Danielle Kendricks, yet you're fast becoming a huge puzzle to me. How do I solve that puzzle, hmm?"

Before she could reply, he turned and walked away. Danielle raised her hand and placed the tips of her fingers to the spot still warm from his touch. How could she help him solve his problem, when her own life was just as mystery-laden?

The afternoon passed quickly for Danielle. She finished lining the kitchen cupboards with new shelf paper and did the grocery shopping she'd been putting off. At the supermarket she ran into a number of old friends. Once they got over the surprise of seeing her and welcomed her back, she could tell they were fairly bursting to ask if she and Zack were getting back together. One even went so far as to ask if she'd seen Zack. By the time she got back to Oaklaine, Danielle felt like she'd been put through an emotional wringer.

Dinner, to Trish's delight, was hot dogs grilled on the barbecue outside. While they were concentrating on getting the fire started, Zack rode his black stallion, Satan, onto Rosewynn property. The horse came to a halt beneath the low limbs of an oak tree, and its rider's attention became wholly focused on the woman and little girl.

From time to time the man caught the sound of Trish's childlike chatter. He saw Danielle bend down and hug her daughter. Their blond heads were together as they talked and laughed, and the man knew a moment of such intense pain it took his breath away. There was one vital part missing from the picture... him. He should be with them, one arm holding Trish and the other one keeping Danielle close against his side.

Zack jerked the reins, causing the powerful stallion to instantly respond to his touch. They raced across the sloping wall of the meadow, not stopping until man and beast were both drenched with perspiration.

When dinner was finished, and after Trish had her bath, Danielle patiently waited while the child said her prayers.

"And please, God," Trish said as she began to wind down her lengthy monologue after blessing everything she could think of from frogs to her mother, "if you won't let my daddy come back and live with us, will you think about sending me a new daddy? Susie Summers told me today that she plays with her daddy. Do you think Uncle Zack can be my daddy? He plays with me. Amen."

Danielle didn't know whether to laugh or cry as she went through the nightly ritual of tucking Trish and several of her stuffed animals into bed. The prayer was so simple and honest, yet it reflected a sense of confusion in Trish's mind. Danielle bent and kissed one tiny, rosy cheek.

"Good night, sweetheart."

"Good night, Mommy. Is Aunt Chalie still coming over? Can I get up and see her when she comes?"

"Aunt Chalie isn't here yet," Danielle explained. "You'll be asleep long before she arrives." She turned and walked toward the door, stopping when Trish called her.

"Will the mailman bring my new daddy tomorrow?"

Danielle did smile then—she had to! In spite of Trish being in earnest, it was really comical thinking of a man being delivered with a label around his neck reading that he was Trish's new daddy.

"Er . . . I really don't think so, honey."

"But I asked God. Didn't he hear me?"

"Of course he heard you, sweetheart," Danielle was quick to reassure her. "But sometimes we have to give God a little time on some requests. It will take a while for him to find the right daddy for you," she answered, hoping desperately that her explanation would satisfy Trish.

"Oh."

"Good night, honey."

"Night."

A short time later, Danielle recounted the story to Chalie. "I'm afraid she's not going to be very happy with God if he doesn't come through for her."

"That's precious." Chalie laughed. "Were you aware that she felt so strongly about wanting a daddy?"

"No," Danielle said firmly. "Frankly, I think it's a combination of her hearing Susie talk and having Zack take up so much time with her. Perhaps in her own little way, she's just begun to realize what daddies really do."

"I wonder what Zack would say if he knew Trish was asking for God to let him be her father?"

"Who knows? But I hope you won't tell him. What with Trish in his lap the minute he appears and his helping me with Elizabeth and Lenore, I'm sure he wishes I'd disappear."

"Oh, I seriously doubt that," Chalie said. "You know Zack doesn't do anything he doesn't want to."

"I hope not," Danielle said, shrugging. "What happened with the doctor this morning?"

"Nothing. I'd had some tests done in Houston, and George got the results back."

"Any change?"

"None. The prognosis is still just as depressing as ever."

Danielle took a sip of wine, then leaned back, letting the stemmed glass lightly rest against the arm of the sofa. She looked at Chalie, who was curled up in a comfortable old chair opposite her. It was beginning to get late, but neither of them was sleepy.

"I'm afraid I still don't understand you," Danielle said softly. "Why are you depressed with the doctor's report? You've known for a couple of years that you can't have children. Did you have reason to think something had changed?"

"Not really." Chalie shook her head. "But...I didn't want to believe that. The doctor in Houston was my last hope. He was also very frank. He merely confirmed what George has already told me. He told me to accept the fact that I would never have a baby, and to get on with my life."

"I agree." Danielle nodded. "But what does Dane have to say on the subject?"

"Oh, he's being gallant and steadfast," Chalie murmured bitterly.

"You sound like some disenchanted heroine in a Victorian novel. If you're saying Dane refuses to stop loving you simply because you can't bear children, then fine. In my opinion it shows he has great taste. You're a really neat gal, Chalie Carlsley."

Chalie closed her eyes, her lips compressed into a tight, trembling line as she fought back the tears, tears that were finding their way down her cheeks while she grieved in painful silence.

"Chalie, I—"

"Please." Chalie held up one hand. "Please, just give me a minute."

Danielle did as she asked, her heart bleeding for her friend. They'd been raised like sisters. They'd shared everything from comic books to boyfriends. Yet, for the first time, Danielle found herself unable to help. There was nothing she could do or say that would take away the pain Chalie was experiencing, and that saddened her.

"I know you can't understand, but I feel so inadequate," Chalie finally said. "You have no idea how Dane loves children. Do you know he coaches a little-league baseball team?"

"That's a very nice thing for him to do." Danielle nodded. "But even if he didn't work with the children, he would still be a nice person. Just as you, even though you can't have children, are still a nice person. Chalie, honey, the ability to reproduce isn't a yardstick by which we're judged to be nice or not-so-nice people. What we are, the kind of people we are, comes from within us. Dane knows the kind of person you are, honey. He knows the goodness that's in your heart."

"You make it all sound so simple," Chalie said accusingly. She raised the glass to her lips and kept it there till it was empty. "I hear the words and I want to believe them, but I'm afraid..."

Danielle watched as Chalie reached for the wine bottle and refilled her glass. "Don't look so disapproving," Chalie remarked. She sat back, her sad gaze encountering Danielle's concerned one. "I'm not an alcoholic. But this evening...here with you...it's the first time in months I've really let myself go. I can't talk to Birdie. She'd help if she could, but, bless her heart, so much of the time she isn't in any condition to help anyone. Zack, in typical big-brother fashion, wants to protect me. If I were to break down and cry in front of him, he'd want to knock somebody's head off. And since there are no heads available or anyone to blame, he'd only become frustrated. That, my friend, leaves you."

"I gladly accept the position," Danielle said softly. "But you must try to help yourself, Chalie."

"How so?"

"By accepting the truth, and getting on with your life. You work with children every day at your kindergarten. You have to know how many little ones there are today without anyone to care for them. For heaven's sake, start thinking about adopting."

"But that wouldn't be the same as my own," Chalie protested. "It wouldn't have my blood flowing in its veins. There would be nothing of Dane or me in its biological makeup."

"Big deal. I was adopted. What does that make me?" Danielle demanded.

For a moment Chalie looked stunned. Gradually her expression turned to one of acute embarrassment. "How could I have been so rude?"

Danielle smiled and shook her head. "Not rude, Chalie, simply unthinking. You've always accepted me as Uncle Tony's daughter. Haven't you?"

"Of course."

"Why?"

"Because you ... I mean ..." She looked confused. "You *were* Uncle Tony's daughter. It would have been impossible for him to love you any more."

Danielle raised both hands in a gesture of surrender. "I rest my case."

"It's a very good case, Dani, but you've forgotten Dane. Even if I could convince myself to adopt, what right would I have to ask him to forgo the pleasure of fathering children? What right?"

"The right of loving him, Chalie ... the right of loving him. And remember, you aren't holding a gun to his head. If he was as concerned over the matter as you seem to be, don't you think he'd have made some move to sever the relationship with you by now?"

"I don't know," Chalie muttered, her fingers nervously toying with the stem of her wineglass. "At the moment he loves me, and he's trying so hard to do the right thing by me. I think it would kill me if that love turned to hate. And that's what I'm afraid will happen if we do marry."

"Oh, Lord!" Danielle rolled her eyes. "Please give me strength not to choke her! What is it with you? Huh? Have you taken some private vow of self-condemnation?"

In spite of her unhappiness, Chalie had to laugh. "You make me sound like a nut case."

"That's because you're *acting* like a nut case. Stop feeling sorry for yourself and start thinking of little babies or small children without homes."

Whether or not the lecture would do any ultimate good, Danielle knew she would have to wait and see. But at least her strong words momentarily snapped Chalie out of her depression. In fact, Chalie was laughing and talking like her normal self again before she finally went home. Danielle watched the taillights of her car disappear, then closed the door and turned off the outside light.

She stood with her back pressed against the door, thinking about how ironic it was that she and Chalie were each caught up in her own private hell. Years ago, when they'd romped and played as children, it never occurred to either of them that one day they'd be comforting each other while they struggled to cope with such immense problems.

Danielle took a deep, sobering breath. She was recovering from a bad marriage and wanted to know her natural mother. She was also involved in an emotional battle with Zack that was becoming bigger and bigger by the moment. Chalie was distressed because she couldn't have children, and she didn't know how that would affect her life with Dane.

Would fate treat them more gently in the future? Would either of them ever find the happiness they were seeking? Danielle wondered. Thinking about those questions, she tossed and turned all night long.

CHAPTER SIX

DANIELLE, TRISH AND ZACK were at one of the local hamburger chains where everyone in Natchez seemed to congregate on pleasant summer evenings. Trish was outside playing on the merry-go-round and slide provided by the restaurant, and Danielle and Zack were alone. He had dropped by Oaklaine earlier, and before Danielle knew what was happening, Zack and Trish had decided on hamburgers and fries for dinner. They'd purposely not discussed an issue that had become a point of pride for them both until Trish had gone outside.

"Are you so well-off financially that you can afford to turn down good old muscle and brawn?" Zack asked in a teasing voice. "I and some of my men will be glad to help you move to the main house."

"You know the answer to that," Danielle replied. "But still, I don't want you to feel you have to look after Trish and me. I've been doing a pretty good job of taking care of us."

Zack turned his head toward the window and looked out to where Trish was playing. His expression was thoughtful. "Your marriage wasn't a happy one, was it?"

"What brought that up?" Danielle asked curiously.

"I honestly don't know," Zack confessed. "I suppose it could be this fierce independence I'm seeing in you, or the confident manner in which you run your home. I see those very admirable qualities in you now, and wonder if you really are the Danielle I used to know, or an impostor.''

Danielle smiled at the comparison. ''I'm the same person, Zack. I simply learned, rather harshly, that life is a great deal different from what my father and Precious Love raised me to believe. Once I recovered from the shock, I knew I had to survive. And, by then, I had my baby to think of.'' She glanced at Trish, who was talking with another little girl. ''But hey,'' she said quietly, looking once more at Zack, who hadn't taken his eyes off her, ''why are we getting so serious? You offered your, er, brain and brawn, didn't you?''

''I never welch on a promise,'' he said, grinning.

''Then I accept. And I think you'd better brace yourself. Trish is about to join us, and I'm sure you'll get an earful about her newfound friend.''

A moment or two later, Trish bounded into the booth on Zack's side and, just as Danielle had predicted, began telling him all about the little girl she'd played with, as well as the playground equipment.

Danielle sat back, watching and listening. Life really could be confusing, she decided. Years ago she'd left Zack, declaring him to be the most insensitive man in the world. Yet there was her own daughter, sitting beside him in the booth, her small face wreathed with a huge smile as Zack listened, then began teasing her.

What was there in their relationship after they married that had caused each of them to act so differently? Danielle wondered. What had made them change so drastically toward each other? They'd gone from friends to lovers to enemies.

Zack, glancing across the table at Danielle as he listened to Trish's constant chatter, saw the flashes of sadness in her eyes. Without thinking, he reached out and touched her hand resting on the table. "We don't allow sad faces at this table, lady," he said gruffly.

Trish giggled at the remark, and Danielle smiled. It also occurred to her that, to the casual observer, they looked like an average family. One part of that thought was pleasing to her, but another part of her pulled back from such an involvement—even an involvement that was, so far, mostly in her mind.

For the remainder of the outing, Danielle drew a number of speculative looks from Zack because of her quietness. When he left them at Oaklaine, Danielle walked him out as far as the front porch.

"What happened back there at the restaurant to make you so quiet all of a sudden?" he asked. He was standing so close to her that her natural body heat mingled with the cologne she was wearing and filled his senses. He lifted a hand to cup her nape. "What's bothering you?"

"Nothing...you, me," Danielle said in a perplexing tone. "I didn't come back to Oaklaine...to Natchez...just to become involved with you, Zack."

"Frankly, I wasn't too pleased to hear that you were coming back," he freely admitted. He bent his head then and dropped a light, gentle kiss on her lips just as Trish popped through the door.

"Why are you kissing my mommy?" she demanded to know.

"Because I wanted to." Zack smiled. "She's a very pretty lady."

"Why don't you marry her?" the little girl asked, continuing her direct line of questioning.

"You told me the other day that I was silly. Your mother doesn't want to marry a silly man. Princess, marrying your mother would be a decision she and I would make. We couldn't do something like that just because you wanted it, no matter how much we love you. Marriage is a very important thing. Besides," he continued, suddenly swinging her high over his head and bringing a childish shriek of enjoyment from her, "if I were to marry your mother, that would mean you could tease me all the time. That would be terrible." He shuddered, pretending to be displeased. When he set Trish gently on the floor, he patted her affectionately on the head. "Good night, honey."

"Night," Trish said over her shoulder as she scampered back into the house, her thoughts already focused on something entirely different.

Danielle looked up at Zack and shrugged. "I'm sorry. Sometimes she comes out with the darnedest things. You handled that very nicely."

"Don't apologize, Dani," Zack said quietly. "She's a normal child, as yet untrained in the art of concealing her feelings. I find her totally refreshing. By the way, we'll get that furniture moved tomorrow. Okay?"

"Okay."

"Take care," Zack said softly as he took one last look at her, then turned and walked to his car.

Danielle watched till the bright red of his taillights faded out of sight, then slowly entered the house. She felt like she'd certainly established herself as a mature individual rather than a dependent female looking to Zack for constant help. At least she hoped she had. Yet his feelings were so controlled, she doubted anyone every really knew what he was thinking.

ON THE SURFACE, Danielle and Trish couldn't have been happier. Living at Oaklaine was everything Danielle had hoped it would be—for her and for Trish. Her state of mind, however, was troubled because of Zack, who still seemed to be a huge unsettled problem in her life.

As the days went by, there were moments when she vowed she never wanted to see Zack again. Yet each time he appeared at Oaklaine, she found her heart racing and her palms wet with nervous perspiration. And even though he and Danielle quite often tore into each other with words or looks, he was always incredibly patient and gentle with Trish. In fact, Danielle found herself having to caution him about spoiling the child.

The situation came to a head sooner than she anticipated.

One sunny October afternoon, Danielle was planting tulip bulbs in two long earth-filled containers on the patio when she heard a car coming up the gravel drive. Trish, who was playing with Dolly nearby, immediately ran to investigate.

"It's Uncle Zack, Mommy," the child yelled, then disappeared.

Fully expecting Zack and Trish to join her at any moment, Danielle found a stopping place, then removed her gardening gloves. She poured herself a glass of lemonade and sat down at the table.

She wasn't sure how long she waited, but after a while it became obvious to Danielle that Zack and Trish had found something very interesting in the front yard. She rose to her feet and went to see for herself what could be holding their attention so completely.

The sight of Trish perched on the seat of a spanking new bicycle, complete with training wheels, and Zack striding alongside, one hand on the handlebars, the other at the back of the seat, brought Danielle to a complete halt.

"Look, Mommy," Trish yelled excitedly the second she caught sight of her mother. "See my new bicycle Uncle Zack brought me? It's got training wheels on it, too."

"How nice," Danielle said tightly. Although she smiled, she was already rehearsing what she was going to say to Zack regarding the subject of his extravagant gifts to her daughter the minute they were alone.

When Trish went inside, Danielle asked him point-blank. "What's the idea of buying my child a bicycle?"

"How can you stand there and ask me something so ridiculous?" Zack practically shouted at her, his dark eyes glowing with anger. Danielle was tempted to whack him over the head with one of her gardening tools.

"I ask, Mr. Carlsley," she returned spiritedly, "because it's a good question. It's gotten to the point that every time you stop by, you have some little surprise tucked away in a pocket. I realize you think I'm para-noid on the subject, but that can't be helped. I don't want Trish growing up thinking she's entitled to a sur-prise—or a bribe, if you please—each time she sees you. It's a habit I don't care for. I do hope you see what I'm talking about."

"Well, I'd have to be damn nigh deaf, dumb and blind not to see it," was Zack's stinging reply. "She'll be disappointed if I don't bring her something," he said after a moment's silence.

"A little disappointment won't kill her." Danielle tried to be patient, the beginnings of an astonishing idea taking root in her mind. "Are you afraid she won't love you if there are no surprises?" The question was gently put because suddenly Danielle's heart was full of empathy for him. Zack got to his feet and began pacing. It seemed that each day she learned something new and interesting about his complex makeup. What a shame, she thought sadly, that she hadn't taken the time and trouble to get to know him years ago.

Zack came to a stop in front of her, his hands shoved deep into the back pockets of his faded jeans, his head thrust forward in a meditative pose. With the plaid shirt he was wearing and the old scuffed boots he wore when working on the plantation, he looked like he'd just stepped out of the saddle—which he probably had. He stared fiercely at Danielle, a frown deepening the lines across his broad forehead.

"Is that such a crime?" he snapped. *Now let her make something out of that,* he thought savagely.

"Not at all," Danielle said gently. "It simply shows what a deeply caring man you are, Zack. I'll be the first to admit that our situation is unique, but I'm delighted Trish has you as the dominant male figure in her life right now. Frankly, I didn't dream of such a thing happening when I moved back to Oaklaine, but now that it has, there doesn't seem to be much I can do about it. And if that's to be the case, then you have a responsibility to her, one of helping to teach her values."

"She's too little to be concerned with values," Zack said crossly. He knew in his heart Danielle was right, but he didn't want to hear it. Trish had become very important to him in a short period of time. He was also aware that part of the reason Trish was so special to him was—aside from his genuinely liking kids—that she was Danielle's child. He freely admitted it . . . but only to himself.

"I disagree," Danielle continued stubbornly. "An occasional toy is fine, but stop bringing her one each time you visit."

"And if I don't?" he challenged her, his dark eyes never wavering as they held equally determined blue ones.

"You'll leave me no choice but to ask you to stop visiting Trish."

"Do you realize we sound like a divorced couple discussing my visitation rights?"

"Yes, it does sound like that, doesn't it? But I hope we can be more adult about it than some of the couples I've known who really have faced such problems."

"Hearing you speak of maturity and values doesn't fit in with my mental picture of you." Zack was angry, and he wanted to throw her off stride just for the pure hell of it. She'd called him down, and now he wanted to hurt her.

"That's your problem." Danielle surprised him by replying calmly. "After our second meeting, I realized that nothing I was likely to ever do would change your opinion of me. You still have me pegged as an uncaring, unfeeling twenty-year-old. I'll admit I was those things, and spoiled, to boot. But I've grown up, Zack. And if you don't choose to get to know the real Danielle, then it will be your loss. As for my daughter, I set the rules in her life. Understand?"

Zack's only response was to glare furiously at her for several long, uncomfortable moments, then turn and barrel his way from the house. He slammed the door with such force that the windows actually rattled in their casings.

Two or three days went by before Zack returned to Oaklaine. When he did arrive one morning, astride Satan to take Trish for a ride, there was no surprise in his pocket. Nor was there one the next time, or the next. The treats for the child tapered off to a once-in-a-while thing rather than becoming a feature of each visit.

And that in itself, Danielle decided, was a small miracle. She knew from experience that Zack wasn't one to be deterred once he made up his mind. Looking back, she could see now that their mutual stubbornness had figured heavily in the breakup of their marriage.

The ever-present problem of her feelings for Zack was put on hold momentarily when Harvey Graham called and asked her to meet with him. Upon Danielle's arrival at the law offices, the first thing to be discussed was the possible custody suit. Harvey's sources were still investigating the Kendrickses, and as soon as there was anything to report, he assured her, he would let her know immediately.

However, before Danielle left his office she was in possession of certain pertinent facts regarding her birth mother, the most important one being Elizabeth's name. She was Mrs. Nathan Harrison. They were also facts Harvey Graham warned her to think long and hard about before coming to a decision. That decision would be made somewhat easier because Elizabeth and her husband were on a cruise.

"I've only been involved in one of these cases, but I'm familiar with several similar to yours, Danielle," the short, stocky attorney told her. "I wish I could tell you that they've all turned out happily, but I can't. Each one is unique."

"Do you think I should drop it? Let well enough alone, so to speak?" Danielle asked curiously. "Zack thinks I should forget about it."

"That's because he's afraid you'll be hurt. Actually, it's a decision only you can make," he told her. "Let's just say, I can certainly understand you wanting to know. I hope it works out the way you want it to."

So do I, Danielle thought grimly, *so do I.*

"You might also have to face the rather humiliating fact that at first Mrs. Harrison will suspect you of contacting her because of her wealth."

The look of surprise on Danielle's face brought a chuckle from Harvey. "Surely you're kidding," she said.

"Not at all. Remember, you're a stranger. She doesn't know anything about you other than the fact that you were raised by her cousin."

It was a sobering thought, one that stayed with Danielle all during the drive back to Natchez.

When she stopped at the mailbox, the only thing she found of importance inside was the *Times Picayune,* New Orleans' daily paper. She'd begun taking it when Birdie told her that she thought Elizabeth was in New Orleans. However, during her meeting with Harvey, he'd told her that Elizabeth and her husband had a home in Houston, as well.

She eased the car away from the mailbox, then continued on to Oaklaine, where she parked in the garage at the rear of the house. Once inside the kitchen, she immediately kicked off her shoes and went straight to the fridge and something cold to drink. Even though the fall season had officially arrived, the afternoons were still warm—especially in the city.

The sound of a car door slamming brought a soft moan of dismay from Danielle. She was tired. The last thing she wanted was company. But no amount of wishing could negate the sound of the footsteps crossing the patio. She reached the door at the same time that Chalie did, bringing a laugh of surprise from both.

"Thank goodness it's you," Danielle remarked. She closed the door behind Chalie. "I'm beginning to think everyone I know in Natchez wants to visit me. Hardly a day goes by that I don't have company." She nodded toward the can of diet pop in her hand. "Care to join me?"

"Why not," Chalie replied. She pulled out a chair from the oak table and sat down. "I stopped by to see if you'd found out anything interesting about Elizabeth. Zack said Harvey's legal eagles were hard at work and had turned up a couple of leads."

"Glass?" Danielle asked, grabbing a couple of napkins on her way to the table.

"The can's fine," Chalie said impatiently. "Tell me what's going on before I die of curiosity."

Danielle joined Chalie at the table. "Well," she began, "Elizabeth married Nathan Harrison twenty-four years ago. Harvey gave me a copy of the marriage license this morning when I was in his office."

"Harrison," Chalie murmured, her brow furrowed as she tried to place the name.

"How about the Calvert grocery chain with stores throughout the south?"

"Nathan Harrison owns the Calvert stores?"

"Every single one. Seems Calvert was his mother's maiden name."

"Wow!" Chalie quietly exclaimed. "Are there children?"

"I'll be back in a sec," Danielle murmured, bounding to her feet. She was only gone a few moments. When she returned, she had a magazine in her hands. "Remember me telling you about subscribing to everything about New Orleans that I could find? Well, look on page thirty-three. Of course, without Zack's lawyers finding out who she was and where she was, this wouldn't have meant a thing to me. At any rate, it seems the family divides their time between Houston and New Orleans." She handed the magazine to Chalie. "At the moment they're on a cruise."

Chalie quickly flipped to page thirty-three and found herself staring at several photos of men and women in formal dress. The occasion was a charity ball, a ball to which the Carlsleys had received an invitation for as long as Chalie could remember. "We missed this one. Birdie wasn't feeling well, and Zack didn't want to leave her."

"It's a pity she was ill. Otherwise, she could have renewed her acquaintance with Elizabeth. That's Elizabeth, her husband, Nathan, and their son and daughter in the upper-right-hand photo."

Chalie felt a scattering of goose pimples rush over her skin as she stared into the face of the tall, slender blonde. She shivered. Not a hair on Elizabeth's head looked out of place, and her makeup was flawless. Chalie wondered why the words *icy* and *cold* kept skipping through her mind. But they did. The son was handsome, but the daughter was on the plain side, seeming to take after her father. Somehow Chalie couldn't quite picture warm, vivacious Danielle with the people in the photo.

"What will you do now?"

"What do you mean?"

"Being so wealthy and all, do you suppose she'll think you want money from her?"

"Harvey mentioned that. Frankly, I haven't the faintest idea." Danielle sighed. "However, rich or poor, it makes no difference. My next problem is to decide how best to approach her. I mean, precisely how do I introduce myself to a mother I've never met?''

''Darned if I know,'' Chalie answered, chewing thoughtfully at her bottom lip. ''I know Zack's been helping you; what does he say?''

''We've ... discussed it,'' Danielle replied guardedly.

''Am I safe in assuming the two of you aren't in agreement on the subject?'' Chalie asked, with a knowing grin.

''Quite safe.'' Danielle nodded, her expression grim. ''In fact, we get into an argument each time the subject comes up. He isn't exactly opposed to the idea—he just keeps bringing up situations he hopes will discourage me.''

''He's concerned.''

''I'm not so sure.'' Danielle sighed. ''I think he enjoys tormenting me.''

''Several months ago, even before you came back to Natchez, you accused me of refusing to face life by not marrying Dane,'' Chalie reminded her. ''Now I think it's time for you to take some of your own advice. You know Zack cares for you, and he adores Trish.''

''I know you believe what you're saying, Chalie, and in a way, you're correct. Zack does still care for me in some weird fashion that neither of us understands—at least I don't. But instead of making him happy, it's having the opposite affect. He deeply resents the fact that something in his makeup can still care for me even though I was a lousy wife and divorced him. If there was such a thing as punishment for crimes against the male ego, I'd probably have been tried, convicted and shot seven years ago.''

Chalie tipped her dark head to one side in a thoughtful pose. "Perhaps that's what's been eating away at him lately. I knew there was something, but..." She looked at Danielle. "I'm sorry. I know I said I wouldn't interfere, but I was hoping—"

Was she secretly hoping, too? Danielle wondered. She smiled then, albeit slightly off balance. "Hope for something else... such as you and Dane getting married and raising a house full of kids. You can't keep that man dangling forever, you know."

"He keeps making the same noises," Chalie retorted somewhat resignedly. "I just want to be sure... rather, I want him to be sure."

"Nothing's ever a sure thing, honey. I'm living proof of that."

"But at least you're moving forward with your life."

"What other way is there? I have a child to raise. I can't afford the luxury of vacillating. So right or wrong, I have to decide on a course and stick with it."

AS THE CONVERSATION was taking place between Danielle and Chalie, another individual, seated in a lounge chair on the deck of a luxury cruise ship in the Caribbean, was staring at a photo from a magazine. The magazine featured an article and pictures of several of the antebellum homes in and around Natchez that were still occupied by direct descendants of the original owners.

It couldn't be! It simply couldn't be!

But the longer Elizabeth Harrison studied the snapshot of the smiling features of the young blond woman and the little girl at her side, she became more and more convinced that this stranger was indeed Danielle, the baby she'd given away. Her gaze quickly dropped to the caption accompanying the photo, where it was explained that Oaklaine was presently occupied by Ms Danielle Kendricks and her daughter, Trish—descendants of Samuel Lorman, original owner and builder of the house.

Kendricks? Was her name Kendricks now?

Suddenly a hollow, aching feeling began gnawing at Elizabeth. Her slender hands, the nails painted a rosy pink, trembled slightly. And for the first time in years, she knew a moment of cold, icy fear. Fear, and at the same time, avid curiosity. She was staring into a face that was remarkably like her own. Her own...her daughter!

Danielle.

The name wasn't one she was accustomed to using. In fact, she'd always avoided it when possible. It made her uneasy and left her with an uncomfortable sense of guilt.

It had been Claire's choice of names. She'd even asked Elizabeth if she liked it.

Claire...kind, soft-spoken Claire. She and Tony had been a perfect match for each other back then. Elizabeth sighed. She'd liked them well enough, but found them incredibly boring.

Claire had her volunteering and her gardening; Tony, in his spare time, spent countless hours reading his precious classics and cleaning and caring for his gun collection. Their life had been boring and humdrum to Elizabeth, but she'd known they would make good parents.

"Found something interesting, dear?" Nathan Harrison asked, glancing over the dark rims of his reading glasses at his wife. He was a distinguished-looking man, his olive complexion a perfect foil for Elizabeth's fairness.

"Rather an interesting article on some of the old homes in and around Natchez," she replied, smiling at him, then dropping the magazine beside the lounger. She closed her eyes and adjusted her sunglasses. "I think I'll take a nap. Make sure you wake me in forty-five minutes, Nate. I promised to play bridge at three."

But sleep evaded her, for her mind was filled with picture after picture of a tiny baby girl with a smithering of golden curls on her head and a perfect dimple in her right cheek.

THAT EVENING, AFTER Trish was in bed, Danielle curled up on the sofa in the den. She'd just had her bath and was wearing a pair of yellow pajamas. Her thoughts were totally immersed in the few facts she'd accumulated on Elizabeth. But as she looked at the opened magazine and at the family picture of the Harrisons, she thought back to the remark she'd made to Chalie.

Was the course she'd set regarding Elizabeth the correct one? She felt a rush of doubt as she stared at the picture. How would the sophisticated woman in the photograph react to being contacted by an illegitimate daughter she'd given up for adoption years ago?

Only the day before, Danielle had read an article in a leading magazine, courtesy of a stern-faced Zack, about a woman only a couple of years older than she was, who had found her mother. The results, while satisfying the daughter's need to identify with a mother figure, left a lot to be desired in other areas. The newly found mother wasn't as anxious to become a part of the younger woman's life as her natural child had expected. Even friendship was denied them because of the sensitivity of the situation. In the end, although they'd met and would have liked it to have been otherwise, they were still strangers, with nothing in common but the blood that flowed in their veins. "But that should have been enough," Danielle muttered to herself. "It should have been enough."

Would sharing the same blood in their veins be enough for Elizabeth and her? Could it forge a bond between them strong enough to offset the twenty-seven years they'd been apart?

A sharp scraping noise against a window caused Danielle to jump off the sofa like a shot. She stood in the middle of the floor, the magazine clasped against her chest, her frightened gaze darting from one bare window to the other.

How stupid of her.

Instead of drawing the draperies, she'd wanted to enjoy the openness uncluttered windows offered. Except in the bedrooms and bath, she'd left the draperies on all the windows as open as possible.

So much for enjoying nature!

Now she was shaking like a leaf, surrounded by the light in the room, while whoever was outside was able to amuse himself at her expense.

Before she could draw a steadying breath, her ears picked up the sound again. She looked around for some sort of weapon. What if a stranger were to get inside and harm Trish? The third time she heard something it seemed to come from the French doors directly behind her.

Danielle swung around, fully expecting to see some horrible monster leering at her. But instead of a monster, she saw Zack's scowling features glaring at her through one small, square pane of glass.

She practically flew across the room to the door and flung it open, a loud "Ouch!" bursting from her lips when the edge of the door scraped across the top of the big toe of her right foot. It started burning like the very devil.

"Do you realize you scared me half to death?" she demanded angrily, her chest heaving as if she'd been running for miles. Her heart was pounding like crazy, and her face was as white as a sheet.

"Good," Zack replied tersely. He stepped inside, then closed the door. Without stopping or asking her permission, he walked over to the windows and began drawing the draperies. "I couldn't believe my eyes when I saw you perched on that sofa like a damned fool."

"Fool? What on earth are you talking about?" she demanded, hopping along behind him like a small, infuriated chicken.

"You were a perfect target for any pervert that might happen along," Zack snapped. "Even though the magazine spreads encourage letting the outdoors in, I suggest you use a little common sense. I know you think you're isolated here, but you have neighbors a half mile down the road. They also have two teenage sons who, boys being what they are, prowl around at night." Zack became aware of her uneven gait for the first time, his frown deepening. "Why the hell are you hopping around like a damned rabbit?"

"Thanks to your cute little tricks, I've probably broken my toe," she informed him. To be honest, the pain was beginning to subside. However, the fear she'd been feeling moments ago now exploded into a full-fledged rage. All of it aimed at Zack.

Danielle placed her hands on the back of the sofa in order to take her weight off her injured foot and glowered at him. "Just what gives you the right to sneak around at night scaring the daylights out of people, Zack Carlsley?" she demanded.

At any given time of the day she was beautiful, Zack was thinking, but at that precise moment she was breathtaking. Her hair, freshly shampooed, was loose and wispy, her face scrubbed clean. She looked vitally alive and incredibly sexy in her yellow silk pajamas. Zack could feel his control slipping...leaving gut-aching desire in command of his mind and body. He'd waited so long . . . so damned long. . . .

He began walking toward her, pausing only to turn off the lamp. Each step he took was a deliberate action bringing him closer and closer to the object of his undivided attention.

Soon, barely six inches separated them. He moved closer and the six inches became less and less, till it was reduced to nothing. Breathing became deep and labored when the rigid crests of her breasts nestled against the material of his shirt. Zack marveled—briefly—at the inexplicable hold Danielle exercised over him and his senses. He wasn't ready to analyze his reactions.

He had no ready excuse for what he was doing then or probably would do in the moments ahead. He was simply on a course that resulted from a recurring thought involving a certain woman, a woman who had spoiled him forever for any other female. A woman whose whispered endearments and small, perfect body held the power, with its clean lines and shape and movement, to control him till eternity and beyond.

A lightly abrasive palm slid smoothly beneath still-damp blond hair and cupped a slender nape.

Brown eyes merged with blue ones, coming together... blending effortlessly into a collage of feelings and sensations.

Another hand reached out, the fingertips lightly caressing the edges of a breast, then feathered their way to the excited nipple that crouched like a tiny silken bud beneath his touch.

Danielle felt desire breaking over her, saturating her body with each beat of her heart. Breathing seemed to have become unnecessary, till she became aware of the pain in her chest. She exhaled, then immediately sucked the life-sustaining air back into her lungs in a huge gulp when she felt cool air hit her skin and knew the wonder of Zack's warm hands palming the weight of her breasts.

She looked down in wonderment at her naked breasts resting so innocently in wide, capable hands. She saw her pajama top, a soft yellow heap, against the dark stained wood of the floor.

She looked back up at Zack and some instinct made her place her hands on his chest. Somewhere in the swirl of desire encircling her was the taste of fear. "Zack," she whispered. "I—we..."

A tan square-tipped forefinger came to rest against her dry lips. "Shh." The gentle sound was remarkably loud in the utter stillness of the room. A crooked grin, partly happy, partly filled with pain, pulled at his lips. "Danielle." The sound of her name rolled off his lips like a caress. "I want you. Do you understand?"

"Oh, Zack," she murmured, her lips trembling with emotion, her eyes glistening with unshed tears. "Wanting each other was never a problem for us."

Zack bent his head to the breasts he was still holding and touched his lips to the tightly swollen firmness, made that much tighter from that mysterious core of need as old as man. The words *warm* and *firm* floated through his mind, as if he were discovering her for the very first time. The moist tip of his tongue curled around one sensitive nipple, taking it between his lips, then beginning an exquisite sucking motion. He moved from one breast to the other, coaxing, teasing, his dark head becoming a blur before Danielle's unseeing eyes.

His hands eased inside the elastic waistband of her pajamas. Slowly, with such incredible lightness of touch as to seem dreamlike to the desire-intoxicated Danielle, the single spot of yellow on the floor was joined by its mate.

Zack stepped back then, his hands resting heavily on the slight flaring of her hips. Though the room was in darkness, a faint glow from a light in another part of the house enabled Zack to follow the outline of her body. From her breasts his gaze followed the curve of her waist, and on down over a flat tummy to the dark gold shadow shielding that feminine counterpart to his male sexuality.

"You're beautiful . . . so very, very beautiful." The words burst unbidden from Zack's lips. Nonetheless, in that moment of intense pain that gradually grows into mind-numbing ecstasy, there was unspoken doubt about the wisdom of their lovemaking. But before the doubt could take hold and shatter the moment for him, Zack picked Danielle up in his arms and placed her on the sofa.

Suddenly he was gone, and Danielle felt lost and alone. "Zack?" The edge of panic was in her voice when she spoke his name.

"I'm here," he said, materializing beside her as suddenly as he'd disappeared. "I closed the door." He remained standing over her, staring down at her while he removed his clothes. When he was naked, Zack knelt beside her, his hands caressing and smoothing their way over a body as familiar to him as his own.

Danielle touched him then, her fingers eager to reacquaint themselves with a hair-coarsened chest. That same raven-black hair arrowed its way down his body to form a dense background for that part of him that was pressing hard and hot against her thigh.

She caught his head and brought it down till their mouths were fused, their tongues curling together, darting and delving into dark, sweet troves of sensitivity, till their heads swam with need for a greater release than they could find in a kiss.

Danielle clasped the proof of his manhood, and heard the sharp gasp from Zack. She didn't need light to know his head had dropped back or that his teeth were clenched as he fought for control. She'd touched him the same way before and watched his reaction. She'd gotten the same response many times in the past.

They'd always touched...and died a little bit each time they came together, Danielle thought dazedly. Touching and dying.

Zack caught her wrists and held them over her head with one hand while he moved into place over her. Danielle felt the probing hardness against that most secret part of her. She opened to him, taking him inside her, momentarily forgetting how completely he filled her, then remembering with a muted cry of satisfaction.

Restraint. Zack repeated the word soundlessly. He wanted Danielle to enjoy their lovemaking as much as he was, but she was so hot...so tight. Suddenly his intentions to begin slow and easy were dashed when

Danielle's body arched to meet his, matching him stride for stride, refusing him the slightest mercy as she gave and demanded equal pleasure.

When that sudden, desperate climactic victory began rushing over him, Zack fought it with all his might till he pulled Danielle to the summit with him. They were completely one for a brief moment, lost in a world where thought was impossible—where emotions were near delirium.

They were helpless as the bold gods of sexual love laughed at their mortal attempt to tame the rush of passion, and flung them without mercy into the mysterious world from which one awakens exhausted, yet sated.

CHAPTER SEVEN

THOUGH HER EYES WERE CLOSED and her breathing was deep and regular, Danielle had never felt more awake in her entire life. She'd known the instant Zack slipped from the bed to get dressed. A few minutes later, when she sensed his presence beside the bed, she continued to hold the pose. She felt the touch of his lips against her cheek, then heard his almost silent footsteps as he left her bedroom. He went a few feet down the hall, stopped for a moment at Trish's door, then quietly let himself out of the house.

Danielle opened her eyes then, her hand going out to touch the indentation on the pillow where his head had rested. She clasped the pillow to her. It still carried the scent of Zack's after-shave...the scent of his body, a scent that never left her mind no matter how long they were apart.

Suddenly, Danielle threw back the covers and stood, then walked the few steps to the window that faced Rosewynn. She pulled back one edge of the drape and stared into the darkness. For a moment or two she was unable to find what she was seeking. And then, just as he emerged from the shadows of several oaks, she was able to see Zack as he moved along with his long, brisk stride, his head bent slightly forward, his hands tucked in the front of his jeans.

Even at that distance, he gave the appearance of a troubled man in deep thought. And Danielle could certainly understand his pensive mood, since her own mind was still reeling from what had taken place between them.

They'd made love, and it had been indescribable. In each other's arms it had been as if time stood still, as if those years between had never happened, as if the unhappy months of their marriage never existed.

Danielle sighed as she watched Zack walk farther and farther away and finally disappear from view. She knew a few moments of ecstasy should in no way be confused with day-to-day reality. And the reality of the situation between her and Zack was the stark reminder that years ago, she'd mistaken a lifelong friendship for love. She'd allowed family and familiarity to govern her decision to become Mrs. Zachary Carlsley.

Deep in her heart, Danielle felt she wasn't ready to become intimately involved with Zack. Yet, another part of her was looking at him through the eyes of a single woman, who saw an extremely attractive man in every respect, a man any woman would be a fool to ignore.

While Danielle was staring pensively out the window, Zack pulled the collar of his windbreaker closer around his neck, instinctively hunching his broad shoulders against the crisp, cool breeze stirring the skeletal shapes of moss hanging from the limbs of the oak trees.

He paused, then turned and stared at the house he'd just left—the house where Danielle was sleeping.

If he were to follow the dictates of his heart, he'd go back inside and slip into the bed he'd carried her to, then pull her sleepy-warm body close and hold her in his arms for the rest of the night. But common sense told him that he was three kinds of a fool for allowing himself to become caught up in her affairs, much less making love to her.

He rubbed at his chin with a wide hand, exhaled noisily, then turned toward Rosewynn. It was best that he go home—or at least not go back to Danielle tonight, Zack reasoned. Making love to her had but momentarily assuaged his appetite for her. It seemed he'd never get enough tasting and touching and feeling Danielle's body.

He could still smell the scent of her shampoo drifting upward from the heated skin of his chest. She'd gone to sleep with her hair spread over him like a golden cape.

When Zack came to the narrow footbridge fording the small trickling creek between the two properties, he stopped again, his hands braced on the railing. He stared down into the rivulets of running water, glistening like lengths of crystal in the moonlight.

There was a quick brilliance of tears in Zack's dark eyes, tears that were a reflection of the intense pain inside him, tearing him apart. More than anything in the world he wanted to believe that Danielle was a different person. He wanted to believe that what he was seeing was the real woman she had become. He wanted to believe that he could take her into his heart and his life, and that she would never leave him.

But his heart and his mind were eons apart. He couldn't believe any of those things and his distrust was keeping him a prisoner.

He thought back to their lives before they married, trying to recall the moment when he'd first fallen in love with Danielle, but it evaded him. It seemed she'd always been there. Always laughing with Chalie. Always getting into mischief. Birdie had been right, Zack thought sadly; in her youth, Danielle had attracted trouble. More times than he cared to remember, it had been his lot to rescue her.

No, he thought, and sighed roughly, there was no way he could pinpoint or chart the growth of his love for Danielle. She'd always been a part of his life. And when she left him, it was like losing an arm or a leg.

Since their divorce, his involvement with women had been handled so that each lover knew from the very beginning what to expect. A wall of granite surrounded Zack's heart, and nothing anyone did seemed to make the slightest dent in it. When he walked away from an affair with a woman, there were no regrets, and there was no pain.

He thought of the future. Now that he and his ex-wife had made love, how would it affect their relationship? Would they fall into the habit of casual sex? Unable to let each other go, yet unable to build a life together? No, he answered without hesitation. There would never be anything casual about their making love. And he was forced to admit that, whether or not he could ever trust her again, nothing stood in the way of his admiration for her.

A rough groan of pain drifted past his rigid lips as he cursed the demons inside that refused to let him believe. Zack looked one last time toward the sleeping quietness of Oaklaine, then disappeared into the shadows of the trees.

AT NOON THE NEXT DAY, just as Chalie was leaving the kindergarten where she taught, Dane's car stopped at the curb beside her.

"Need a lift, lady?" he asked, smiling a smile at her that had her heart flip-flopping like crazy.

"I usually don't ride with strangers," she returned teasingly, "but since you look so *safe* I don't suppose this one time will hurt."

"Safe?" Dane spluttered as he waited for her to get in, then leaned across and quickly kissed her. "Just wait till I get you alone. I'll make you think safe."

"Promises, promises," Chalie returned in a singsong voice, the tip of her tongue lightly running over the surface of her lips where his mouth had touched hers. Their gazes met and held for a moment, the love they felt for each other shining in their eyes.

It was Chalie who looked away first.

Why?

Why had she suddenly felt guilty about exchanging a loving look with Dane? What could there possibly be in the depths of his eyes that made her want to look away, that made her want to try to conceal something from him, that made her want to jump out of the car and run till she was exhausted?

This was Dane. Her Dane. Why was she feeling so uneasy in his presence?

"Chalie?"

She turned her head and looked questioningly at him. "I'm sorry?"

"I asked if you have an appointment or anything. Were you headed somewhere in particular?"

"Oh . . . no," she answered, shaking her head. "Actually, I'm through for the afternoon. I'm not sure how it's happened, but I've managed to finally hire a really competent staff. These days I don't have to stand guard over everything that's done in order to make sure it's handled properly."

"That's because you're an excellent business-woman," Dane told her.

In spite of her unsettling thoughts, that remark brought a smile to her lips. "You're really lavish with your compliments today, aren't you?"

"I'm in a good mood. But even if I weren't, you really are a good businesswoman."

"Thank you. However, are we going to sit here all afternoon or are we going to lunch? I assume that is why you offered me a ride, isn't it?"

"All in good time, my darling, all in good time," Dane remarked as he pulled away from the curb, his expression and tone of voice conveying a hint of mystery.

Ordinarily Chalie would have been pleased with Dane's behavior. But lately she was finding it harder and harder to concentrate on the good things about their relationship. Her thoughts were more often than not occupied with the disturbing fact that she could never have children.

Idle conversation passed between them till Chalie realized they were a mile or so out of town and that the car was slowing down. She looked around, realizing the only house in the vicinity was the one sitting some distance from the road. It was a rambling ranch-style building, surrounded by trees.

She turned and looked at Dane. "You didn't tell me we were going to visit someone."

"We aren't."

"But we are going there—" she nodded toward the house "—aren't we?"

"Correct."

"Would you mind explaining?"

"Certainly," Dane said, looking pleased as punch with himself. He stopped the car before the double carport, his hands resting on the steering wheel as he gazed at the house. "I'm thinking of buying this."

Chalie couldn't think of a single thing to say. Her tongue was suddenly thick as a four-inch board, and she wanted nothing more than to get as far away from the house as possible. No matter what it looked like inside, she knew she wasn't going to like it. She just knew it.

"That is, if you approve of it. The owners were transferred, and they're practically giving it away." Dane was aware of Chalie's hesitation, but he chose to ignore it. He was afraid that if he pounced on her every single time she acted out of character, they'd do nothing but fight. However, lately her emotional distress over not being able to have children was putting an enormous amount of pressure on their relationship. He pocketed the car keys, then smiled. "Let's go have a look-see. Okay?"

Ten minutes later, Dane knew he'd made a mistake. Chalie was nervous, making no comments unless asked a direct question.

"Am I to assume you don't like the house?" Dane finally asked, an irritated edge to his voice.

"It's all right," she said coolly.

"Then what's your problem? You act as if you're being forced to walk through a torture chamber."

"I just can't figure out why you're so anxious to buy a house."

"Anxious?" he repeated. "I'm thirty-three years old, Chalie, not eighteen. I hardly think wanting to buy a house at my age makes me anxious."

"Why do you need a house?"

"Why do *we* need a house, Chalie," he corrected her, his direct gaze challenging her wavering one. "We are *supposed* to be getting married. Have you forgotten?"

"There's no need to be insulting, Dane," she snapped, turning on her heel and storming out.

Dane stood in the middle of the empty room, a sense of hopelessness creeping over him. He could feel the gulf between him and Chalie becoming wider and wider, and there didn't seem to be a damned thing he could do about it.

DANIELLE WAS NERVOUS.

In approximately forty-five minutes she would be hosting her first dinner party at Oaklaine. Admittedly the guest list was small, but it was a dinner party just the same.

Dane and Chalie were coming. Danielle sighed as she thought of the topsy-turvy situation in their lives. Chalie was still struggling to come to grips with her inability to have children. Danielle often marveled at Dane's patience, and hoped he wouldn't become disenchanted before Chalie made up her mind.

Birdie and Zack made up the remainder of the guest list. Birdie because Danielle genuinely wanted her to visit . . . and Zack?

Because he'd been so helpful to her?

It was nice to let people think that. But Danielle knew better.

She was convinced that seven years ago part of her attraction for him had stemmed from the fact that she was so used to him. She'd been able to do and say things with Zack that she would never have done with any other man. Now she'd been thrown into a very similar situation. Was this new sexual attraction she was feeling for Zack enhanced by the fact that he was—once again—handy? Was the attraction made even more appealing this second time around because he was so kind to Trish? Was there any real substance to her feelings, or was she experiencing emotional despair?

Several days had passed since they'd made love. But even so, Danielle was still stunned by the response he'd drawn from her. She still couldn't believe she'd actually done some of the things that stood out so vividly in her mind. Those were the moments when she would close her eyes in embarrassment, as she remembered the abandonment with which she responded to him. Moments that were responsible for her now feeling a twinge of awkwardness in his presence.

And even he hadn't been untouched by those few hours they'd lain in each others arms and loved—letting the depth of their passion override the problems that existed in their relationship. The two or three times she'd seen him since that night, Zack had seemed extremely preoccupied for the most part—except when Danielle would catch him staring at her, a frown furrowing his brow. His was as thorough a scrutiny as she'd ever endured, and she found it most disconcerting.

Was his preoccupation his own form of self-protection? Was he silently denying the reaction she'd seen—trying to convince himself that they'd simply afforded each other physical release and nothing more? Or was he, like her, afraid to delve too deeply into the complexities of the situation? Was he afraid of becoming trapped again in a relationship bred of familiarity?

The buzzer on the oven went off. Danielle gave a start as the sharp noise interrupted her perplexing reverie. She quickly collected her thoughts, then dutifully peeked through the square of glass in the oven door at the spinach Madeline. As she stared at the thick, bubbling sauce, it occurred to her how the more mundane chores of daily life demanded their due time and energy from a person, regardless of the emotional problems that person faced.

Living. It was called living, Danielle thought as she caught the corner of her bottom lip between the sharp edges of her teeth. The ups and downs of day-to-day living—bringing happiness and grief at will. In her opinion, she'd had enough grief, even though some of it had been brought about by her own doing. Now it was time to get on with the happiness part—she hoped.

For the fourth or fifth time, she hurried into the dining room to check the table. She moved an imaginary speck from a napkin, then eased a glass forward a fraction of an inch. She turned the centerpiece, a low basket of fall flowers, to another angle, only to change her mind and put it back in its original position.

When she answered the door a while later, Danielle found tall, blond Dane Ewing standing on the porch, a lovely bouquet of flowers in one hand, a bottle of wine in the other and a charming smile on his good-looking face.

"Oh, my goodness." She chuckled. "I do hope all that's for me." She stepped back and waved him inside.

Dane frowned with mock seriousness. "Gee." He sighed. "I'm not sure. I was told to give the flowers to the lady of the house, a short, plump, matronly lady."

"You rat!"

He laughed as he bent and kissed her on the cheek, then handed her both wine and flowers. "Chalie will be along with Bertie and Zack. They'll be fifteen or twenty minutes late. Some minor crisis at Rosewynn, I believe. Where is your daughter?'' he asked, speaking nonstop.

"Spending the night—maybe—with Susie Summers, Cathleen's little girl. We figure they'll make it to eleven o'clock. And the emergency at Rosewynn is an unexpected visit from a not-too-favorite relative. Chalie called,'' Danielle explained, not bothering to add that Chalie had said she and Dane weren't on very good terms. "This person only visits them once a year or so. Always manages to arrive at the most inopportune time imaginable.'' she patted Dane's arm. "Come into the kitchen with me. That way we can gossip like crazy while I put these flowers in water and take care of last-minute details for dinner.''

As they made their way through the front parlor, Dane looked around with interest. "You've really spruced up this place. It looks great. There's only one problem. A little bird told me you hadn't been to the liquor store,'' Dane teased her with a rueful twist of his mouth. "I hope that situation has been corrected? You do know I'll kill if you offer me cooking sherry, don't you?''

"One shares what one has, you ungrateful fink.'' Danielle tried for a stern voice, failing miserably. "I should serve you prune juice.''

"Cooking sherry is pretty close to prune juice.''

When they reached the dining room, she stopped before an antique sideboard. After shifting the wine and flowers to one hand, she bent down and opened a bottom door with a small flourish. "Ta-da!'' she announced in her best trumpet voice. "While certainly not as extensive as your supply,'' she remarked with suspect meekness, "I think you'll find a decent enough bourbon and Scotch to satisfy even your discerning palate.''

"Looks like you've got everybody covered," he remarked as he entered the kitchen close behind her, holding a bottle. "Care to have a bourbon and branch water with me?''

"Surely you jest?'' Danielle, who was checking baby carrots simmering in a saucepan on the countertop range, eyed him suspiciously.

Dane looked properly horrified as he suddenly remembered Danielle's very low tolerance for hard liquor. "Sorry, kid. Forget I offered." He began fixing his drink, softly whistling as he got ice from the fridge.

Danielle glanced at him. "You seem in excellent spirits this evening. Has some rich uncle died and left you millions?''

He looked over at her and shrugged. "Nothing so auspicious, I assure you. I'm just normally a cheerful person.''

"It shows.''

Dane leaned against the counter, one hand holding his drink, the other braced on the surface of the counter. "Thanks for trying to help by talking to Chalie. She's told me about some of your conversations. Maybe being able to confide in you will enable her to see that she isn't some sort of subhuman simply because she can't have a baby. Who knows?''

"Ah, Dane,'' Danielle said wistfully. "Try, if you possibly can, to give her a little more time. I know you're tired of hearing reasons she thinks she shouldn't marry you. But the ironic thing is, Chalie is concerned for you, and to her, infertility is a very real problem. She has it in her head that you will either come to hate her because she will deprive you of your natural right to father children or that if you two were to decide to adopt, there would be a barrier between the child and you or her, because it wouldn't be blood related.''

''I've talked to her till I'm blue in the face, Dani,'' he said resignedly. ''Yet she refuses to believe me. I really do wish she would seek professional help. I think it would do wonders. Chalie means the world to me, but my patience is running out.''

Danielle didn't have any quick-fix advice to offer him. She wished she did, but it was something Dane and Chalie were going to have to work out together. She was torn between her loyalty to her friend and the truth of what Dane was saying. To her, it was the saddest thing in the world that two lovely people were being kept apart because of such simple reasons—simple to an outsider. To Chalie, Danielle quietly reflected, her reasoning made complete sense and in the end, since it was Chalie's problem, it was she who had to be satisfied within herself before she could ever participate in a meaningful relationship with Dane.

People and their problems, she thought as she took the fruit salad from the fridge and added the dressing. What was abhorrent to one could be readily accepted by another. Something painful to another was ignored by yet a different person. The problems in life were legion, but one couldn't stop trying to understand, to learn, to mature.

Danielle remembered those thoughts later after all her company had arrived. She'd caught a glimpse of Chalie's face as she was talking to Dane at dinner. The love in her eyes was there for all the world to see. They were so perfect for each other, yet so far apart. How sad it would be if they were unable to work out their differences.

"You've done a fantastic job, Dani, with your re-decorating," Birdie remarked, as Danielle was removing the dinner plates before serving dessert. "I was telling Chalie before dinner what a nice job Walter Smith did for you."

"Thank you," Danielle said, smiling. "He did do a good job." Danielle glanced at Chalie, then wished she hadn't, when she encountered the amused glance. She whisked a silent Zack's plate from before him and hurried to the kitchen, smothering her amusement on the way. She'd no more than made it to the sink when she heard his heavy tread.

"What was that all about?" he demanded.

Danielle turned and looked at him. She saw a tall, broad-shouldered man with dark hair and eyes. Even with a heavy scowl on his face, his rugged features were still striking. *He looks terribly unhappy,* she thought.

"I'm sorry," she said after a moment. "What did you say?"

"You and Chalie. What's so amusing about Walter Smith hanging wallpaper?" He walked on over to stand beside her. They were so close that each time she moved her arm, it brushed heavily against the muscled hardness of his.

Zack could barely keep his eyes off the mint-green dress she was wearing, for it was made of a soft, clinging material that did fantastic things for her figure. The outfit had his desire rising to the boiling point.

Danielle swallowed the disturbing sensations gathering in the pit of her stomach, and in other sensitive points of her body. She took a deep breath and explained to Zack what had taken place between Birdie and Mr. Smith. "I can look back on it now and laugh," she said, grinning. "But then, all I could think of was being sentenced to a life of papering and painting."

"You didn't do so bad in here," Zack said huskily. It was a degree of huskiness that implied an intimacy between them, an intimacy neither of them was ready to deal with. "Even the shed has taken on a new look."

When he'd accepted the dinner invitation, he'd made himself a promise to keep the evening on a strictly impersonal level. If possible, he'd decided not even to be alone with Danielle. So much for promises.

"Th-Thank you." Oh, sweet heaven! His eyes were like deep, dark pools. She could drown in them. She felt herself going warm, hot and moist.

"I like your hair down." He lifted one hand to her shoulder, his fingers tracing up against her neck and through her hair. When his hand slowly moved away from the golden mass, single strands of it clung to his skin, as if reluctant to let him go.

"It's . . . it's hard to manage this evening," she stammered, pushing at her hair. "I just shampooed it." She saw the tiny pulse in the side of his throat throbbing wildly. For the first time since they'd made love, Danielle saw a crack in that granite wall surrounding his heart. She knew he was remembering.

Without thinking, she reached up and placed her fingers against the fluttering pulse. Her eyes merged with his. She knew.

Zack caught her wrist when she would have moved it. He held it so that her palm moved with excruciating slowness midway along his chest. He stopped then. His own fingers closed over hers just as his body had covered hers when they made love. He guided flesh against flesh beneath the opening of his oxford-cloth dress shirt. His skin was hot, his heart beating rapidly.

"Wear it down tomorrow evening," Zack said hoarsely.

If he'd said to go nude tomorrow evening, at that precise moment Danielle knew she would have nodded in agreement. It would have been impossible to have done otherwise. "What's tomorrow evening?" she asked, but knew the answer without him saying a word. Awareness was flowing between them like the headlong rush of a raging river.

"Dinner at my apartment in New Orleans. We'll be late. Get Chalie to keep Trish."

"She might have plans," Danielle said, trying to calm the flutter of nerves attacking her. "I'll check with Cathleen tomorrow and see if she can recommend a sitter."

"No." Zack shook his head. "Don't leave Trish with a stranger. I'll speak with Chalie."

"*I'll* find a sitter," she corrected him. That small matter of defining her authority broke the spell and reminded Danielle that she had guests waiting for dessert.

Zack smiled gently down at her and Danielle's heart skipped a beat at the look. It had been years since she'd seen a look like that from him directed toward her. "I know you're a good mother, Dani. You don't have to keep reminding me."

"But I do have to keep reminding you, Zack. And of other things as well. We both know I'm constantly on trial with you."

"I know," he murmured, "I know."

"How long, Zack? How long? Six years have passed, you know. I'm not the same person I was when I married you, or when we were divorced."

He didn't need to be reminded of those years that had elapsed, or of anything related to them. Every day had been a slow, cruel passage of time that left its mark upon his heart. He pressed her fingers firmly against his chest for a moment, then reluctantly released them.

"I hear the words...and I know you mean them. But words have nothing to do with it. Can you understand?"

Danielle felt the excitement of only moments ago leave her like a narrowing swirl of water rushing down a thirsty drain. "Why not?" She stepped away from him, then turned to where a chocolate pie and dessert plates were waiting on the counter. "I spend considerable time fighting my own ghosts, Zack, past and present."

Zack's thoughts immediately went to Theo Kendricks and the man's suspected suicide. Zack wanted to relieve her mind on that point. But so far Harvey Graham—in putting together a defense for her, in case the elder Kendrickses did push the custody suit—hadn't found any evidence to support or deny Danielle's fears.

"Would you mind carrying in the dessert tray?" Danielle asked without looking at Zack. "I'll bring the coffee. By the way, I forgot. I've already made tentative plans for tomorrow evening." She picked up the carafe of coffee. "Shall we?"

Zack had no choice but to follow. But he knew his time would come. If he didn't get a chance to correct the situation after dinner, then he'd definitely take care of it in the morning.

Of one thing he was certain. Unless the world came to an end before then, tomorrow evening Danielle would be dining with him in New Orleans.

CHAPTER EIGHT

THOUGH HER HEART WAS heavy as stone, Danielle wore a pleasant smile when she entered the dining room with Zack in her wake.

"Did you think we'd run away with dessert?" she asked teasingly.

"Something like that," Chalie agreed. "I was about to send out a search team," she said, continuing in a lighthearted vein. "Not to find you two, mind you, but to recover the pie."

"Hear, hear," Dane chimed in.

Later, as they were clearing the table, Chalie looked at Danielle. "I couldn't help but pick up on the tension between you and my dear brother. Problems?"

"Yes and no," Danielle murmured. "But then, isn't there always trouble between Zack and me?"

"Need to talk?"

"I don't suppose it would hurt, but I—"

"Don't worry. I'll wait till Zack is on his way to New Orleans."

"New Orleans?" Danielle repeated. He hadn't said anything to her about going *tonight*.

"He has a business appointment later this evening."

Danielle's expression revealed her disbelief. "Business appointment?"

Chalie shrugged. "That's what he said, Dani. I have no reason to doubt him."

"Must be some kind of business."

Danielle picked up the tray of dirty dishes and carried them to the kitchen, Chalie following with the soiled table linens.

Chalie gave a brief shake of her head. How could she have been so dumb? "I'm sorry. I shouldn't have mentioned it."

"Why not? Zack certainly doesn't have to clear his every move with me," Danielle said, her tone brittle. A business appointment at this time of night was one of the worst excuses she'd ever heard. Why didn't he just say he was meeting a woman? And why did that bother her? Hadn't she been telling herself only an hour or so ago that she didn't want to fall into a trap of convenience with Zack? Well, apparently, he didn't either.

If he'd only mentioned his other plans earlier, Danielle silently fumed, she certainly wouldn't have expected him to come to dinner. That way, he and his friend could have eaten at a decent hour.

"If you say so."

Danielle looked crossly at Chalie. "What's that crack supposed to mean?"

"Only a blind and deaf person could fail to see the looks in both your eyes."

"I doubt that," Danielle stubbornly maintained.

"Doubt it all you like," Chalie told her, "but it's true."

"I'm . . . oh, you're right," she said, sighing. "It's there, but it's also very confusing."

"What do you mean?"

"My explanation is a bit redundant, but let me try anyway. You know that when Zack and I married, he practically turned into a recluse, and expected me to do the same thing. When I began toying with the idea of returning to Oaklaine, the only thoughts directed toward Zack were ones where I imagined us both still feeling much the same about each other as when we divorced.''

"And you don't?''

"Not at all. From the minute I saw him in the hardware store it was as though an entirely different man was standing before me. There was something then, and still is, about him that's... mystifying. I saw him two other times that same day. Each time I saw him, I was amazed at how attractive he was. I couldn't believe what I was thinking.'' She lifted one shoulder in confusion. "I had divorced the man, for pete's sake. To suddenly find myself wondering if he was still a good lover... what it would be like to have him kiss me... if he was seeing anyone at the moment... All those absolutely ridiculous things began cropping up in my mind. I felt like an idiot.''

"They aren't ridiculous thoughts, Dani,'' Chalie said softly. "They're merely feelings and thoughts that should have been present in your relationship before, but weren't.''

"I suppose you're right.''

"Have you thought about solving part of your curiosity by sleeping with him?''

Danielle was quiet for a moment. Finally she looked at Chalie. "Your advice is a bit late, honey. And it didn't solve a darn anything. He's still a fantastic lover, he kisses like every woman's dream man should, and I have no idea about whether there's another woman in his life. When we're together I'm too busy trying to analyze my feelings where he's concerned to question him. Till tonight, that is. Now I really do wonder if there's someone else. The thought that there might be hurts like hell, and I don't know why."

"Oh, Dani," Chalie murmured. She slipped her arms around her friend and hugged her. "I wish—"

"What's going on?" Zack asked as he walked into the kitchen. He watched Danielle step back from Chalie. He saw the mask of indifference slip into place on her face and knew a moment of utter frustration. Dammit! She was still angry with him because of what he'd said to her earlier. "Would you and Dane mind dropping Birdie at Rosewynn?" he asked Chalie.

"No problem." She squeezed Danielle's hand. "No problem at all," she told her as she stepped around him and left the room.

Danielle met his gaze defiantly, though she felt as if her insides had been wound into a tiny, tight ball. "Hadn't you better be on your way? It's not nice to keep your friend waiting, you know." She started for the door, stepping well around Zack's imposing hulk.

He was faster, though. Five fingers of steel clamped themselves to her arm and jerked her against him, the force of impact bringing a sudden whoosh of air from her lungs.

"What the hell's wrong with you?" Brown eyes were sparkling with anger.

"I beg your pardon?" Blue eyes met brown ones with equal spirit. Something inside her urged her to come right out and ask him if he had a date, but her pride held her back.

"What kind of game are you playing, Danielle?" he asked gruffly. His free arm slipped around her shoulders, his hand going to the back of her head. "You're driving me crazy. Do you know that?"

"I seriously doubt that." She steeled herself against the passion-making, desire-inflicting glow in his eyes. She wasn't about to give in to the sensuous lips reminding her of how deliciously they'd trailed feathery kisses from her lips to the tip of her toes and teased that tiny core of femininity that triggered explosion after explosion of ecstasy within her body.

No. No way.

"What's Chalie been telling you?" Zack asked. His head was tilted to one side while he watched her. Dear God! he wanted her. Pride or no pride, he wanted to bury himself in that womanly softness of hers. He wanted to die that special little death with her. He wanted to awaken in her arms, then begin all over again.

"Chalie? Really, Zack, I haven't the faintest idea what you're talking about."

"Oh . . . you know, damn you." He stared at her for a moment longer, then took her mouth in a deep, bruising kiss that transmitted his frustration, a frustration that bespoke his lack of control over the situation. When he raised his head and looked down at her, they were both breathing like long-distance runners. Short, hurting gasps inflicted physical pain, emotional pain. "Remember, we have a date for dinner tomorrow evening."

He released her, then turned and strode from the room.

Like a mechanical robot constructed of nuts and bolts and plastic and metal, and performing at the command of its human creator, Danielle went through the motions of bidding her guests goodbye. She even managed to murmur to Chalie that she'd take a rain check on their talk.

However, once she was alone, the tears of frustration slowly stole down the smoothness of her cheek. She was confused and she was hurting. She wanted to find some dark corner and curl up while the world passed her by.

But even that small but much-needed release was denied her by Trish's tearful arrival.

Danielle thanked Cathleen and apologized for the inconvenience.

"I missed you, Mommy," Trish murmured in a small voice a short time later as she walked beside Danielle to her bedroom.

"And I missed you," Danielle said, smiling down at the woebegone expression on her daughter's small face.

"I think Teddy missed me, too," Trish told her.

Danielle willed her mouth not to give in to the smile threatening to break through any second. The poor baby. She was trying so hard to be the way she thought a big girl should be. "I'm certain he did. As well as all your other friends," she said, indicating the numerous stuffed animals in Trish's attractive bedroom.

After tucking covers snug around Trish and Teddy, Danielle sat on the edge of the bed and listened to the little girl's prayers, which included blessing everything from the frogs croaking in the creek to Dolly the golden retriever. "And God, please...if you won't send my daddy back to live with us, send us a new one. Susie says her daddy plays with her. Uncle Zack plays with me. Amen."

The amusement that had been lurking just beneath the surface of Danielle's expression only a moment ago was replaced by a look of compassion. She leaned over and kissed Trish on the cheek, then made a big fuss of doing the same for Teddy. "Good night, honey," she said softly as she turned and began walking toward the door.

"Do you think the mailman will bring my daddy tomorrow?"

Danielle stopped, then slowly turned. "Er, I don't think so, honey," she murmured.

"Don't you think God was listening to me?"

"Oh, yes, honey, he was listening. But, as I've told you before, sometimes it takes longer for some of our requests to be filled. We'll just have to be patient."

Trish turned over on her side, clasping Teddy tightly in her arms. "Now I remember."

Wishing with all her heart that she could say something that would brighten the child's world, Danielle walked back to the bed. "I've just thought of something really neat, Trish. Would you like to go on a picnic with me down by the creek?"

"I guess."

"Great."

"Can Uncle Zack go with us?"

"I suppose so. But he might be busy working."

"Will you ask him?"

"Of course. I tell you what. The next time you see him, why don't you ask him?"

"Okay. Night, Mommy."

"Good night, Trish," Danielle whispered, accepting that she'd been dismissed by her daughter.

But outside in the hallway, Danielle waited a moment or two in case Trish called her. Her baby was hurting, and there wasn't a darn thing she could do to take that hurt away.

At Rosewynn, Chalie waited in the car while Dane saw Birdie to the door. When he returned, he glanced at his watch, then at Chalie.

"How about a drink at Dewey's?" He was reluctant to see the evening end, considering Chalie had acted friendlier this evening than any other time since their fight over the house. He loved her, and watching her grow distant was tearing him up.

"Sounds nice." She nodded, then lapsed into silence. As much as she loved Dane, Chalie honestly didn't want to be alone with him. When they were alone, he invariably brought up the subject of marriage, a subject she was becoming more and more convinced simply wasn't in their future.

"Something on your mind?" Dane asked as he drove down the tree-lined driveway. Dammit! She was withdrawing from him again. He could feel it, and there wasn't a darned thing he could do about it.

"I was just thinking about Danielle and Zack." Chalie spoke the lie with amazing calmness. How could she tell him that she thought it would be best if they didn't see each other for a while? How could she suggest that to him, when she loved him so deeply?

"They're two mature people," he told her. "They'll work it out eventually."

"I'm not so sure," Chalie murmured. "There's no trust between them. Zack is terrified that if he lets go and shows his love for her, she'll leave again. Danielle is equally afraid they're falling into the same old trap of convenience. That's part of what happened before. Danielle was bowled over by Zack. And once the families realized what was happening, they really got behind the idea. I honestly think that once the hubbub died down and Danielle came out of the daze, she wondered why in this world she'd married Zack. Of course he didn't help the situation by trying to keep her all to himself.''

"Did he tell you that?"

"In a manner of speaking. This afternoon he and I were working with those two new horses he bought last week. He was in one of his talkative moods, and I listened. Tonight Danielle was just as miserable. She's afraid to trust her instincts. I think it will take a major miracle to get them together."

"And what will it take to get us together, Chalie?" Dane asked the question in a soft, quiet voice she knew very well. It was a careful voice, one he used when he was extremely upset or angry or barely in control. He was tired of being put off, tired of being told that she loved him, but...

She slowly turned her head and stared at him. "What do you mean?" She knew exactly what he meant, but hoped that by pretending ignorance, she could sidetrack him.

"When are we going to set a date for our wedding?"

"Dane, please. You know I need more time."

"Time? Time for what?" he demanded. The reflection of light from the dashboard revealed the hard, glittery gleam in his eyes. "You're beginning to sound like a broken record, Chalie. I don't know about you, but I want more out of life than I'm getting at the moment. I want a wife. I want a home, and I want a family. I want those things with you. I ask you again, time for what?"

The crazy way he was talking bothered Chalie. This wasn't the sweet, patient Dane she'd always known. He'd been so kind to her as she'd gone from doctor to doctor in hopes of finding something that would enable her to have children. How could he change so drastically?

"Time for me to...to accept that I can't have children."

Before she knew what he was about, Dane pulled the car onto the shoulder of the road. He slammed the gear selector into park, then turned to face her. One arm rested on the steering wheel and the other lounged along the top of the seat. "Then let me *help* you accept that fact. You...cannot...have...children! There," he said harshly, "that's all there is to it."

"Dane!" Chalie said his name in a thoroughly shocked voice. What on earth was wrong with him? "Why are you acting this way?"

"Why?" Dane repeated in a raised voice. "I'll tell you why, Chalie. I'm acting this way because I'm tired of waiting. I'm tried of watching you refuse to accept reality. I'm tired of watching you put yourself through endless torment by going from one specialist to the other in hopes one will say what you want to hear. You pity Zack and Danielle. Don't. Either of them has more daring in their little finger than you do in your entire body. At least they're in there fighting it out. While you, you're doing nothing but running around like a little girl, holding your disappointment to your breast, cherishing it, nurturing it."

Chalie's face was deathly pale. She could feel her body trembling with rage. How dare he! How dare he! "I don't think anyone has ever spoken to me in my entire life as you've just done. You can't possibly know what I'm going through. And I can't possibly imagine how I ever thought you to be a caring, considerate person. What you've said is unforgivable."

"I'm glad," Dane said firmly, refusing to back down an inch. "Maybe it will shock you into realizing that you have a lot of things to be thankful for, Chalie. You chose to work with children. You own and operate a very successful kindergarten. What is there in your makeup that refuses to let you see that loving a child is really quite simple? There are so many children out there, just waiting for someone to adopt them. Be thankful that you aren't seriously ill, and let us get on with our life."

"The only thing I'm thankful for at the moment is that I'm beginning to see the real Dane Ewing," Chalie lashed out in a stinging voice. "Loving someone means you're supposed to support that person during their sorrow as well as sharing in their happiness."

"Sharing, yes." Dane nodded. "I agree. As for support, of course that holds true, also. But in your case, how long am I supposed to support you, Chalie? Do you want me to join you in the Order of Sorrow you've established in your mind? Would it make you feel better if I were to wear sackcloth and ashes in support of what I'm sure you consider a curse placed upon your body? But there's something else. What about me? When are you ever going to start thinking that *I* might be hurting a little bit also? Not because you can't have children, but because I'm only just beginning to realize how self-centered you really are."

"That's a horrible thing to say to me."

"But true."

His words cut into her like thin, cold steel, leaving her emotions in ribbons, leaving her bleeding. He couldn't possibly be hurting as she was, could he? Certainly not. She was the one whose body wasn't normal, not his. He was a whole person, she wasn't. "Please, Dane. Take me home."

"And that's all?" He saw the tortured look in her eyes and wanted to reach out and take her into his arms. But if he were to do that, then every word he'd just hurled at her would have been in vain. He had to believe that something he said would eventually get through to her.

"That's all."

"Very well," Dane muttered through clenched teeth. He checked for traffic in the rearview mirror, then made a sharp U-turn. "If you walk away from this, Chalie, it's over between us." He said the words, hoping against hope that she wouldn't get out of the car when he stopped. Hoping against hope that she would come into his arms and tell him that he was right, and that they could be married as soon as possible.

"Is that a threat?" she snapped.

"No. Simply the truth." And another truth, Dane told himself, was that he'd most likely gone too far. But he'd been desperate. For months he'd tried everything in the world to shake her out of the notion that she wasn't a whole woman. Yet no amount of sympathizing or gentleness or loving her had done the trick. And now, apparently harsh words delivered in an insulting fashion served no purpose but to make her incredibly angry with him.

When they reached Rosewynn, Dane turned and watched her, gauging the look in her eyes. He saw her hesitate and for a moment hope was reawakened in his heart. And then he watched as she took a deep breath and opened the car door. She looked him straight in the eye, her chin held at a defiant angle.

"Goodbye, Dane."

Dane felt a knife slice through his heart. "Goodbye, Chalie." He watched her as she made her way up the walk and across the front porch. His hands gripped the steering wheel when he saw her open the door, enter the house, then close the door behind her.

She was gone.

WHILE DANIELLE AND CHALIE were wrapped up in their own personal miseries, in New Orleans, Harvey Graham was working late, trying to gain a step or two on the eternal bête noire of the legal profession, stacked-up caseloads.

He leaned back in his chair, his feet, sans brown loafers, propped comfortably on the corner of his desk as he perused the information his staff had compiled on Elizabeth Harrison and the late Theo Kendricks.

Quite a while elapsed before Harvey felt confident that he'd digested everything. When he was finally satisfied, he reached for the small, square microphone and began dictating a brief reminder to get Danielle Kendricks in the office as quickly as possible.

Zack had wanted him to uncover all he could on Theo Kendricks. If the elder Kendrickses chose to pursue the custody suit they'd threatened Danielle with, Zack wanted enough ammunition to stop them cold. There'd been no ifs, ands or buts about it; Zack had been adamant. Well, Harvey mused as he paused to form his next sentence, in his opinion he'd found the ammunition. And unless the Kendrickses were fatalists, they weren't likely to want their dirty linen aired in public.

FOR SOME STRANGE REASON, after seeing Danielle's picture in the magazine, Elizabeth Harrison had lost a great deal of her original enthusiasm for the cruise.

Her husband, Nathan, noticing how quiet she'd become, had marked it up to her trying to *come down* with something, and insisted that she see the ship's doctor. Elizabeth had done as he asked, and of course the doctor had found nothing wrong.

When the cruise ended, and she'd arrived alone at the apartment in New Orleans, Elizabeth had welcomed the few days of solitude that would be hers. Both her children were in school in Texas, and Nathan was away on business. But she might just as well have had constant visitors for all the good it did her, Elizabeth decided one morning as she sat at the breakfast table, unable to eat.

Instead of solitude, she found her mind taken over with the events of a summer some twenty-eight years ago. Events that would always haunt her in the form of the baby she'd chosen not to keep. A child would have been an inconvenience to her and the modeling career she was determined to have, and especially because the father of that child was the only man she ever really loved.

James Enoch.

He'd been so handsome, Elizabeth remembered, sighing as she looked out over the terrace. So handsome, so young and so poor, with only his struggling career as an engineer to support him. Part of her had wanted to settle for that, but another part told her not to be a fool. Hadn't she watched her mother struggle to raise a family with nothing? Hadn't she vowed never to let that happen to her? James would always be on the move, and she—as his wife and mother to his children—would always be on the move with him. There could be no room in such a relationship for a modeling career.

The career was moving along slowly but steadily when Elizabeth met Nathan. Six weeks later he'd asked her to marry him, and she'd accepted.

Other than the usual trials of raising two children, her life as Nathan's wife had been very comfortable. He wasn't the most exciting lover in the world, Elizabeth thought, but that was of little consequence. The consideration that came with being Mrs. Nathan Harrison meant more to her than sexual gratification.

She rose to her feet then walked over to the French doors leading onto the terrace. Why were James Enoch and their daughter, Danielle, occupying so many of her thoughts lately? Was it the magazine picture? Or was coming across the picture of Danielle and her little girl just the catalyst needed to break open the floodgates of her mind to the past?

DANIELLE WAS HAVING her first cup of coffee well before seven o'clock the morning after her dinner party when she got the telephone call. Excitement quickened in her veins when she heard Harvey Graham tell her that he had information on Theo's case he thought she should hear.

"Is it something that will help with the custody suit?"

"I think so."

"Good. Have Elizabeth and her husband gotten back from their cruise?" she asked. She'd known the day would ultimately arrive, but still . . . she was nervous at the thought of coming face-to-face with the woman who had been on her mind so much lately.

"They're back. My sources tell me Mrs. Harrison will be staying in the apartment here in New Orleans, as is their custom, till after Thanksgiving. Seems the Harri-

sons and some close friends spend Thanksgiving together in the city."

"That means she'll be in New Orleans for several
weeks yet," Danielle said, thinking out loud.

"Correct," Harvey replied. "Can you get in today?"

"Eleven o'clock all right?"

"Fine. See you then."

As soon as she got a dial tone, Danielle called Chalie.

"Of course I'll keep Trish, but are you sure you don't
want me to go with you?" her friend asked.

"Thanks, but I'll be fine."

"All right, but I want to know everything the minute
you get home. By the way, how long did Trish hold out
at Cathleen's?"

"Almost midnight." Danielle chuckled. "Once she
was tucked snug in her bed at home, she became quite
brave again. She said next time would be different."

"Poor baby," Chalie murmured. "She's trying so
hard to be a big girl. Doesn't that break your heart?"

"Yes...and no," Danielle said honestly. "As I watch
her growing and learning new things, I think there's a
natural tendency to want to keep her a baby all her life.
But common sense takes control, thank goodness, and
I find myself making decisions that are best for Trish."

"You make it sound so simple."

"No...not simple," Danielle told her. "Just adapt-
ing to the ever-changing ebb and flow of life, Chalie.
Nothing stays the same, you know."

"Neither do people."

Were they talking about the same thing? "Are you
and Dane arguing?"

"You might say that. We broke up."

"Oh, Chalie," Danielle cried. "Why?"

"Apparently I'm not as adaptable as you are."

"I ... see."

"I'm sorry, Danielle," Chalie said softly. "That was uncalled for."

"No apology necessary. If I remember correctly, I was a little sharp-tongued myself last night. If you need someone to listen, come on over—after I get back from New Orleans. Need me to pick up anything for you while I'm down there?"

"A good-looking man."

"You have that in Dane, honey, even though you're having problems right now."

Later, as she was rushing Trish through getting dressed and fed, Danielle wondered what had transpired after Chalie and Dane left her house. When he was talking to her last night, Dane had made some remark about patience. He and Chalie were made for each other. Yet Chalie couldn't expect the man to wait forever.

When Danielle dropped Trish off at Chalie's kindergarten, she was shocked at her friend's appearance. Charlie looked pale and drawn, as if she hadn't slept.

"I could try to act as if everything is fine and ignore the obvious, but I'm not," Danielle remarked as soon as they were alone. "We've known each other too long for either of us to resort to such polite nonsense. You look awful," she told Chalie.

"Oh? Don't you care for the hag look?"

"No. It doesn't become you. Do yourself a favor and call Dane. Work out whatever it is that's keeping the two of you apart. He loves you, Chalie. I know he does."

"When did you say you'd be back?" Chalie asked, politely ignoring all references to Dane.

Danielle sighed resignedly. "I hope around four or four-thirty."

"Well, don't rush it. If you aren't back when I get ready to go home, I'll take Trish with me. Okay?"

"Sure."

"By the way," Chalie said as Danielle started to walk away. "Are you ignoring the fact that Zack asked me to keep Trish this evening?"

"No, actually. He knows I'm not having dinner with him. I told him I had other plans before he left my house last night."

"Then he obviously wasn't listening," Chalie replied, a wide grin on her face in spite of the heaviness of her heart. "Big brother has been known to do that, you know."

"That's too bad," Danielle murmured. "Thanks, Chalie. I'll be back as planned."

The drive to New Orleans was uneventful, if one ignored the heavy traffic. By the time Danielle got to Harvey Graham's office, she was a nervous wreck.

She opened the door and walked into the reception area then found herself looking straight at Zack, who was in a leaning-sitting position against the front edge of the blond receptionist's desk. His long arms were crossed over his chest, and his gaze was squarely trained on the door.

Today he was wearing a dark suit, white shirt and tie. The executive Zack Carlsley, Danielle thought fleetingly. Had he worn a similar suit for his appointment last night? She wondered what role he'd assumed then.

The dark rose suit added color to her cheeks, Zack decided. Color he wished had been put there because of his lovemaking. With fire in her eyes and her hair loose and slightly windblown, she reminded him of one of the mythical Sirens who lured sailors to their deaths. She was beautiful. She was... He shied away from completing the sentence, but that failure in no way deterred him from beginning the course he'd decided upon at some point during the night.

He had to have her.

He pushed to his feet and walked across the plush carpet toward her. "You're late. I was worried."

His voice was deep and thick and suggestive of remembered caresses. The memories hit her with stunning accuracy.

"My appointment isn't until eleven o'clock," Danielle told him, then somehow managed to glance down at her watch. Finally she had to look back at him. "What are you doing here?"

She was trying desperately to ignore the tremors already attacking her body. *Be strong*. She began a silent litany. *Be strong*. Don't give in to those eyes and that voice and the presence that could start an avalanche of desire without the slightest effort.

She had to start making plans for her future. She had to make plans for Trish's future. She had to remember that.

"Which is in thirty minutes," Zack told her, never taking his eyes off her. "In case you've forgotten, Harvey is my attorney. We had what is so often called a working breakfast, during which he told me that he hoped to get you in today. Let's go help ourselves to a cup of the firm's coffee." He looked at the receptionist and smiled while Danielle watched the poor woman all but melt on the spot. "When your boss wanders in, tell him we'll be in the lounge."

Zack caught Danielle's elbow and hustled her across the room and down the corridor past staff offices. He opened a door to an attractive room with a table and chairs, a sofa and several occasional chairs. The aroma of coffee teased her nose, and there was a box of doughnuts on the counter.

Danielle walked over and dropped her purse on the table. She reached to pull out a chair just as Zack's hand closed over her wrist. He kept a steady pressure on her arm till she was forced to turn and face him.

With moves motivated by a combination of determination and a certain defiance to her withdrawal, Zack slowly folded her into his arms, ignoring the less than pliant feel of her body. That would come, he kept telling himself, that would come. He could tolerate her being angry at him for a while, but he refused to allow her to shut him out of her life and thoughts. It wasn't clear to him exactly when he'd arrived at that conclusion, but he had, and he meant to be a very visible part of her existence from now on.

"Don't be angry with me, Dani," he said huskily. Her body was warm against his. The heady scent of her perfume was invading his senses, leaving him dizzy with wanting her.

His hands framed her face, his thumbs teasing the corners of her mouth, straying to the fullness of her lips. He was watching her, gauging her reaction to his touch, to the fires of desire he knew he was kindling within her.

"Kiss me," he commanded in a rough, hoarse whisper.

Danielle briefly closed her eyes against the raw need she saw in his gaze. She fought desperately to ignore the white-hot core of desire flaring throughout her body... fought the blatant reminder of his arousal riding hard and intimate against her stomach. "No." She forced the word past the pads of his thumbs gently tracing the outline of her lips.

"No?" He repeated the word with humorous disbelief in his voice. "No?" His hands moved from her mouth, one to cup the back of her head, the other to the small of her back. There was the barest hint of a smile on his sensuous mouth as he gave her a kiss that refused to accept anything less than total response.

His tongue ruthlessly scored the tender inside of her lips, then demanded entrance into her mouth to taste the sweetness of that dark and sensual cavity.

Danielle felt her resolve vanishing. She had no defenses against the weapon of Zack's studied seduction. She welcomed his touch, the feel of his body and the scent of him.

Their mouths were fused as one.

Breathing was disregarded. It occurred to Zack that he might be hurting her, but he was unable to correct the situation. He wanted to devour her, to absorb her into his very being. Then and only then would he be satisfied that he wouldn't wake up one morning and find his world an empty shell again.

Slowly, his gaze dulled with desire, Zack raised his head, some small part of him remembering where they were, and what was surely going to happen if he didn't ease back.

Tonight...ah. Tonight there would be no pulling back, he reminded himself as he dropped tiny weightless kisses on Danielle's still-closed eyes, her moist, slightly parted lips. He bent and nuzzled the soft curve of her neck, then watched her for a moment longer. "Snap out of it, honey," he whispered softly.

Danielle opened bemused eyes to the face only inches above hers. She was floating...weightless...and Zack was trying to stop her. Shame on him! But no matter how hard she tried to hold on, the incredibly arousing sensations began to fade. "Killjoy."

Zack's deep chuckle rumbled in his chest, sounding familiar and strangely comforting to her ear. "This is true. But I really don't think you want to shock old Harvey that badly, do you? And even if you do," he teased, his forefinger following the arch of her eyebrow, "I can't let you. What we just shared needs to be continued in a more accommodating setting."

Caution was momentarily thrown to the wind. "Just how accommodating?" she asked huskily. Most likely—no, not most likely, most definitely—she'd hate herself later, but Zack was right. What they'd just shared wasn't something that could be pushed aside and forgotten.

"My apartment."

She remembered the apartment well. They'd stayed there occasionally when they were married. They'd also spent their wedding night there before flying to Acapulco. "I distinctly remember telling you that I would be busy this evening."

"I know."

"That's why you're here now, isn't it?"

"Yes." No evasion...no pretense. Simple and straightforward.

"Why?" she asked curiously, hoping his answer would shed some light on her own lack of understanding of their situation.

"One day at a time, Dani," he said as he stared down at her. "At the moment we don't need speeches about crazy damned things that probably wouldn't mean anything in the long run. I've been empty for six years. That emptiness is beginning to be replaced with something else now. It feels good, and I don't want to analyze it.''

Danielle reached up and placed her palm against his cheek. "Sometimes, Zack, a person has to do a bit of self-analysis, even if she isn't too pleased with herself in the end. I know that's been true in my case. And the really tragic thing is, I never intended to hurt you. We married for all the wrong reasons. Even now I keep thinking we're drawn to each other because we're convenient ... we're familiar to each other. Trish is going through an emotional crisis at the moment because she doesn't have a father, and I feel guilty because I might have helped toward Theo taking his life. So your suggestion of one day at a time is very well taken. I can't even begin to think of making any definite plans for the future till I've sorted out my own personal problems.''

"You say we married for all the wrong reasons," Zack murmured gruffly. "I disagree. I loved you, and in my book that was reason enough."

"I'm so sorry," she whispered, "because I know now that I married you without loving you." She didn't add that her feelings for him had undergone a puzzling change. She wasn't sure she knew what love was.

"Don't be sorry. I appreciate your candor. Let's just concentrate on the future—one day at a time. You have to know by now that I, too, have my doubts to deal with. But we're doing things together now that we didn't do before. And we're even talking out our disagreements, our differences of opinion, as it were. That must count for something. As I said, let's just take our time and let the future surprise us.''

But what kind of a future was it going to be? Danielle wondered just as there was a knock on the door.

Zack stepped back, keeping a hand at her elbow.

The door opened and Harvey Graham stood in the aperture. He paused for a moment, his shrewd gaze taking in slightly mussed blond hair, flushed cheeks and a mouth that hadn't quite recovered from being thoroughly kissed.

"Plan on standing there all day, Harvey?" Zack asked dryly, knowing perfectly well what was going on in his friend's mind.

Harvey, an expert when it came to reading people, grinned and closed the door. "It's a pleasure to see you again, Danielle," he said, nodding at his client. He walked over and sat down at the table, placing two folders before him on the shiny surface. "When you and I set up this appointment, we didn't include Mr. Carlsley. Do you mind him being here, or would you rather he left?"

The dramatic entrance and his remarks had given Danielle a little time to regain her composure. She liked Harvey Graham—she'd liked him even when he represented Zack during their divorce. He and Zack had been friends for years, and trusted each other completely.

"I'm staying." Zack spoke up before Danielle had a chance to open her mouth.

Harvey looked questioningly at Danielle.

She nodded. "He stays."

"Now I wonder why your response doesn't surprise me," Harvey murmured, chuckling softly.

He waved them to chairs, then opened the first of the folders. "The last time you were in, Danielle, we were still waiting for a copy of the report from the FAA." He paused for a moment, then handed her a single sheet of paper. "As far as they can tell, there were no mechanical problems with the plane. Your husband neither radioed for help nor reported any trouble. His last conversation with the tower in Knoxville ended one minute and forty-five seconds before the crash.''

CHAPTER NINE

DANIELLE FELT HER HEART PLUMMET as she listened to Harvey Graham's voice. She'd so hoped that there would be conclusive evidence in the report to show that some mechanical malfunction had caused Theo's death.

She looked at Zack, who was sitting to her left, his dark eyes telling her that he knew what she was thinking...what she was feeling.

He understood. She really wasn't sure why that fact gave her comfort, but it did.

Mechanical failure would have relieved the feeling of guilt dogging her, Danielle reasoned, and, at some much later date in the future, would have been easier for Trish, Danielle concluded. It seemed to her it would be far kinder for Trish to think that Theo had died accidentally, rather than wondering if he'd committed suicide.

"I was hoping—"

"There's more,'' Harvey interrupted her. He, too, was feeling compassion for Danielle. From all he'd learned, the Kendrickses had really run roughshod over their daughter-in-law. For a moment he stared thoughtfully at the file spread out before him. "Were you aware that Theo was embezzling funds from clients?''

Danielle's eyes grew round as saucers as she stared at Harvey. "You're kidding me,'' she finally managed, her astonished gaze swinging from the lawyer to Zack, then back again.

"I'm afraid not," Harvey said.

"But why? How?"

"We've learned—through our own investigative means, and from rumors circulating among lawyer friends in the Memphis area—that Theo was systematically bilking varying amounts of money from certain estates he handled. Scuttlebutt has it...he was also into gambling." He named a financial figure that brought a gasp of dismay from Danielle.

She couldn't believe what she was hearing. Yet the more she thought about it, the more it made sense. She looked at Harvey. "Believe me when I tell you that I'm floored by all this. Yet," she said, frowning, "now that you've pointed it out, certain things are much clearer."

"Such as?" Zack spoke for the first time since Harvey began talking. He was relieved to see some color coming back to Danielle's cheeks, though he knew that was precious little comfort, considering the news she'd just gotten. When he thought of Lenore and Simon Kendricks and what they'd put her through, he wanted to kill them.

"Theo spent an unusual amount of time with his friends, and sometimes they played cards. We argued about it on several occasions. However, nothing I said made the slightest difference. He always went anyway. I honestly never knew to what extent he was involved. They just seemed to enjoy playing cards together."

"That's one of the subtle traps of gambling," Harvey mused. "It all seems so innocent at first. But that's another story. Go on." He nodded to Danielle.

"That's really about all there is to it. Other than Lenore and Simon assuring me that their lawyers would handle everything when Theo died. Now I realize they were really blocking any effort I might have made to take matters into my own hands so they could keep Theo's secret. At that time, though, Trish was having a particularly rough spell, with red throat and ear infections, so I didn't put up too much of an argument. I merely assumed their odd behavior to be an extension of their grief. Lenore was extremely possessive of Theo, and he was their only child."

"They never hinted that anything was wrong?" Harvey questioned.

Danielle shook her head. "Never. Being a legal secretary helped me to know—to a degree—the usual procedure for settling an estate. And every question I asked regarding Theo's practice was met with a legitimate answer. Of course, I had sense enough to check any papers that required my signature. Though there really weren't that many...just the life policy and our banking business. I was able to get rid of the condo easily enough, so there was no problem there."

"What made you decide to move back to Natchez?" Harvey asked.

"Lenore began spending day after day with me, refusing to let Trish out of her sight. The woman was driving my daughter and me out of our minds. She was continuously making some reference to the fact that Trish was all she and Simon had left of Theo, that she was the most important thing in their lives." Danielle paused and took a deep breath. "Their smothering attention was beginning to cause behavioral problems with Trish, and I was ready to pull my hair out."

Harvey rubbed at his chin with one wide hand, nodding as though pleased with what he was hearing. "And when you told them you were coming back to Natchez, that's when the talk of a custody suit began, correct?"

"Correct."

"Perhaps it's time for me to tell you that the chances of them winning their case are slim to nil. You are aware of that fact, aren't you?"

"Certainly. But even though I know they aren't telling the truth, and you know they aren't telling the truth, there will be one or two people out there who will believe them. I resent like hell having to defend myself against something that is a lie. And of course, there's the financial angle. I know they're hoping to deplete my finances to such a degree I'll be forced to return to Memphis. That's really the only reason they're entertaining such an idea."

Harvey smiled, and he reminded Danielle of the Cheshire cat. "I'm sure you're right, and I can't guarantee you that one or two people won't believe them— if the case ever does get to court. If that happens, then you will come out the winner. Trust me."

"The Kendricks name is quite powerful in and around the Memphis area."

"But I seriously doubt they want their only child, their only son's activities to be made public. You see, Danielle," Harvey told her, "your in-laws paid back every cent Theo embezzled. But the fact remains...he did embezzle. They even took care of his gambling debts. Now you tell me—are they the kind of people to want information of that sort circulated about their son?"

"They'd die first."

"My point exactly."

"But . . . but that's blackmail." Danielle looked at Harvey, then turned to Zack. "That's blackmail," she repeated. "Isn't it?"

"Not if the information is used carefully," Zack told her. "Besides, I don't have the slightest qualms about blackmailing your in-laws." He caught her hand gripping the edge of the table, forcing her fingers to interlace with his. "Hear Harvey out, honey, he knows what he's doing."

"If, and when, the Kendricks make good their threat of a custody suit, we'll be happy to let their lawyers know they can get ready for a real fight. And of course it will be my responsibility, as your legal counsel, to go to great lengths to show how they harassed you . . . how they threatened you . . . how they, by paying enormous sums of money to keep their son's name from being dragged through the mud, would be questionable as really responsible adults to raise a four-year-old."

"What you're implying," Danielle said slowly, "is that once *they* know what *we* know, you think they will give up."

"I couldn't have put it better." Harvey grinned. "Now, promise me you'll try to put this out of your mind. I can't tell you they won't file suit. From what I've learned about the people, they probably will. But . . . we will prevail." He closed the file, then opened the other folder. He looked at Zack and Danielle. "Ready to talk about Elizabeth Harrison?"

"Yes," Danielle said, casting Zack a nervous smile. "We're going from one extreme to another, aren't we?"

"Looks that way, honey," Zack replied, grinning. "But the only thing I want is for you to remember that Harvey is the expert here. Follow his advice, no matter what he tells you."

"What Zack is really saying," Harvey was quick to add, "is that he would be just as happy if I advised you to drop the idea of contacting Elizabeth. But since I represent you, and since we've already discussed the situation, we'll remind Zack that it really isn't any of his business."

There was a wicked grin on Harvey's face as he regarded his friend of many years. Zack's answering scowl brought a soft chuckle from Danielle.

"You sound like Ann Landers instead of a lawyer," Zack said coolly.

"Please." Danielle held out one hand. "I appreciate your concern, but I would really like to hear what has been learned about Elizabeth."

"Mrs. Harrison," Harvey began, ignoring Zack's less than friendly glare. "As I told you this morning, Elizabeth Harrison is now at her apartment." He named a location only a few blocks from Zack's place. "And if everything goes as is the custom, the family will spend Thanksgiving with friends here in New Orleans. Afterward, the Harrisons will return to Houston, while visiting the Crescent City frequently. I also have a schedule—we think it's fairly accurate—of her comings and goings, along with her telephone number, which is unlisted."

"Do you think I should call her first or pretend to bump into her or simply go to her apartment and tell her who I am?" Danielle asked. She was so nervous, she was honestly beginning to feel light-headed.

Harvey was quiet for a moment. Finally he looked at Danielle. "I think I'll have to answer that with a question. If you were in the same situation—I mean, in Elizabeth's shoes—how would you want a daughter, one you hadn't seen since she was an infant, to present herself to you?''

"I thought it would be best to call her first," Danielle told him. "No matter what I do or how I do it, it's going to be a shock to her."

"True." Harvey nodded. "On the other hand, I can't help but think that most women who give up babies for adoption must subconsciously prepare themselves—at some point in their lives—for just such a thing that's about to happen to Elizabeth Harrison."

Approximately an hour and a half later, a still-rattled Danielle was seated at the table in Zack's apartment. He saw her hand tremble as she raised the fork to her mouth. The emotional strain she was under was getting her down, and Zack didn't like that. He didn't remember that he was very fond of Elizabeth those few times he saw her that summer years ago, and thanks to the stress Danielle was under, he still didn't like the damned woman.

"That's only your third bite in almost five minutes," he reminded her gruffly.

Zack had taken Danielle to his apartment so that she would have some privacy when she made her first telephone call to Elizabeth. But instead of calming down, she was becoming more nervous by the second. Any moment she chose, she could dial the number Harvey had given her and hear her mother's voice...her honest-to-God mother's voice.

"Are you keeping count?" she asked, smiling at him in spite of feeling as strung out and taut as a violin string. Would Elizabeth be happy to hear from her? What would she do, Danielle wondered, if Elizabeth hung up on her? Would she go around to her apartment? What if she never got a chance to see the woman who'd given birth to her? What if . . . ?

Stop it! the little voice inside her head yelled in protest.

Danielle briefly closed her eyes, then tried to think of more pleasant things than the possibility of her unknown mother failing to acknowledge her.

"I certainly am. Although you're built on rather smallish lines, you do require a bit more food than a bird." Zack was becoming more concerned by the minute with her emotional state. The pulse in her throat was beating rapidly, and she was as pale as a ghost. He still wasn't convinced she was doing the right thing. But his hands were tied. Danielle was her own woman, and she was determined to find her birth mother.

"Your tactfulness never fails to amaze me," Danielle remarked with a perfectly straight face, although her eyes were brimming with amusement. She'd needed him today, and he'd been there. Even when she thought she'd outsmarted him, he'd calmly planted himself in Harvey's office and waited.

Zack sat back in his chair, his dark head tilted slightly to one side as he regarded her from beneath stern black brows. Never having been in her particular position, he really had no idea what she was feeling, but he sympathized with her. "I'll be tactful another time. At the moment, I'm more concerned with keeping you healthy. You've been under a hell of a lot of strain lately. And from where I stand, I can't see it getting better any time soon. Meeting Elizabeth is going to make things ten times worse."

His honesty tugged at Danielle's heart, that and his concern for her welfare. Dear sweet heaven. They were poles apart in so many areas, yet closer than most married couples in other ways. He watched over her and Trish like a broody hen with two errant chicks. But even though she was not at her best emotionally, Danielle was wise enough to realize that, at some point, their relationship must progress to a point where obligation and guilt and convenience took a back seat and allowed two people the space to make a normal decision.

Would they ever find that normal, happy medium or would they, one day soon, be forced to call a halt to a situation that was fast getting out of hand awareness-wise, but one without a future otherwise?

"I know you are, Zack. Thank you. As for meeting Elizabeth—my mind boggles at the thought." She took a sip of iced tea, the cool liquid like velvet against her dry throat. Her mouth was dry. Even her lips were dry. She was beginning to feel like a darned desert. "I simply couldn't put down that diary and forget what I read. I had to do it, you know—or at least try."

"No, I don't know," Zack said thoughtfully. "At the risk of sounding trite, I've never been in your particular situation. All I know is that I don't envy you. And yet, I have to admit I'm somewhat in awe of your courage. I'm also afraid for you."

"So am I," Danielle admitted, "afraid, that is. But getting to know Elizabeth became an obsession with me the moment I read what Claire had written." She touched her napkins to her mouth, then reached into the pocket of her suit jacket for the small piece of paper with a telephone number scrawled across it in Harvey's dreadful handwriting. "This telephone number is my link to a woman I never knew existed until a few weeks ago, but, I hope, a woman who will play a very important part in my future."

Zack felt a stab of jealousy hit him. He didn't want Elizabeth Harrison coming into Danielle's life and monopolizing her time. He needed time to be alone with Danielle...time they needed to get to know each other, something—he was beginning to realize—they'd not done before. And from what he remembered of Elizabeth, she was a very demanding woman.

"Be sure, honey," Zack said quietly. "Once it's done, there can be no turning back. It truly is a case of opening Pandora's box."

Danielle slowly shook her head as she smiled across the small table at him. "Stop being such a worrywart, Zack. Do you honestly think I haven't thought about how difficult this is going to be? I mean—" she gestured with her hands, palms up "—I haven't the faintest idea what to say."

"Just say what's in your heart," Zack told her. What he didn't say was that he was afraid her heart was going to be broken before Elizabeth got through with her.

"But I don't know what's in my heart," Danielle admitted with a wry grin. "I don't want to be blunt to the point of cruelty, nor do I want to try to be so subtle as to make an ass out of myself."

"How about starting off with telling her who you are. Let her take it from there," Zack suggested.

"You make me sound like a total idiot."

"Not at all, honey. Merely a person with a very huge problem."

"Are you sure?"

"Positive."

"I'm glad you're with me...rather, I'm glad I'm here at your..." She shook her head. "Ignore me. I don't know what I mean."

Zack leaned forward and grasped her hand. He coaxed the slender fingers open, his stronger ones hovering protectively. He looked at how they intertwined. Her hand, so slender and fragile, his wide and strong. That's the way he felt about her, he thought fleetingly. He was afraid for her. He wanted to protect her.

"Don't worry," he said huskily. "I know what you mean. Why don't you quit torturing yourself and go ahead and make that call?"

"Now?" Danielle said sharply, panic edging her voice.

"Is there a particular time of day that you think will be better?"

"No."

"Well?"

"I suppose now is as good a time as any." She started to get up, but Zack stopped her.

"Stay where you are." He waved her back into her seat. "I'll bring the phone to you. I'll even give you some privacy. There are a couple of errands I need to run. Will an hour be long enough?"

"No!"

Zack watched her for a moment, trying to gauge the fear he saw in her eyes. Panic was more accurate. "Okay, okay," he murmured soothingly. "I'll stay."

Danielle sat like a statue while Zack left the room, then returned with an ivory-colored phone. He placed it on the table before her. "Want me to dial for you?"

She shook her head. "No. I'll do it."

Stiff fingers flexed, hoping to loosen taut muscles. For a moment she couldn't even focus her eyes. Breath rushed in and out of her lungs, as if she were a long-distance runner.

Danielle punched in the numbers, then slumped back in the chair. There was such a roaring in her ears, she wasn't even sure she could hear her, should Elizabeth happen to answer.

"Harrison residence."

Dear Lord! She'd actually gotten through.

Don't be such a sap, she berated herself. Harvey wouldn't have handed out a bogus telephone number.

"Mrs. Harrison, please."

There! She'd actually done it. Now she was waiting to speak with her mother. Goose pimples scampered over her skin in an icy rush, and she wasn't sure she was going to be able to say a single intelligent word to Elizabeth.

"Whom shall I say is calling?"

"Mrs. Kendricks," Danielle replied in a cool, firm voice. A grinning Zack gave her the thumbs-up sign as he resumed his seat. She might sound in control, Danielle thought, but she was far from feeling that way.

"Just a minute, please."

There was a long pause. Finally Danielle heard a faint rustle as the receiver was picked up. "Hello?" The voice was cool, distant. For one wild and incredible moment, Danielle was tempted to hang up. What was she supposed to say? How was she supposed to act?

"Mrs. Ha-Harrison?"

"Yes?"

"My name is . . . Danielle Kendricks."

"How may I help you, Ms Kendricks?"

You're my mother, Danielle wanted to yell into the receiver. I want to see you. I want to touch you. I want to sit and just look at you. "Mrs. Harrison," she said instead, "I don't know any other way of saying this, other than coming right out with it. I was adopted as an infant by Tony and Claire Lorman.''

A long silence settled over the telephone line connecting the two women. One, young and vulnerable and wanting desperately to be accepted by the other, sat pressing the receiver to her ear, waiting with such open longing in her face that the rugged individual seated across from her felt a knot forming in his throat.

In the master bedroom suite of a plush apartment six blocks away, a tall, slim blonde sat at a French provincial desk. She was known in her circle of friends as being always in control. The unflappable Elizabeth, they called her. But the words that spilled out of the receiver sent fear spreading throughout her body. At that precise moment she was anything but unflappable. She was in total shock!

For years she'd worried that one day she would come face-to-face with her past. Face-to-face with questions she didn't want to answer. Answers that, no matter how she said them, would show her up as being uncaring. Well, now it had happened, and she was stunned.

Her spine was ramrod straight, her body icy cold as she struggled for control.

"What...what do you want...Danielle?" The name sounded stiff on her lips. Oh, God! This couldn't be happening to her after all these years. But it was, Elizabeth told herself as she tried to deal with the numbness flooding her.

"I'd like to meet you," Danielle said before she lost her nerve. Her throat felt like it was about to close. If she was this nervous talking to Elizabeth on the telephone, how on earth would she act when she met her in person? "Could we have lunch or dinner one day soon?"

"Yes . . . yes. Yes, I think we should. About Tony—is he aware that you're getting in touch with me?"

"I lost my father four years ago."

"I'm sorry," Elizabeth murmured, her mind whirling with shock. "Why don't we have lunch together tomorrow? How about Visko's in the Brewery? About eleven-thirty?"

"Sounds great. I'll be there." Danielle started to say something else, but the line went dead. She slowly replaced the receiver, her blue eyes meeting Zack's.

"Well?" he prompted.

"Give me a little while to get used to it," she whispered shakily, her hands going to her face, her fingers pressing against her warm cheeks.

"Was her response what you expected?"

"She sounded surprised. I suppose stunned is more like it."

"That's certainly understandable." Zack nodded. "She does have another life, you know."

Suddenly Danielle found his negative attitude more than she could handle. The entire world was closing in on her—tomorrow she would be facing Elizabeth for the first time, and all he could do was remind her of the dark side of the problem. "Will you stop it?" she practically yelled at him as she bounded to her feet.

The outburst was unexpected—by both of them. They stared at each other for what seemed like an eternity, but was actually no more than a minute or two. The silence in the room was deafening.

"I'm sorry," Danielle finally whispered, amazed to find herself leaning forward over the table, her body supported by her hands gripping the edge. "I don't know what came over me."

With the flick of a wrist, Zack dismissed her apology. "Forget it." But he knew what had come over her. Elizabeth Harrison.

"I can't forget it," she murmured. "You've been like a rock through all this, yet here I am yelling at you like a shrew." Tears gathered in her eyes, spilling over onto her pale cheeks. "How can I possibly make you understand? How can I get through to you that what I'm feeling right . . . right at this very moment is unbelievable. I'm happy. I'm sad. I'm terrified. Can you possibly imagine what it feels like to know that in a few hours you're going to meet your mother for the first time?"

"I don't have to understand, Danielle," Zack said gruffly. He ran one large hand over his face, then curled it into a fist that came to rest on the table. It was a gesture Danielle knew from old that showed how uptight he really was. "If I seem to come on like the voice of doom, then it's because I want you to be careful. You can be hurt."

"I know that," she said shakily. "But it's a chance I have to take. I also have to think of Elizabeth. When I was talking with her just now, I could tell she was just as unnerved as I was. Neither of us knew what to say. But I think agreeing to see me tomorrow is an excellent sign. Don't you think so?"

Zack nodded, a gentle smile softening the rugged features of his face. "Sure, honey. And tomorrow you'll look back on all this anxiety and worry, and wonder why it ever happened." *And pigs will fly!* he thought derisively. Nothing in the world would ever convince him that Elizabeth Harrison was about to welcome an illegitimate daughter into her life. But how could he say so to Danielle?

"Thank you, Zack." Danielle smiled gratefully. "You've been such a help. Perhaps after tomorrow you and Elizabeth and I can go to dinner or something. Maybe then you wouldn't be so antagonistic toward her."

"What do you mean after tomorrow?" He frowned, ignoring the invitation to get to know Elizabeth better. Frankly, he knew all he wanted to know about Elizabeth Harrison. He got to his feet and walked around to where Danielle was standing. There was gentleness in his arms as they slipped around her, his fingers lacing against her back at the waist. That move brought her hips to press intimately against his. The way his body responded to hers still amazed him. The hold she wielded over his emotions was incredible. "I'd like to be with you tomorrow when you meet Elizabeth."

"But that's not possible," Danielle told him. She saw the inflexible set of his chin...saw the curious glitter of rebellion gather in his dark eyes. It had practically become his permanent expression during their marriage. "Please, Zack," she murmured. "This is something I have to do on my own. Something I *will* do on my own."

"You're no match for Elizabeth Harrison," Zack said harshly, his resolve not to be critical of the woman gone. From listening to Birdie, and the bits and pieces he remembered from that summer when Elizabeth was in Natchez, he was of the opinion she was a pro when it came to using people and always managing to land on her feet.

"Zack!" Danielle stared sternly at him. She even tried to wiggle out of his arms, but found he wasn't about to let her go. "What on earth did Elizabeth ever do to you?"

Pulling on every ounce of self-control within his reach, Zack gave a brief, tight shake of his dark head. "You're right. I'm sorry." He looked down into her eyes, seeing the same Danielle he'd sworn to love till he died—the same one he'd swore to hate till death as well. She fit into his arms the same as always. She even smelled the same...like wildflowers on a lazy spring afternoon.

Yet no matter how hard he tried to convince himself that the woman in his arms was the same uncaring person he'd once known, he was beginning to think differently.

Inwardly she seemed to have changed. Gone was the immature, pleasure-seeking woman who was mainly concerned with her own comfort. In her place was a warm, loving woman. A woman who gave every appearance of trying to meet her responsibilities in life head-on. And though he was totally against this latest venture, he had to admire her courage.

"I have a suggestion," he said, breaking the tense silence, damning Elizabeth Harrison to hell and back for destroying this time he'd looked forward to spending with Danielle. These days he was anxious to be alone with her. In many ways it was as though they'd only just met when she took up residence at Oaklaine. Maybe he was playing a silly game—a fool's game. But even if he was, the game was helping him come to grips with the wealth of bitterness that had been festering in his heart for too many years, and Zack welcomed the release.

"What?"

"Though it goes against everything I believe in—" he ruefully sighed "—why don't we scratch the plans I'd made for this evening. You like antiques, so why don't we spend the afternoon browsing through the shops on

Magazine Street. Afterward, we'll have an early dinner, then I'll drive you home. I have several appointments in the morning, so it'll be no problem for you to come back to New Orleans with me tomorrow.''

"But what about my car?'' The idea was tempting, Danielle thought. As nervous as she was about talking with Elizabeth and the prospect of meeting her tomorrow, she didn't relish making the trip home and then driving back by herself the next morning.

"It can stay right where it is in the garage. I keep four spaces.'' He tapped the tip of her nose with one long forefinger. "You won't be robbing anyone of a parking place, so don't start worrying about that. Sound okay?''

"What if I said no?'' Danielle teased. What he'd just suggested sounded perfect. She was deeply touched by his caring. And though they both knew the fires they'd started back in Harvey Graham's office would have to be put out at some point in the near future, she was deeply touched by Zack's offer. Besides, a tiny voice whispered inside her, making love with Zack at this point in her life held its own complexities.

They were both searching, sifting through the ashes of a burned-out relationship in hopes of finding direction for their future, and a purpose for the invisible ties still binding them. On the surface they seemed to be getting along beautifully. But in her heart, Danielle knew that they were both scared—afraid to trust their own judgments in affairs of the heart.

Zack regarded her through half-closed lids, feeling the electric silence surrounding them. "Don't tease, honey,'' he murmured huskily. "I'm trying to be strong, but I'm afraid I'm putty in your hands.''

His mouth touched hers, their lips sensitive to the merest touch, their tongues hot and moist as they curled around each other.

"Not quite all of you is putty, Zack," Danielle whispered into his mouth as the hard thrust of his desire pressed against her stomach. "Not quite all."

Several hours later, after Danielle found a lovely cherry muffin stand, which Zack gladly paid for, and after they'd gorged themselves on raw oysters and dark, thick gumbo and French bread, they headed back to Natchez.

When Zack stopped the car in the drive at Oaklaine, he turned to Danielle. Her face was in shadow. He heard her sigh, and knew she must be tired.

"It's been a long day, hasn't it?"

"Yes, but one of the most exciting I've ever lived through," she readily admitted. "The only black cloud on the horizon is wondering what tomorrow's meeting with Elizabeth will bring."

"It'll bring you happiness." Zack spoke reassuringly. But he, too, was worried about the meeting, which he was powerless to stop. He had no choice but to sit by and wait for fate to take its course.

CHAPTER TEN

"I CAN'T BELIEVE YOU'RE back home so early," Chalie said to Zack, a slow grin curving her lips. "You are supposed to be in New Orleans. I do hope you know that you've spoiled Trish's and my evening. We'd planned on staying up all night. I'm disappointed."

"Ha!" Zack hooted. "From what Danielle told me, Trish and Susie tried to do that last night." His dark gaze followed Danielle's retreating figure till she disappeared into Trish's bedroom, then swung back to his sister. "What are you looking so smug about?"

"Isn't it obvious?" she asked. "Feeling flows between you and Dani like crazy. Yet each of you denies it to high heaven. I'm beginning to think you're both idiots. And those denials certainly can't be because of Trish. I've seen the way you are with her. You love her, and she adores you."

Zack walked slowly over to the fireplace and propped one elbow on the mantel. His hand was resting on his hip and there was a thoughtful expression on his face. "I suppose you could say Danielle and I are . . . overly cautious, squirt." He gave her a measured look, unconsciously reverting to his pet name for her. "We were experts at making each other miserable during our marriage. Neither of us wants to go through that again. I agree with you that there's feeling between us, but we both know *feeling* isn't enough. And who's to say we wouldn't have the same kind of marriage we did the first time? As for Trish . . .'' He shook his head. "Trish isn't the problem, believe me. How could I not love her? But what kind of a father would I make for her?'' he asked. ''The simple act of loving a child or a baby is easy, unless one doesn't like children to begin with. But becoming a parent to a ready-made family is an awesome responsibility.'' He shrugged. ''However, since Danielle and I aren't discussing marriage, I really do think this conversation is pointless. How's Dane these days?''

The question was a low blow, and Zack knew it. But he was willing to do just about anything to jolt Chalie. Besides, he'd felt just the tiniest bit out of sorts with her for forcing him to voice his thoughts on fatherhood and the ambiguous feelings between himself and Danielle. Certainly he'd wondered what it would be like to have Trish for a daughter, just as he'd fantasized about Danielle as his wife again. But he was sensible enough to realize that fantasies were, more often than not, just that . . . fantasies. Something to be lived and nurtured only in a person's mind.

''Cheap shot, brother dear,'' Chalie told him sternly. ''You know quite well Dane and I aren't seeing each other anymore.''

''I also know you aren't seeing each other because that's the way you want it. How long are you going to hide, Chalie?''

''Is that what you call what I'm doing? Hiding?'' she remarked, sneering. ''Exactly when did you become the great mystic? Don't you care that Dane said some really insulting things to me? And just for the record, Zack sweetie, is it by choice that you watch Danielle with pure raw hunger showing in your eyes? Is it by choice that neither of you seems the slightest bit interested in going out with other people? Haven't you ever wondered why?''

"That's none of your damned business—''

"Hey.'' Danielle's voice cut into the argument, effectively silencing the two combatants. She slowly walked over to where they were standing before the fireplace, glaring at each other with looks that could kill. "I won't pretend I don't know what was being said. I heard practically every word. And, I might add, so did anyone else in the area who happened to be listening. Don't you think you're being pretty hard on each other? I mean . . . right now, we're all, Dane included—'' here she gave Chalie a challenging look "—we're going through a trying time. Even if we can't agree in principle, the least we can do is not attack each other.''

Brother and sister looked rather sheepish, both ashamed of the swipes they'd taken at each other. Without saying a word, Zack reached out and locked an arm around Chalie's neck and pulled her up against him. He planted a comically loud, smacking kiss on her forehead, then released her. "I'm sorry, squirt. Forgive me?''

"Sure,'' Chalie said, shrugging as she smiled up at him.

"I've got to make some calls,'' Zack told them, stepping back. "Chalie, do you want to ride back to Rosewynn with me?''

"I don't think so. Danielle has to fill me in on every word Elizabeth said.''

"But it's almost midnight,'' he reminded her.

"I know,'' she replied. "But she still has to fill me in on the details.''

"And you defended her?" Zack asked, looking at Danielle with dark brows arched. "See what you've let yourself in for?"

"No problem." Danielle laughed. "When I get tired, I'll simply tell her to go home. This comes from being friends since the cradle. Besides, considering the way I'm feeling right now, I seriously doubt I'll be doing much sleeping tonight."

"Probably not, but you should at least try," Zack said, frowning. "You shouldn't be forced to spend the rest of the night answering questions put to you by your nosy friend." He caught her hand in his warm, slightly callused grasp. "Walk me to the car," he murmured.

"Walk me to the car," Chalie mimicked, sticking out her tongue at her brother. "If you're so concerned with Dani's rest, why not say good-night at the door?" she asked innocently, unable to hide the mischief in her eyes.

"Because we want to get away from your prying eyes," he told her bluntly, pulling Danielle along behind him.

"What time do you want to get started in the morning?" Danielle asked as they walked across the front gallery and down the wide cypress steps where generations of Lormans had walked.

"Between six-thirty and seven. Is that too early for you?"

"No." Danielle shook her head. "Sound's fine. I'll probably be ready way before that."

"I'm sure you will," Zack murmured, smiling down at her. She was so vulnerable where Elizabeth was concerned it almost tore out his heart. Some sixth sense warned him that she was going to be terribly hurt, but he couldn't get her to listen. "Why don't you take something to make you sleep? Excitement is one thing, but at this point, you're running on nothing but raw nerves.''

"Quit worrying, Zack," Danielle told him. She stopped at the wrought-iron fence, then looked up at him, a look of amusement in her eyes. "I'm twenty-seven, not seven. I know you think getting to know Elizabeth isn't the wisest thing I've ever done. And you may be right. But I have to find that out for myself, don't I?"

"I suppose so," he said wearily, exhaling roughly. "There are moments—brief ones, mind you—when I'm not so sure I approve of this cool, confident Danielle I'm constantly seeing."

"Then I'm afraid you're going to have to make adjustments in your thinking, Zachary," she told him, "because she's here to stay."

"Oh?"

"Yes."

"Then I suggest you take a dose of your same medicine," he said decisively. "You can be as independent as you like, but it doesn't keep me from worrying." He caught both hands in his, suddenly feeling like a young boy again. He realized then that having him concerned with her welfare really was something she was going to have to become accustomed to. He'd been doing it too long to think of changing now.

But why? his conscience asked. To which Zack quickly responded that it was because Danielle was Birdie's godchild...because, as her ex-husband, he felt a certain obligation to see that she was protected. But even as he was trying to convince himself of those two really miserable reasons, his heart was telling him something else.

Zack pulled back, not sure...not brave enough to face the truth, only to have Danielle put the word in the form of a question, a question Zack was dreading. "Why?"

"Because I am a special friend of Trish's, and it's my obligation to look after her mother," he said gruffly, his choice of words as evasive as the fear deep in his heart.

Danielle pulled a hand loose from his, then reached up and touched his face. "You're really a very gentle man, Zack Carlsley," she told him. "Why do you go to such great lengths to hide it?"

He leaned down then, and captured her mouth with his. The kiss was deep and stirring, transmitting their desire for each other, yet lending a certain emotional comfort separate from the sexual aspect of their relationship.

Zack raised his head, the high-riding moon throwing one side of his face into rough relief; the other side was a dark shadow. There was a glow in his eyes, and he seemed happier than she'd seen him since her return to Natchez.

"You're smiling," she murmured, as if that fact alone was something of a miracle. "Why?"

"All in good time, honey," Zack said roughly. "All in good time." He squeezed her hands. "Sleep well," he whispered, then turned and walked to his car.

Danielle slowly walked back to the house, the moonlight lending a special brilliance to the house and grounds. She loved the crisp nip in the air, the falling of the leaves. Danielle hugged her arms around her upper body and closed her eyes for a brief moment. It was her favorite season. But even the season couldn't make everything right.

She thought back to Harvey's news. She'd so hoped to learn that Theo's plane had developed mechanical trouble . . . but it hadn't.

"And I'll never know for sure, will I?" she murmured.

There would always be a small fragment of guilt tucked away in the back of her mind. But whatever the reason behind the crash, she reasoned, now she no longer felt totally responsible for his death just because she'd asked for a divorce. If there'd been the slightest chance of it being found out that he was embezzling funds from clients, Theo would have panicked. Even the gambling debt could have pushed him over the edge.

She reached up and brushed back a wisp of hair that had fallen over her forehead as she retraced her steps over the brick walkway. Unfortunately, Danielle thought sadly, there'd been no way to help Theo. He'd been lost in a world of utter helplessness long before she had come into his life.

Before mounting the steps, she bent and broke off a yellow mum from the mass of color in the two beds flanking the entrance, then looked up at the moon. In her heart, she wanted to remember the laughing Theo she'd first met, not the shell of a man he later became. In a sense, because he was weak, Theo was sacrificed. It was tragic, she thought sadly, but it was the way of the world, and in his case so very true.

"Goodbye, Theo," she whispered, then turned and went inside.

Chalie wanted to know every word, sigh and breath that had passed between Elizabeth and Danielle.

"What do you think?" she finally asked, after she'd heard the entire story twice.

"What do you mean?"

"Her voice...you can tell a lot about a person by the sound of the voice. At least I think I can," Chalie told her. "Did she sound warm—friendly?"

"She sounded frightened, stiff," Danielle said and nodded thoughtfully. "I'd say her tone was a mixture of absolute astonishment and a kind of fear."

"And she recognized your name right off, hmm?"

"I don't think so. When I said I was Danielle Kendricks, I thought there was a slight reaction, but I can't be sure. And then of course, when I mentioned the Lormans, she knew. At any rate, I'm so nervous about finally meeting her tomorrow, I'm honestly feeling sick to my stomach. Zack suggested I take something to make me sleep, but I don't think I will. Even the anticipation is unlike anything I've ever known, Chalie."

"What does Zack think about tomorrow?" Chalie asked curiously.

"At first he was furious when I told him I wanted to meet Elizabeth alone. But he finally came around. He's really been a rock through all this. By the way, Harvey had some rather interesting, but sad, information about Theo's death."

She related the story to Chalie, gaining a certain sense of release as she talked.

"I'm sorry there was no evidence that the plane malfunctioned," Chalie said quietly.

"So was I," Danielle admitted. "But I think I've finally come to grips with that situation. Oh," she said, then shrugged and gestured with her hands, "there'll always be that niggling little doubt, but after learning what Harvey found out, a divorce was the least of Theo's worries."

"Of course," Chalie reminded her, "no one knows what Lenore will do."

"This is true. But one of the nice things about the situation now is that I no longer fear her. At least I've grown beyond that point."

"You've grown in more ways than just that one, Danielle. As I watch and listen to you, I find myself wondering when and how you became so smart."

Danielle couldn't help but smile. "You make me sound like some kind of unknown quantity under a microscope."

"Not at all," Chalie pointed out. "You're a very self-assured lady now. If you weren't like a sister to me, I'd be green with envy at the way you handle the problems that crop up in your life."

"Believe me, Chalie, I didn't become self-assured overnight," Danielle said, thinking of the irony of her own words.

"NERVOUS?" ZACK ASKED the next morning, looking over at her and smiling as the miles fell away, taking them closer and closer to New Orleans and Elizabeth.

"Petrified," Danielle replied in a breathless voice. "I keep thinking, what if we don't get together? What if each of us were to sit at a table waiting hours for the other one to show up? You see things like that happening on comedy shows, but what if it happened to me in real life?"

Zack chuckled, knowing clear thinking wasn't her strong suit at the moment. "I'm sure whoever gets there first will tell the hostess that they're expecting the other one."

"Oh," Danielle said slowly as if his suggestion carried overtones of brilliance rather than common sense.

"Don't be so hard on yourself, honey," Zack told her. He dropped a heavy, warm hand on her thigh.

"Just think what a lucky person Elizabeth is to be meeting you. You're a fantastic individual. She can't be anything but pleased."

"I wonder," Danielle murmured, chewing pensively at her bottom lip, his compliments passing completely over her head. "Now that I've actually made the first move toward getting to know her, I'm beginning to think of a hundred different reasons I shouldn't have."

"That's nerves talking," Zack offered reassuringly, though he would have liked nothing better than to have turned the car around and taken her back to Natchez. "You'll be singing a different tune this afternoon."

Danielle turned in her seat and stared at him. "Do you really think so, Zack?"

"Of course I do," he said, smiling at her. He was lying with a perfectly straight face. In his opinion, Elizabeth had cut the conversation mighty close yesterday. He hoped such brevity wasn't an indication of the way the relationship would continue.

For the remainder of the trip, Zack kept a steady conversation going, entertaining Danielle with amusing stories related to his work and the different parts of the world he'd been to.

Danielle knew what he was trying to do, and she was grateful. She even responded when he asked her a direct question and tried to take part in the conversation, but she was terribly afraid that talking to her just now was about as interesting as talking to a post. Which was rather unusual, because she found her senses incredibly alert—even if her mind had gone on vacation. The sun seemed brighter, the air crisper, the color of the leaves on the trees sharper. She glanced at Zack. He was even sexier—more appealing, if such a thing was possible.

Once they reached New Orleans, Zack drove straight to the outrageously expensive complex where his apartment was located, and the underground garage where Danielle had left her car.

"You know I don't like this, don't you?" he said, gruffly.

"Yes, I know," Danielle softly replied. "But I'll be fine, I promise. If the slightest thing goes wrong, I'll phone your office or Harvey's."

Under his disapproving eye, Danielle made the switch from the Mercedes to her Datsun as quickly as possible. In his own way, and for different reasons, Zack was just as uptight as she was, and she didn't want to argue with him. He'd been too kind to take a chance on there being sharp words between them.

As she began weaving her way in and out of the heavy traffic, she couldn't help but grin at the look of frustration on his face when he'd kissed her goodbye. Being told no was something Zack was unaccustomed to.

AN HOUR BEFORE IT WAS TIME to meet Danielle, Elizabeth was nervously pacing around the living room of the Harrison apartment. She'd been up and dressed for what seemed like hours and hours, and had consumed gallons of coffee.

"Is there anything I can get for you, Mrs. Harrison?" Martha Cooly, the housekeeper, asked.

"No, thank you, Martha. I'll be leaving shortly, so if there are any calls, just tell them I'll get back to them later this afternoon."

The housekeeper nodded, then went about her business.

Elizabeth resumed her pacing, thinking of nothing but the voice she'd heard on the telephone yesterday.

Danielle.

She remembered the picture in the magazine she'd stumbled across while on the cruise. At the time, she'd known in her heart that it was too much of a coincidence for a young woman named Danielle to be mistress of Oaklaine, and not be the former Danielle Lorman.

But the last name had thrown her, Elizabeth thought, and frowned. She assumed Danielle would have taken back her maiden name when she and Zachary Carlsley divorced. How did the name Kendricks fit in? And how did the child fit in? She gave a confused shake of her blond head. Why waste so much energy on idle conjecture, when in less than an hour she'd know the answers?

Less than an hour.

The phrase kept repeating itself in her mind. In less than an hour she'd come face to face with the child she'd given up. Was there really any way she could make Danielle understand the reason she'd been adopted by Tony and Claire? Would she think it selfish when she learned a career had been the first consideration in Elizabeth's life?

With anxiety running rampant, Elizabeth picked up her purse and walked toward the front door.

IN ONE WAY, ELEVEN-THIRTY came much faster than Danielle wanted it to. In another, she thought it would never arrive. She took the elevator to the fourth floor, where Visko's was located, her hands trembling, her palms damp.

As she walked toward the smiling hostess, Danielle wondered if the woman could see how dreadfully nervous she was. Frankly, she felt as if the entire world had focused its attention on her and the meeting with Elizabeth.

"Hello. Table for one?" the attractive brunette asked.

"Er...no. I'm supposed to be meeting someone. Mrs. Harrison. Has she arrived yet?"

"As a matter of fact, she has. Just a few minutes ago," the smiling hostess told her. "This way please."

Danielle followed, her body numb, her eyes glued to the back of the woman in front of her. She was terrified of looking to her right or to her left, afraid she would look straight into Elizabeth's eyes.

Even more doubts began to assail her.

Was her pink dress okay? Zack told her yesterday that she looked good in pink. Would Elizabeth think so?

"Here you are." The hostess stopped as she turned and indicated a small table. It was in front of one of the numerous windows overlooking the River Promenade. Beyond the promenade was the river itself, ambling its way past the crescent curve toward the Gulf of Mexico.

"Thank you," Danielle murmured, her lips moving mechanically.

The hostess walked away.

Danielle suffered the ultimate humiliation of having the corners of her mouth begin to twitch, as though she were the victim of some mysterious tic.

She tried to smile at the attractive blonde already seated at the table. Her bottom jaw felt slack, and for one horrible moment, she found herself blinking back a rush of tears from her blue eyes. The same shade of blue eyes were looking back at her from the other side of the table, going over every inch of her, from the top of her shiny blond head to the tips of her taupe leather heels.

"E-Elizabeth?" she asked huskily, taking a hesitant step forward. Dear Lord! What was she supposed to do? Should she kiss the woman, hug her neck, or both, or neither?

"Danielle?" the woman said, offering a tentative smile. Maybe she should stand up, Elizabeth thought worriedly. At least it would look like she was welcoming her daughter. But she was terribly afraid her legs wouldn't support her.

She's so pretty, Elizabeth thought in amazement . . . so pretty. She saw features she and Danielle shared. The resemblance was remarkable. But as if to remind her of that summer long ago, she also caught the ghost of James Enoch hovering on the edges of Danielle's young, pretty face. Mocking her in the wide forehead, the slight upward tilt of eyes and the fullness of her lips. Oh, yes, she told herself, James was indeed visible there.

James. The only man in her life she'd been unable to control.

"Yes, I'm Danielle."

Perfect. That one word ran through Danielle's mind. Elizabeth Harrison looked perfect in every way.

Blond hair was caught in a neat twist at the elegant nape, blond hair the same color as her own. Makeup was skillfully applied—nothing garish or outstanding—beautifully blended, one step slipping unnoticed into the next to create a face that was a quiet study of understated beauty and elegance. That same style was carried over into the deep burgundy suit and eggshell-colored silk blouse.

How odd, Danielle thought. She'd worn pink and Elizabeth wore burgundy. Unaware of the other's taste, they'd both chosen clothes from the same color grouping. Could that be an omen of good things to come?

"Please, sit down," Elizabeth said softly. "Coffee?" She reached for the carafe to her right.

"Coffee sounds nice," Danielle told her. She would have accepted mud at that particular moment and downed it without quibbling. "H-how are you? I mean . . . did my calling you cause you problems?"

Elizabeth placed the cup and saucer before Danielle. "You didn't cause me any problems," she told her. She smiled then, and Danielle felt her heart swell with happiness. "You did, however, surprise me."

"I'm so sorry," Danielle replied. "But I hope you can understand how I felt when I read about you in my mother's diary. I felt I had to know you, no matter what."

"Is that how you learned that you were adopted?" Elizabeth asked curiously, finding it difficult to believe Tony had kept the secret from Danielle all those years. He and Claire had made that promise to Elizabeth years ago, but she honestly hadn't thought they could or would keep it.

"Yes. I've recently returned to Natchez from Memphis. I'm living at Oaklaine. At any rate," she rushed on, only slightly calmer than she'd been five minutes ago, "I was storing boxes in the attic when I found the diary. I went to see Birdie, and she told me what she knew. I'm referring to Birdie Carlsley. Do you remember her?"

"Oh, yes," Elizabeth said. "I remember the Carlsleys. You married their son, didn't you? I was sorry it didn't last for you."

This time it was Danielle's turn to look surprised. "How did you know those things about me?"

"An account of the wedding was carried in the *Times Picayune*. Zachary Carlsley's name was well respected in business circles even then. Now he's considered to have made it. When you divorced him, there was speculation as to why."

"That's odd," Danielle murmured, studying Elizabeth over the rim of her cup as she sipped the hot coffee. "You read about my wedding in the paper and I saw your picture in a magazine." She mentioned the ball where the four Harrisons had been photographed.

"You have a lovely family," Danielle said.

"Yes, I do," Elizabeth agreed, and a tiny voice inside reminded her that she didn't want anybody causing that family problems. But the warning was so unexpected, Elizabeth tried to put it out of her mind. "Rod is twenty-three and just now becoming interested in the family business. Cory is nineteen. At the moment her greatest concern is who she'll play tennis with tomorrow. I think she's immature, but Nathan tells me that I worry too much."

"Don't you think a certain amount of worry comes with motherhood?" Danielle asked gently.

"It must. Do you and your husband want children?"

"My husband died several months ago. As for children, I have a lovely little daughter. Trish is four years old, and delightful. I can't wait for you to meet her. Needless to say, I'm the typical proud parent."

"Good heavens!" Elizabeth exclaimed a trifle uncertain. "Then I really am a grandmother."

"Yes, you are," Danielle said a little slowly, "but I don't understand."

"At the risk of trying to play one-upmanship, I, too, saw your picture in a magazine, featuring photos of several antebellum homes in and around Natchez. You were shown in front of Oaklaine, with a little girl beside you. I thought it too much of a coincidence for you not to be the Danielle I knew about, but your last name and the little girl threw me."

"Does being a grandmother bother you?" Danielle asked as she opened her purse and took out a small, flat photo case. She opened it and handed it to Elizabeth. "I've been told that she favors me."

"Oh, she does, and she's precious," Elizabeth murmured as she looked at the different poses of a tiny sprite of a girl, her face aglow with mischief and energy. Her heart began pounding like a sledgehammer. Her granddaughter. An expression of sadness flickered across the classic features.

"Does it bother you, knowing you have a granddaughter?" Danielle asked again, picking up on Elizabeth's apparent discomfort.

"I'm not sure."

Well, at least she was honest, Danielle thought. Though she wished she'd been just a wee bit more enthusiastic.

Elizabeth closed the folder and handed it back to Danielle. She sat back then, taking a deep breath into her lungs. "Are you curious as to why I gave you up for adoption?"

Danielle wasn't expecting the question. Of course she was curious. Hadn't she and Chalie spent a good part of the last few weeks imagining any number of situations wherein a young woman, alone in the world, might be forced to give up her baby? "Yes, I am. I'm very much interested in knowing why."

"I bet you've been very generous with me, haven't you? You probably assumed I was strapped financially and, rather than see you do without, I finally made the agonizing decision to give you up for adoption. Pretty close?"

"That was probably first on my list."

Elizabeth took a deep breath, started to speak, then paused. Her friends knew her to be a very outspoken person. However, looking across the table into such overwhelming emotion as was reflected in Danielle's face was disconcerting. "I'm afraid, Danielle, that I don't have a very *good* reason. I was young...yes. Young and very selfish. And for your sake, I wish I could tell you that money was a problem or that I was thinking solely of your welfare. But I can't tell you that, because neither of those reasons was true. As I said, I was young...and selfish...." She paused for a moment, then continued. "I was anxious to get on with my life. At the time, I thought a baby would hold me back. I was ambitious and eager to get ahead as a model. It's a tough, demanding career, and I wanted to succeed. That's when I thought of Tony and Claire. Tony was a third cousin, and we'd always gotten along well. They jumped at the chance to get you and...well, you know the rest."

Danielle masked the disappointment the confession left with her. Somehow she'd imagined some small part of Elizabeth as having always regretted her decision, as secretly longing to see the child she'd given up. To know that wasn't entirely the case threw her off stride.

"I appreciate your candor," Danielle said quietly.

"But you're disappointed in me, aren't you?"

"Somewhat."

"Don't think I didn't miss you and that I didn't have time to regret my decision, Danielle. I did...plenty of times. But you were already settled in with Tony and Claire, and I was doing...well, there just never did seem to be a good time to try and get you back. Besides, I didn't have the heart to hurt Tony and Claire. However, I did toy with the idea of reappearing when Claire died. But something held me back. I knew you were well cared for and loved, so I left well enough alone."

A rush of happiness replaced the disappointment Danielle had felt only moments ago. Her instinct hadn't been wrong. Elizabeth had missed her. She did regret giving her up.

"Please," Danielle said quietly, "no more explanations. I understand. All I care about now is that we've found each other. And all I want is for you and me to be able to spend some time together. I want to get to know you, and you to know me. I want to be able to introduce you to my friends as *my* mother. I want to do things with you, simple things...shopping, laughing, eating lunch together. I want Trish to have a chance to know her other grandmother. And perhaps someday— when you feel the time is right—I can meet your family. Are those impossible, illogical dreams of mine, or can they become realities?"

Elizabeth felt the cold hand of fear clutching her heart. This daughter she'd given birth to was a beautiful, poised woman now, thanks to Tony Lorman. Dare she take advantage of the second chance fate was offering her? Dare she reach out for Danielle's hand and say, "Welcome into my life?"

Dare she?

CHAPTER ELEVEN

"WHAT DO YOU MEAN, she doesn't want to see Trish yet?" Zack demanded.

"Exactly what I've just told you." Danielle's reply was also curt. "Can't you understand? The poor woman has suffered an enormous shock."

They were sitting in the breakfast room at Oaklaine. It was almost midnight, and although she was ready for bed, Danielle wasn't the least bit sleepy. Zack's appearance at her back door had been unexpected, but welcome. He'd been on one of his nightly prowls, which quite often ended with them sharing a cup of coffee and talking.

"Enormous shock or no, I can't understand her reasoning," he added.

"By the time we see each other again, I'm sure she will have changed her mind." Rather than take exception to Zack's remarks, Danielle ignored them. She was still operating on a high beyond description. In her mind she'd gone over every word that passed between her and Elizabeth. Examining the meaning, the tone...storing away bits of information that were priceless to her.

She'd learned that Elizabeth was a patron of the arts, particularly the ballet. She collected Steuben glass, and enjoyed traveling with her husband. From what Danielle gathered, Nathan Harrison was several years older than his wife. Danielle couldn't help but be a little disappointed at Elizabeth's insistence that they keep their relationship a secret for a while longer.

"Well, now that the shock has been eased, I certainly hope she'll want to meet her granddaughter. What could it possibly hurt?" Zack continued with his typical mulish intent.

"We're having lunch again next Thursday, and I imagine at that time we'll get into how best to introduce her family to Trish and me."

"So Nathan Harrison doesn't know that years ago she had a baby and gave it up for adoption, hmm?"

"Apparently not," Danielle replied. "She didn't say so, but I got the impression that he was rather a possessive man. Perhaps she felt if he knew about me it would hurt her marriage."

"If he really loved her, it wouldn't matter," Zack remarked, his dark gaze resting on Danielle's animated features. Suddenly he felt like he was a million miles away from her instead of no more than three feet. Elizabeth had created that schism, and Zack wasn't in a particularly forgiving mood.

Danielle was quiet for a moment. "You really don't trust her, do you?" At first she'd thought his attitude toward Elizabeth had something to do with him knowing her when he was a young boy. But after asking Zack, and learning that nothing out of the ordinary had happened to make him dislike the woman, Danielle was really stumped.

"I don't trust or distrust her," Zack prevaricated. "How can I? As I've told you before, I don't know her. Oh, I remember her from years ago, certainly. But that can hardly be called knowing. About all I remember is a slim, pretty blonde. Want to hear the kicker?"

"Of course," Danielle said eagerly, thinking he was going to tell her something he'd suddenly remembered from the past.

"I've met Nathan Harrison a couple of times, but I had no earthly idea he was Elizabeth's husband. He and I are members of a club in New Orleans, made up of businessmen. Our yearly dues are used to pay a lobbyist in Washington to watch certain legislation we think will help us. However, neither of us is as active as some, since our homes are away from the city."

"Elizabeth didn't mention that today," Danielle said slowly, going back over the conversation that related to Zack. "She did mention seeing the announcement of our wedding in the *Times Picayune*, and that she remembered hearing of our divorce." She grinned at Zack. "She was quite complimentary of your financial success."

"I do regret that she didn't see you as a bride," Zack said gently, almost broodingly. "You were lovely. Do you know your wedding dress is still in my closet?"

Danielle was stunned. "You're kidding! I thought I'd gotten everything. Birdie agreed to call Precious Love if I missed anything." She naturally assumed the dress was in the cedar-lined closet in the attic. It disturbed her to learn otherwise.

"The closet's large," Zack reminded her. "That particular garment bag the dress is in happens to be the same color as a couple of others. It was easy enough to miss. In fact, it was months before I discovered it."

How could he tell her that he'd taken the dress out of its protective covering during one of his darkest bouts of depression and held it to his face? That the only mark on the virginal white satin and lace were faint outlines where his tears had dropped unnoticed... Those were thoughts that were personal—more than personal, actually. They were part of his soul, a soul he wasn't ready to bare to such close scrutiny by Danielle.

"Why didn't you send it to Oaklaine when you found it?" she asked. Knowing he'd kept her wedding dress was disconcerting. It was as if he'd held on to some part of her.

"That's a good question," Zack said briskly, embarrassed at the memories talking about the dress stirred. "Do you have any idea why I might have kept something like that around all these years?"

"No." The single word slipped softly from Danielle's lips.

Oh, please, she silently implored to whatever gods were sketching her future. What was happening with Zack? Tonight he was acting like a jealous lover. Yet, since her telephone call to Elizabeth the day before, he'd run hot and cold. One minute he was caressing her with his eyes, his voice and, at moments, his hands, while the next minute might find him regarding her moodily, snapping out at some innocent remark. The only time he'd been his old self was when he was with Trish.

"Perhaps you kept it around as a reminder of what not to do again," she told him as she pushed to her feet and walked over to the cupboard where the glasses were kept. She took down one, then opened the fridge and poured herself a glass of juice, watching Zack over the rim as she drank.

A wry grin pulled at his mouth at the briskness of her tone, his warm gaze watching the way the pink robe clung to the sway and movement of her body. He liked her spirit.

"Perhaps I did do that. But what happens now if I decide to disregard the warning? Would that be wise, do you think?'' He, too, rose to his feet, and began walking toward her with a long easy stride.

When he was close enough, he calmly took the glass from her and placed it on the counter, then drew her into his arms and tucked her head beneath his chin. Her body still carried the crisp, clean smell of soap from her shower; her hair was still slightly damp from being shampooed.

Danielle closed her eyes and let her senses go slightly wild. He smelled of leather and the woodsy fragrance of his cologne. It was his own personal scent, and she would have recognized it anywhere in the world as belonging to Zack.

''You haven't answered my question,'' he murmured, his lips moving against her hair.

She rubbed her cheek back and forth against his chest with intimate ease, the solid beat of his heart sounding in her ear. ''Your heart sounds like a huge drum beating,'' she whispered.

''Deliberately ignoring the issue, Dani?'' He asked huskily. A hand found its way beneath her chin, forcing her to look at him. ''Do you love me?''

The question was so completely unexpected that Danielle could only stare stupidly at him for several long minutes. ''I refuse to answer on the grounds it might incriminate me,'' she eventually managed to say lightly.

Zack threw back his dark head and laughed, the sound filling Danielle's heart with a joy she hadn't known in years. When he looked down at her, the expression in his eyes was gentle, indulgent—the kind of look a man reserves for the woman in his life. ''We're both a little battle-scarred, aren't we?''

''Yes. But scars heal.''

"So they do." Zack nodded. He dipped his head and captured her lips. The hot tip of his tongue traced the outline of her mouth, then stormed that sensitive darkness, engaging her own tongue in an erotic skirmish of touching and clinging.

Wide tanned palms and long, square-tipped fingers conformed to the shape of a slender midriff, slowly moving up and down, up and down. Each exciting sweep carried the light pressure of his thumbs against the rigid protrusion of her nipples, causing them to tighten and contract, till her breasts felt ready to explode from the hot, sweet pressure of passion running through the veins of her body.

Every part of her was aware, participating in the overwhelming fever of their kiss, in the pliancy of her body as it molded itself to Zack's, in the beat of their hearts, which were thudding in unison like the rugged burst of thunder before a storm.

When Zack lifted his head, he saw dazed blue eyes and full, moist lips that were still slightly parted from where his tongue had just been. Zack knew if he wanted to, he could make love to Danielle and she would welcome him.

It took unbelievable willpower for him to resist, but something held him back. In his heart he knew their relationship had now reached a point that required more than just making love occasionally. Love being the operative word, he told himself.

He loved Danielle, though at the moment, he was only able to admit it to himself.

No matter how he fought it, he couldn't get around the plain truth. She was still in his blood, and always would be. To deny it simply because she'd hurt him once before would be foolish. Such an admission elic-

ited a peculiar warm feeling, which spread out over his
body. He'd deal with his doubts of whether or not he
could trust her some other time.

"What if I were to tell you that I care for you?" The
words burst from his lips with a will of their own. Talk
about saying something on the spur of the moment, he
thought rather grimly.

Danielle smiled at him. She touched her fingers to his
lips, then cradled his face with her hands. "Poor, poor
Zack." She shook her head. "Are you finally admit-
ting what I've been thinking for weeks now?"

"Oh, have you?" Zack tried to look fierce, but
wasn't quite able to pull it off. It was a little bit embarrassing for her not to be shocked—or at least to show
some surprise. Yet why should she be surprised when
he'd been acting like a kid in love for the first time?
Even the most simpleminded person could have figured out his problem.

"Yes. And in case you're interested, I care for you
very much."

"And where does that leave us?"

"Very cautiously making our way into the future, I
should think," Danielle said bluntly. "At this precise
moment, I'm terrified of trusting this feeling I have for
you. I'm afraid to call it love. Believe it or not, I remember the past, too. There's something else I have to
consider."

"What's that?"

"Trish. I heard what you said to Chalie last night,
about not being sure what kind of father you'd make.
Well, Trish wants a daddy, and you happen to be at the
top of her list. In fact, you're the only name on her list.
Any relationship I might form in the future will have to
be of my own choosing, not my daughter's."

"Ah," Zack murmured, nodding his head as he remembered certain moments from the past. "Pressure. It happened to us once before, didn't it?"

"Yes."

"Well, at least we can drop the pretense we've tried so hard to keep going," Zack remarked. "I suppose that's progress...of a sort. Whatever the future brings for us, at least we won't be enemies anymore." He watched her for a moment. "Are you going to miss me while I'm gone?"

"Gone? Where?"

"South America. Brazil, to be exact. I've already sent one of my advance teams down. They'll do all the legwork and get everything into position."

Suddenly Danielle felt lonely. She wasn't ready for him to go away. But common sense told her it was probably for the best. They each needed some breathing space. Only, did it have to be so far away? "Will you be having many midnight business meetings such as the one you had the other night?" she asked casually. Caring for each other was one thing. Being able to mold that caring into a workable relationship was an entirely different thing. Twice before she'd been convinced she knew what she wanted. And twice before she'd been wrong.

"Are you implying that you don't believe I really did have a business meeting?"

"Something like that."

"Then you can put your mind at ease," Zack said roughly. "I'll admit I haven't lived the life of a monk since we've been apart. But I can honestly say there's been no one I was serious about. I haven't seen anyone—even casually—since you've been back, and I certainly didn't rush from having dinner here, with you, to New Orleans that night to see another woman. I was finalizing the contract for the job in South America.''

Listening to his explanation left Danielle feeling slightly like an idiot with a ton of egg on her face. ''I'm sorry,'' she said softly. ''It just seemed such an odd time . . . I naturally . . .''

''You naturally assumed I was seeing another woman,'' Zack finished for her. He caught her to him again, forcing her head back against his arm. ''I don't think you have any idea how I really feel about you, do you?'' he asked roughly.

''Maybe I don't,'' Danielle whispered.

Zack stared into her eyes, fighting against the niggling doubts still intertwined with his love. Would there ever be a time when he would be able to look at her and not wonder if she still cared? Could he learn to cope with those doubts and eventually bury them, or would they continue to dominate his thoughts where Danielle was concerned and destroy his chance of happiness? His eyes dropped to her mouth—a mouth he never tired of tasting . . . of kissing.

His head dipped and his mouth took possession of hers. There was a sense of desperation in the kiss, a desperation that transmitted itself to both of them. There was so much still unresolved between them, so much that hadn't been talked through, so many doubts clouding the feelings they'd both freely admitted existed between them.

Could that love overcome all those obstacles, Danielle wondered fleetingly as she gave in to the need gripping her. Could it survive the harsh test of Zack's critical scrutiny? She knew there was no tried and true answer. Only time would tell.

THE DAYS TILL DANIELLE'S second meeting with Elizabeth passed with agonizing slowness. Not only was she anxious and apprehensive at the thought of seeing her natural mother again; she missed Zack. Trish missed Zack. It wasn't until a couple of days had passed that Danielle realized something was wrong with the child.

"Don't you feel well, honey?" she asked Trish at dinner when the little girl refused to eat even a bit of her food. It had been the same thing at lunch.

"Yes, Mommy."

"Would you like to talk to me about anything?" Danielle probed gently. All afternoon Trish had been moping around the house, even forsaking her beloved Dolly.

Trish nodded.

Danielle waited for her to begin.

"I miss Uncle Zack," the little girl finally said. "Will he stay gone like my daddy?"

"Oh, no, honey," Danielle told her. "Uncle Zack will be back just as soon as he's through working."

"You promise?" Trish persisted, not in the least comforted by her mother's adult reassurances.

"I promise," Danielle repeated, amazed at the change that swept over Trish. "And he would want you to eat your dinner." Those words brought instant success, and left Trish happy as a lark.

That evening, just as she stepped out of the shower, she got her first call from Zack.

"Hello," she answered breathlessly, clutching the edges of the towel between her breasts.

"Why are you out of breath?"

The voice was rough and sexy and sent goose pimples scattering across the surface of her skin. "Zack?"

His raspy chuckle set her knees to trembling. She dropped down onto the edge of the bed, drawing her feet beneath her, holding the receiver with both hands, the towel dipping lower and lower...forgotten.

"You sound surprised," he said.

"I am. You didn't say anything about calling me."

"Don't you like surprises?"

"Very much. At least ones like this," she said with simple honesty. Why pretend? she asked herself. Zack probably knew her better than any other person in the world. Pretense with him would be a wasted effort. Besides, she confessed, she really was glad he'd called.

"Are you saying that because you know I want to hear it?" he asked cautiously. "Or do you really mean it?"

"Yes, you awful pessimist," Danielle said with suspect sternness, "I most certainly do mean it. In fact," she added recklessly, "if you were here right this minute, I'd show you just how much."

"That's mighty brave talk, Ms Kendricks."

"'Deed it is, Mr. Carlsley."

"May I have a rain check?"

"Most definitely."

"What are you doing now...this minute?" he asked gruffly.

"Sitting on the edge of my bed shivering. My hair is wet, and the spot where I'm sitting is wet."

"Keep talking and I'll be home in a few hours with an excellent remedy for stopping beautiful blondes from shivering."

"Real cute, Mr. Carlsley," Danielle murmured in a tortured voice. "Especially when you're hundreds of miles away."

"I miss you like hell."

"I know. I miss you, too," she murmured.

"Give Trish a kiss for me. Take care, honey."

"You too, Zack."

Danielle continued to sit on the bed for several long, thoughtful minutes after she replaced the receiver. Was it the distance between them in miles that accounted for the easiness with which they talked to each other?

Whatever the reason, she knew there was little she could do to stop the inevitable showdown waiting for them. Each day, each kiss, each caress, each uncertain thought, carried them closer to the possible hope of the future and the certain fear of the past.

Was she strong enough to endure Zack's troubled doubts? Had she reached that point in her own life where she really did know her own mind? Was she ready for a full relationship between a mature man and woman?

The next telephone call came the following night. She'd already gone to bed and was sound asleep, so her voice was drowsy when she answered.

"You're in bed, aren't you?" Zack rasped, his indrawn breath sounding sharp in her ear. In his thoughts, he was silently damning his profession, which had him strung out in South America taking cold shower after cold shower, and left Danielle in Natchez, both of them wanting each other.

"Mmm." Danielle smiled happily. She'd gone to bed thinking of him, and the minute her eyes closed, she began to dream. In her dream, they'd been making love. Danielle snuggled deeper against the pillows, pulling the covers up around her chin. She stretched, feeling hot and warm in the most delicious places. "What time is it?"

"Late. If I was there, I'd take you in my arms and make love to you."

"You're a mighty brave man, Zachary, when you're miles away," she teased him.

"What are you wearing?"

"A pink nightshirt."

Pink nightshirts—pale yellow pajamas—long silky blond hair—deep blue eyes. All those images kept slipping in and out of Zack's mind with tortured ease. He gritted his teeth with frustration, taking deep calming breaths into his lungs, then exhaling with deliberate care.

He wanted her so damned bad.

But did he want her just as they were, or for another kind of relationship? Zack didn't have the answer to that question.

When Chalie heard that Zack was calling Danielle while he was away, her dark eyes danced with speculation.

"Still going to hand me some old line about how the two of you aren't serious?" she asked one evening when Danielle and Trish were having dinner at Rosewynn. They were sitting in the porch swing, watching Trish and Birdie as they checked on the bed Birdie was having worked up for her fall bulbs.

"Oh...we're serious," Danielle said, and favored her friend with a wry grin. "We're serious enough not to want to make another mistake. And that, my friend, could mean anything. You know what they say, Chalie, about a person never being able to go back? Well, sometimes it's like that with people. In some instances it's best to let go of a relationship."

"Don't suppose anyone can blame you for that," Chalie said softly. Her gaze became fixed on some distant point, and Danielle knew she was thinking of her own problems.

"Are you and Dane still at cross-purposes?"

"Cross-purposes hardly covers it," Chalie said bitterly. "I still can't believe the things he accused me of. It's incredible."

"I'm sorry, Chalie," Danielle murmured sympathetically. "Maybe we shouldn't talk about it."

"I think it would do me good to get it off my chest. Since the last time we talked, I got up enough courage to go see him."

"You mean Dane?"

"Yes. I could have stayed home for all the good it did me. He was like a stranger, Dani," Chalie said harshly, her features rigid and unhappy as she related the story. "Can you believe he actually had the nerve to call me a coward? Said he honestly thought I was using him as an excuse for not accepting reality. And if that wasn't enough, he's been seeing a psychologist. He's discussing our problems, Dani, our very own problems with a stranger, without consulting me. I'll never forgive him."

"Oh, Chalie," Danielle said, slowly shaking her head. "Honey, please don't say things like that. I've never known two people who belong together more than you and Dane do. Right now you're at odds with each other, but with time and patience I'm sure it will work out."

But Chalie was adamant. "He should have told me he was going to see a psychologist."

"Frankly, I think Dane did the right thing," Danielle found the courage to tell her.

"Just whose side are you on, anyway?" Chalie asked challengingly.

"Does there have to be sides?"

"Yes!"

"You don't really mean that, Chalie Carlsley," Danielle scolded her. "Right now you're hurt, and you feel betrayed. But for Dane to seek professional help should show you that he's trying to understand the problem."

"Are you implying that I'm not trying?"

"If the shoe fits…" Danielle remarked pointedly, just as Trish and Birdie came walking up the steps.

"Don't forget, Danielle, if you have plants outside, you should start thinking about where you'll put them when you bring them in. It won't be much longer now before we'll be enjoying a fire in the evening," Birdie said pleasantly as she sat down in a white wicker rocker.

Trish took off in hot pursuit of a yellow-and-white cat, who was the proud mama of three tiny kittens in a basket in the corner of the breakfast room.

"I only have the ferns. But you're right—" Danielle nodded to her godmother "—a blanket is beginning to feel good in the middle of the night. And I love the mornings. It's not quite cold enough to turn on the furnace, yet it's too cool without long sleeves."

This evening Birdie seemed like her old self, Danielle was thinking. She was glad. It had to be extremely difficult for a very active person such as Birdie had always been to suddenly find herself—for days at a time—struggling in a world of vagueness.

"Have you heard from Zack?" Birdie asked, still hoping something would get Danielle and her son back together.

Danielle grinned, knowing perfectly well what was going through the older woman's mind. "He's called me a time or two."

"How nice," Birdie remarked. "How nice." She looked off into the late twilight and sighed. "You know,

I love fall weddings. Everyone feels so much more like getting things done when it's cool."

"Someone you know getting married, Birdie?" Chalie asked, amused by her mother's tactics, in spite of being peeved at Danielle.

"Why...I really don't know, Chalie dear," Birdie answered in a vague voice, for once finding her affliction useful. "But if they are, then I wish them well."

Later, as Danielle was leaving and Chalie was walking with her to the car, Chalie apologized. "Maybe you're right."

"About what?"

"The psychologist."

"Did Dane give any indication that he felt he'd been helped by the sessions?"

"Oh, yes...definitely. He was so enthusiastic, I wanted to clobber him. I was so miserable I felt like dying, and he was going on and on about some shrink."

Danielle slipped an arm around her friend's waist and hugged her. "Chalie, you've spent a small fortune on doctors, trying to find one who would tell you what you wanted to hear. What would it hurt to have a go at one more opinion? But this time, from an emotional point of view rather than a physical one? After all, honey, you are the one who's been unable to accept the situation. Dane's been willing all along."

"I'll think about it, I promise. But right now I'm still hurting from the things Dane said to me, Dani. He was like an entirely different person."

"Don't you think he's hurting also?" Danielle asked gently.

Chalie looked down at her feet, finding it difficult to feel charitable toward the man she loved. There was still a wide gulf separating them. "I suppose so," she said, finally.

"That's a start, Chalie. By the way, don't forget to pick Trish up on your way to work in the morning."

"You know," Chalie began, staring rather sadly into space, "lately our conversations have been dominated with three super-intense topics of conversation—Elizabeth, Dane and Zack. Whatever happened to the two happy-go-lucky gals we used to be?"

"I'm afraid we've become adults, honey...participants in what is so commonly referred to as life."

Several times during the remainder of the evening, and even the next morning as she dressed and then drove to New Orleans for her luncheon date with Elizabeth, Danielle couldn't get Zack out of her mind.

There hadn't been a phone call from him the night before, and sleep had been as elusive as the wind. Worrying about Zack and about her second visit with Elizabeth made for a very restless night. Mainly, she thought about her ex-husband.

Danielle wondered if something could have gone wrong this time when they'd touched off the explosions. During the past few weeks they'd discussed his work, mainly from her point of view about its dangers. Zack went to great pains to reassure her, pointing out the safety precautions he and his men used. But in spite of all those reassurances, she still worried.

He'd given her a number in Brazil where he could be reached if she needed him, and also his private secretary's number at home. Danielle knew without a doubt that if she didn't hear from him by evening, she would be using one or both of the numbers in her possession.

CHAPTER TWELVE

ELIZABETH HARRISON SAT at a small secluded table in the famous old restaurant in New Orleans' French Quarter. The thumb and forefinger of one hand were touching the handle of her cup. Her other hand, clenched into a tight fist, rested against the crisp white napkin in her lap. A good two inches separated her spine from the curved back of the chair. Though strikingly beautiful, she looked stiff and tense.

Her hand shook slightly when she raised the cup to her lips and took a tiny sip of coffee. A deep, deliberately calming breath was pulled into her lungs, one of many she'd taken in the past thirty minutes or so. She exhaled much too quickly, losing the exercise's benefit.

In the days since she'd gotten the explosive telephone call from Danielle, she'd become a bundle of nerves. Sleep had become nonexistent.

Seeing Danielle for the first time since she'd handed her over to Claire and Tony was the greatest shock of all, Elizabeth told herself. Looking into Danielle's eyes was like seeing her own accusing reflection staring back at her.

Guilt as deep and painful as a huge open wound searing her skin tore at her peace of mind. She'd wanted a certain kind of life. Her chances of attaining that life would have been greatly hampered by the presence of an infant.

Twenty-seven years had passed. Twenty-seven!

Elizabeth thought of her son, Rod, and her daughter, Cory. She'd been an excellent mother to them. They were good children. A little spoiled, but good. She wondered what they would say if she were to tell them about Danielle. And Nathan? How would he react? Would a man who aspired to be state senator care for that kind of publicity in his personal life?

Yet, in spite of the negative reasons, could she, a mother, turn her back on her own child?

"Here you are, miss," the white-coated waiter remarked as he and Danielle halted at the table.

Elizabeth snapped out of her reverie to find herself looking up at Danielle and the elderly waiter by her side. "Please—" she smiled at Danielle "—sit down. Thank you, Max," she said as she nodded to the waiter.

As soon as Max moved away, Danielle leaned back in her chair, surprised at how calm she was feeling. Strange. There was none of the fear she'd known the other time. She wondered why.

"How are you?"

"Fine." Elizabeth nodded. "And you?"

"Fine," Danielle parroted, then smiled. "Not a very auspicious beginning, is it?"

"I don't suppose it is. Frankly, I don't know what to say to you."

"Is it that difficult for you?"

"Yes."

"I see," Danielle said slowly, fighting a tightness in her chest that wasn't there before. She'd been calm, yes, but there hadn't been a knot. A knot generating a deep, throbbing pain. Blue eyes stared deep into blue eyes. "You haven't told your husband or your children, have you?"

"No." The word was spoken so softly it was barely discernible over the normal noise in the restaurant.

"Do you plan on doing so?"

A long, tense silence stretched between them. A silence bearing twenty-seven years that one woman was struggling to keep hidden, and the other was trying just as desperately to lay open.

"No."

"Then there's really no need for us to continue this conversation, is there?" Danielle said quietly. She picked up her purse, slipped it beneath her arm, then pushed back her chair. What she really wanted to do was run from the restaurant and down the street till she couldn't run any farther... until the pain from physical exertion blotted out the pain she was feeling in her heart.

"Please," Elizabeth pleaded, half rising from her chair. She reached across the table and placed her hand on Danielle's arm in an effort to keep her from leaving. "Please. Listen to what I have to say."

Danielle stared at her, trying to find something in her mother's face, something in those perfect, unreadable features that would give her the slightest indication of her mood. She found nothing, and that disturbed her.

She placed her purse beside her in the chair, then sat back, her direct gaze meeting the emotionless one across the table. "I'm very sorry now that I got in touch with you, Elizabeth. I can see that it was a huge mistake on my part."

Elizabeth averted her gaze, her head slowly moving from side to side. "You're not clairvoyant, Danielle. You had no way of knowing how I'd react."

"No," Danielle agreed, "but Birdie did try to stop me. For that matter, so did Zack." And she'd brushed aside the advice from both of them, determined to find her real mother.

"Did they ever tell you why?"

"For some reason, they didn't think you'd be too happy to find your past standing on your doorstep. Seems they're right."

Elizabeth looked away from the hurt she saw in her daughter's eyes. Hurt she could wipe away with three simple words. But those words could also destroy twenty-four years of being Nathan's wife. She lifted the cup to her lips. When she placed it back in its saucer, she sat staring into its depths as if fascinated with what she saw there. "Just what did you expect when you found me, Danielle?"

"I suppose it's silly, really, but I've always wanted a mother. I'd more or less reconciled myself to never having one, till I found that diary. When I read that I was adopted, I was stunned. Yet when I cooled down, what I'd discovered began to really hit me. If something hadn't happened to you, then I had an honest-to-God mother." She gestured with her hands. "That's when I felt that it was somehow meant for me to find you. Now I see that it was meant to be only because I pushed it."

"Perhaps it was meant to be," Elizabeth said softly, "even though it's not working out as you expected."

Both women looked up as the waiter approached their table. After a brief discussion they settled on another pot of coffee. At the moment neither was interested in food.

"My husband is seriously thinking of running for the senate next year," Elizabeth began. "He's been an excellent husband, Danielle, and if he wants this political career, then I feel I have an obligation to help him."

"And of course an illegitimate daughter from your past isn't the sort of help he needs, is it?"

What little color there was left in Elizabeth's already pale face drained away.

She suddenly looked her age. She looked like a woman in her fifties—a woman who was very tired—a woman who was very lonely.

"Don't be bitter."

A short, mirthless laugh escaped Danielle. "Bitter?" she asked incredulously. "I'm not bitter, Elizabeth. Disappointed is more like it. I'm very disappointed. I feel that you let me down once, and that you're doing it again."

"Disappointed that I didn't take you in my arms...cry and tell you how much I love you...how much I missed seeing you grow up, and a whole bunch of other meaningless things?" Elizabeth asked in an unsteady voice.

"Yes," Danielle nodded, "I would very much have liked to hear those meaningless things from you. Tell me something, are you affectionate with your other two children?"

"That's a cheap shot."

"Oh, yes, very cheap," Danielle agreed. "But in my opinion it's not very top drawer for you to pit me against a political career and then allow the career to win. On the other hand, I really had no right to bother you, did I? You chose years ago to distance yourself from me. I should have respected your wishes."

Elizabeth looked drawn as she tried to find the words to comfort her daughter, a daughter whose eyes showed their contempt along with the hurt she was feeling. "You must understand, Danielle. When I gave you to Claire and Tony, I put you out of my mind. As I told you the other day, it wasn't the most admirable thing I've ever done, but I can't go back and undo it. I didn't raise you, I wasn't with you during all those years. In order to overcome the guilt I felt for giving you up for adoption, I threw myself into my work. I was a model, and a very good one. I wanted more out of life than I'd had as a child, and I worked hard to get it. When I met and married Nathan, I turned those same energies into being an excellent wife and, later, a good mother to our children. In short, I made another life for myself, a life I find to be very comfortable. One I don't want to jeopardize. Frankly, if I were to try to explain you to Nathan, it would probably end with our being divorced."

Danielle sat very still. Even her breathing seemed to have ceased as she absorbed the impact of Elizabeth's words. Words that continued echoing their hurt long after they'd been spoken.

Zack had been correct in his assessment of the situation. But it was too late to turn back now, Danielle thought grimly. She hadn't listened to Birdie or Zack, thinking she knew so much better than they how Elizabeth would react to hearing from her. She'd based her decision on how she felt she would react in a similar situation. Obviously she and Elizabeth weren't alike in that respect.

"When I called you that day, why did you agree to see me?"

"I was shocked—terrified in part that you were an impostor and, I must admit, I was very curious," she admitted freely. "I also wondered if you were in financial trouble. A few months ago there'd been an article on Nathan and his grocery chain, including speculations on his approximate worth. It occurred to me that you might have seen it and decided to capitalize on it.''

''And now?''

''And now,'' Elizabeth murmured so softly Danielle had to strain to hear her, ''I know you only wanted to know me.''

For the first time since meeting her, Danielle saw a chink in the seemingly impenetrable armor protecting Elizabeth. She saw tears gather in her eyes. Saw the mouth so like her own tremble...saw Elizabeth fight for control. In her heart Danielle wanted to reach out to her, wanted to comfort her, wanted to shower her with the love that was waiting in her heart for the woman. But she held back, knowing her sympathy as well as her love wasn't wanted by Elizabeth. They shared physical features, but their character traits were totally opposite.

''Please forgive me,'' Elizabeth pleaded in a quiet, dignified voice. ''My only excuse for what I'm doing to you is, I'm a coward. I enjoy being Mrs. Nathan Harrison.''

''Is that why you refused to see Trish?''

''Yes. Meeting you has been difficult enough. I might not have been able to carry it through if I'd seen your daughter.''

''Your granddaughter,'' Danielle corrected her, determined to make her at least acknowledge that Trish existed, even if it was only paying lip service. ''Your granddaughter.''

''Yes.'' Elizabeth nodded, her admiration for this determined daughter of hers evident. It had taken enormous courage for Danielle to find her, courage Elizabeth wished she herself possessed. ''My... granddaughter.''

Oh, dear God!

If only she could make herself go to Nathan and tell him the whole story. If he could just see Danielle . . . see how lovely she was. But the moment the thought entered her mind, Elizabeth knew immediately it was impossible. The publicity would be terrible.

And what about Cory and Rod? Did she have the right to ruin their young lives? Of course she didn't. But somehow the answer was given too quickly. Rather than the ring of truth, it seemed to be more an answer of convenience, her own convenience, born out of desperation.

"Would you mind sharing your plans with me?" Elizabeth asked. This would be the last time she would see Danielle. She wanted to have something to hold close to her heart when she thought of this other child of hers, the one she could never really know because she was too torn between a past she wanted to forget and the future of living a life she didn't want to lose.

Oh, she'd tried to imagine that they could possibly meet at some social function in years to come. Depending, of course, upon how friendly Danielle was with Zack Carlsley. Elizabeth knew enough about the world of finance to know that Zack was wealthy in his own right and he'd be at many of the same social functions she and Nathan attended. Any time she'd seen the Carlsley name, she'd paid close attention. But even if they were to bump into each other, Elizabeth knew in her heart neither she nor Danielle would acknowledge the other.

"As I told you the other day, I plan on raising Trish at Oaklaine. In another couple of months I suppose I'll probably start looking for a job."

"Ah, yes." Elizabeth nodded. "You did tell me the other day that you're a legal secretary. You shouldn't have any problems finding a position."

"I'm certainly not anticipating any."

"You've mentioned Zack Carlsley's name several times. Are you seeing him again?"

"Yes, I am." This time she did push back her chair and rise to her feet. She stood, slim and graceful, her movements determined in spite of the aching of her heart. "I think it's time for me to go, Elizabeth. Thank you for seeing me."

"Please..." Elizabeth looked up at her, the word rushing past trembling lips. "Can't you stay just a little longer? I mean..."

"No," Danielle said softly, "oh, no. You have no room for me in your heart or your life, Elizabeth. Can't you understand that your rejection is breaking my heart? How can you ask me to sit here and chat like we're old friends, then calmly get up and never let me see you again? I'm flesh and blood, not a robot without feeling. I came to you, and I gave you a chance to know me. You said no. I'll never come again, Elizabeth." she stepped back, reluctant to finally end the painful meeting, yet knowing it had to be done.

The last thing she remembered as she turned away were the tears streaming unheeded down Elizabeth's cheeks and the stricken look in her eyes.

Danielle walked through the restaurant, her shoulders straight, her chin high. She looked neither to the right nor the left. All she wanted to do was get away from every other human being in the entire world. The only person she wanted to see was Zack, and he was hundreds of miles away in South America.

The door was opened by a hovering attendant, but Danielle swept by him and onto the sidewalk, barely aware of his existence. She turned to her right, in the direction of the parking lot where her car was waiting, and slammed into the solid wall of a warm human chest.

"Whoa there, lady!" a deep, rusty voice said laughingly.

Relief at the sound of that voice snaked its way past the grief threatening to tear her apart. Danielle didn't have to look up. She didn't have to wonder who it was that was holding her with such a hard, yet gentle grip. Only Zack could evoke such a strong reaction within her.

She looked up at him then. And even though he looked tired, she couldn't remember ever being happier to see him.

"Why are you here?"

"Are you going to be angry because I came?" he asked gruffly. They both seemed unaware that they were standing on the street, collecting a number of rather interesting looks from passersby.

"Oh, no," she assured him. "I'm just curious how you knew where I'd be."

"Simple." Zack stared down at her. "Simple. During one of our conversations you told me. At any rate, I got the days mixed up. I tried to get you several times but there was no answer. So I called Chalie from Houston and she reminded me that you were to have lunch with Elizabeth."

"And you, being you, decided to join us?"

"Nothing so crass as that . . . please." He tilted his dark head to one side, drinking in the sight of her. "The job went off without a hitch and, for once, I was able to get home as planned. Since I was going to stop by my office anyway, I simply made another phone call from Houston and reserved a table at this restaurant." He nodded toward the door behind them. "I'd planned on using it in case I felt you needed me."

"In case I needed you," she repeated. "Well...I do need you, Zack Carlsley. You'll never know how much."

Zack's huge body suddenly changed from relaxed to taut, his grip on her arms tightening. "It didn't go well, did it?" His shrewd gaze searched out every inch of her face, going over each feature in careful detail.

"No."

"What do you want to do?"

"Take me somewhere and make love to me. Make me forget. I'm about to explode with pain."

"As much as I want to comply with your request, now's not the time, sweetheart." He frowned. What the hell had Elizabeth said to her?

"It is for me," Danielle told him, her voice wobbly. "Right now, I need to hear somebody say they love me. I have to hear words from another human being that will let me know I'm wanted...even if it's only for a little while. Does that make any sense?"

Zack stared down into her eyes. He saw the pain she was enduring and knew in his soul he could freely and without the slightest qualm literally destroy Elizabeth Harrison.

Without a word, he kept a protective arm around Danielle and led her to his car waiting at the curb. She slipped beneath the steering wheel and over to the passenger side. Though she was staring straight ahead, she saw nothing, her vision blurred by tears that refused to be held back. She felt the vibration of the engine as it sprang to life, and felt motion as Zack blended the Mercedes into traffic.

Had either of them looked back, they would have seen a woman watching them, a slim, attractive blonde with large, dark sunglasses affording her a slight anonymity. The woman saw the tender way Zack treated Danielle and was touched. It made her happy in one sense that there would be someone with Danielle, but in another sense, it left her with a peculiar emptiness inside.

She stepped from the shadows of the entrance to the restaurant and began to slowly make her way to where her car was parked. She'd done it. She'd actually severed the ties with Danielle forever. Her way of life was safe.

Safe and secure, safe and secure. Those words kept running through Elizabeth's mind. But no matter how safe her future was, her heart was heavy as stone.

She forced herself to think of more pleasant things. Nathan, for instance. He was flying in from Miami at three, and they had friends coming over for a small, intimate dinner party that evening. Influential friends who would help his campaign.

Those were the types of things she valued, weren't they? Elizabeth asked herself. The parties, the jewelry, the security... all the trappings that came with being a wealthy man's wife. Those were the important things in life. Weren't they?

Rod and Cory would also be coming home. Each would be dashing off to join the local crowd.

And when the evening was done, and the house was quiet, Elizabeth knew her own private entertainment would begin. An entertainment of thought, featuring memories and thoughts of what might have been and still could be. An entertainment so gripping as to leave her empty and lonely. Entertainment so demanding as to rob her of all sleep. Entertainment so exacting as to leave her a prisoner of her own grief and guilt.

IT DIDN'T TAKE LONG for Zack to get them to his apartment.

The moment he closed the door behind them, he took Danielle's purse from her and tossed it on one of the sofas in the living room.

"This way," he told her, guiding her toward the master bedroom suite rather than allowing her to go into the living room. He glanced down at her, hating the dazed look that had been present in her features from the moment they'd gotten into the car. Shock was never pleasant, and to see Danielle practically in a daze from such an emotional upheaval was something Zack was having difficulty dealing with. He wanted to hurt someone because of the pain she was enduring, wanted to vent his anger on Elizabeth Harrison and her family.

In the bedroom, he led her over to the bed, then gently pushed her down onto the tan-and-mustard tweed spread. "I'll only be a minute," he told her, then reached for the telephone on the bedside table.

Danielle heard him talking with his secretary, but she honestly didn't comprehend a single word that was spoken. Comprehension demanded a certain amount of attention. At the moment, her mind was incapable of giving that attention to anything or anybody. She allowed her head to drop back and closed her eyes.

It was over.

She'd found the woman who gave birth to her, and now she felt completely empty... devoid of emotion.

Danielle opened her eyes just as Zack appeared in front of her. She saw him bend over and grasp her feet, then remove her shoes. "Stand up," he said quietly, catching her arms and pulling her forward. He caught her to him, one large hand going to the back of her head and pressing her face against his chest.

"I'm so sorry this has happened to you," he whispered. "So sorry." He was hurting for her, feeling the pain she was feeling.

Danielle leaned into him, her body curving instinctively to the hard, masculine lines so familiar to her. She could feel the strength of him sustaining her, coursing back and forth, feeding her spirit, comforting her soul.

"Do you know I was wishing for you when we collided outside the restaurant? When you didn't call last night, I thought something had happened to you. I was worried," she said, her cheek resting against the steady beat of his heart. "Then today... I needed you... and you were there."

Zack drew back, his big hands moving around to frame her troubled face. "I've always been here for you, Dani, but you haven't always been able to see that."

"Right at this moment, I don't think I can see anything," she confessed. "All of a sudden I feel completely drained of energy."

"That's why you're going to get a warm shower," Zack informed her as he found the zipper at her back and opened it. He eased the paisley silk dress off her shoulders, then allowed it to fall to the floor. Her slip, bra and panty hose followed close behind. Though admiration was reflected in his eyes, Zack kept his desire under tight rein. Danielle was like a wounded animal, seeking shelter in which to lick her wounds. "Afterward, I'm going to fix you a warm drink, then tuck you into bed.''

"But I need to get back to—"

"You don't need to go anywhere, honey," Zack said, silencing her. He hugged her to him again, reluctant to let her out of his sight. "Trish is perfectly all right. But if it will make you feel any better, I'll call Chalie while you're in the shower and bring her up-to-date."

"Would you please?"

"Only if you promise to stop fighting me," Zack told her, a scowl appearing on his rugged face. He bent his head and kissed the end of her nose. "You're a very difficult lady to do things for, Ms Kendricks. And even though you've been through a bad time today, I sure would like to see a smile on your pretty face—even a tiny one."

The original stone face would have found it difficult not to do as he asked, Danielle thought as she complied with his request, albeit weakly.

"That's better. Now," he said as he turned her around, his wide palm lightly connecting with the rounded temptation of her derriere, "you have exactly eight minutes. Any longer and I'll turn off the hot water."

"Slave driver," Danielle remarked teasingly as she walked into the connecting bath and over to the shower. "You're a cruel man, Zack Carlsley, a cruel, cruel man."

When he heard the sound of the shower, Zack ran a hand over his face, his breath making a whistling noise as it rushed past his lips. He leaned one hand against the wall, palm down, fingers splayed as he tried to collect his thoroughly rattled thoughts.

Holding Danielle in his arms anytime was a pleasure. Holding her naked in his arms was the ultimate torture.

Zack willed his body to return to normal, calling to mind any and all unpleasant details of the job he'd just completed rather than thinking of hovering over her, then burying himself in her as they made wild and passionate love. He tried to concentrate on the fact that she was vulnerable and confused. She thought she wanted him to make love to her, but Zack knew she was simply reaching out for someone...anyone.

He had too much pride and cared too much for her to allow Danielle to use him or herself that way. Later, when she'd rested and calmed down, he fully intended to make love to her. She'd know then more clearly that somebody indeed needed and wanted her.

Cursing Elizabeth Harrison under his breath for being a heartless bitch, Zack made the call to Chalie, shrugging out of his jacket and shirt even as they began to speak.

"It's bad, huh?" she asked.

"Yeah," he muttered. "I haven't asked any questions, but I'd say she's about wiped out. Right now I've got her in the shower. As soon as she's out, I'm giving her a good stiff brandy, then putting her to bed. Keep a close eye on Trish. I doubt we'll be home before noon tomorrow. Okay?"

"You know it's okay. And, Zack," Chalie said, her voice dropping low so that Birdie and Trish couldn't overhear her. "I'm pulling for you, kid."

"For once, I'm not going to tell you that you're imagining things." Zack surprised himself by agreeing. "Frankly though, at this point, I'm not sure what that means. But at least we're discussing things."

They talked on for a few minutes before Zack cradled the receiver. He walked to the door of the bathroom and stood for a moment, watching Danielle's movements through the opaque glass of the shower doors.

Satisfied that she was all right, he changed into a pair of faded jeans, then left the room. A few minutes later he returned carrying a brandy snifter in his palm, the liquid inside creating an amber splash of color against sparkling crystal.

Danielle turned off the water, then opened the door and reached for the huge towel Zack had laid out for her.

Funny, she thought as she smoothed the moisture from the surface of her skin, the Zack she'd been married to at one time and the Zack she'd become acquainted with since returning to Natchez seemed like two different people.

During their marriage he'd been possessive to the point of smothering her, even closing them off socially from their friends. When she tried to talk to him about it, they always ended up arguing. More and more Danielle began looking forward to the times when he was away on a job. That was the only time she saw her friends. When Zack returned, the same old arguments would start anew.

At that time and even after the divorce, Danielle remembered, she considered Zack to be an absolute monster. But now, after being away from him for so long, and picking up on certain remarks Chalie let slip, she'd come to a very startling conclusion. Zack had been extremely jealous, and the differences in their ages merely served to make him a prisoner of his own pri-

vate hell. He'd covered his jealousy so well, Danielle
had simply assumed him to be an overbearing grouch.

She wondered, as she wrapped the towel sarong-
fashion around her body, if he'd changed so drastically. Or had she?

However, the mental effort to actively pursue that
question was beyond her at the moment. About the only
thing she felt capable of doing was moving from the
bathroom to the bed. The idea became more appealing
by the second.

Zack was waiting for her when she entered the bedroom, sprawled comfortably in an old, overstuffed
chair that Danielle vaguely remembered having seen at
Rosewynn years ago. It was huge, and suited his size
perfectly. "Feeling better?" Zack asked, rising to his
feet. He picked up the brandy snifter, then walked over
to her.

"A little."

"That's a start." He smiled down at her. "Drink
this."

Danielle accepted the snifter, regarding the brandy
suspiciously. "In case you've forgotten, my tolerance
for alcohol is still quite low." With any other man she'd
be suspicious. But this was Zack. Right now, she'd trust
him with her life.

"Good." He watched while she took a sip, then
reached out and trailed the tips of his fingers along the
fragile line of her collarbone. "There are still several
habits you've kept that please me very much. But that's
something we'll discuss later. Right now, we need to get
you back to your old self. I imagine you skipped
breakfast this morning, didn't you?"

"Afraid so." She nodded, smiling. She took another sip of the brandy, amazed at how warm her insides were beginning to feel.

"That means the brandy will take effect rather quickly."

He walked over to the bed and turned back the spread and sheet. In spite of the unhappiness brought about by Elizabeth's rejection, Danielle had a silly grin on her face as she watched him gesture grandly, then murmur, "Your bed, madam."

There was something decidedly decadent about being tucked into bed in the middle of the day by a rugged hunk of a man with a hair-covered chest as wide as a mountain, Danielle decided as she downed the last of the brandy, then handed Zack the snifter. She dropped back against the bank of pillows and regarded him through a pleasant fog.

"You are an incredibly sexy man, Mr. Carlsley."

"Why, thank you, Ms Kendricks," Zack replied, smiling at the drowsy picture she made. He walked over to the windows and drew the narrow-striped beige-and-gold draperies, casting the room into cozy dimness.

Danielle watched him through heavy lids, feeling remarkably safe and complete when she saw him sit on the edge of the bed, then felt the warmth of him through the covers as he stretched out beside her.

Zack turned on his side, his arm pulling her close to him, his gaze never leaving her face.

Her eyes were closed, her breathing deep and regular. Zack knew she was drifting off to sleep. Good. When she'd rushed from the restaurant straight into his arms, she'd been so strung out he was afraid he wouldn't be able to calm her down.

But now she was safe, he thought grimly. Safe in his care, sleeping soundly in his arms.

CHAPTER THIRTEEN

DANIELLE AWOKE TO THE MOST heavenly feeling imaginable.

Was she snuggled against a head-to-toe heating pad?

It had to be that, she thought drowsily, because nothing else could possibly feel as good. The entire length of her backside was warm and toasty.

Ah, but wait; another nebulous thought entered her sleep-fogged brain. Her heating pad—undoubtedly the most sophisticated model on the market—was equipped with hands. Hands that were touching her in quite delightful and intimate places.

It didn't take but a moment or two for her to become fully awake in the face of such pleasure. She opened her eyes and found herself staring straight into Zack's dark, smiling ones.

"You give new meaning to the words room service, Mr. Carlsley," she murmured, then raised her arms high over her head and enjoyed a bone-cracking stretch.

"Only for very special guests, Ms Kendricks," he murmured huskily. He was leaning on one elbow beside her, while his free hand continued to torment her body beneath the covers.

She felt his thumb and forefinger capture a nipple and gently squeeze the tight tip. Ripples of desire spread out over her, kindling embers of passion into glowing flames of need.

Suddenly Zack's hand swept over the concave smoothness of her stomach to the juncture of her thighs and the golden triangle that created a protective haven for that most tender part of her, that womanly softness that could take the swollen hardness of him into her being and hold him till his passion was spent.

When his finger touched that tiny, special bud, Danielle felt her body arch upward, wanting his teasing touch to continue. Yet she was torn between what was feeling so good at the moment and what was still to come. Back and forth, up and down...the pleasure went on, till her body followed his hands, greedy for his touch.

She felt hot to his probing fingers—Zack smiled to himself—moist and ready for him.

"Do you have any idea how long I've been watching you sleep?" he murmured as his tongue sipped and tasted its way up and down her body. He even stopped to nibble on her toes.

"Have...no...ooh! Idea!"

"What kind of an answer is that?" He chuckled, his tongue curling around the tiny, sensitive indentation that was her navel. When her body jerked, he laughed again, his hands clamping her hips and holding her against the mattress while he continued to tantalize her with his touch.

"The only kind I can give you," Danielle murmured, her voice thick with emotion.

"I'll take what I can get. When it comes to you, honey, pride doesn't seem to matter," he confessed.

Danielle grasped his head with both hands and drew him up to her, their mouths merging, their tongues indulging in a prelude to the ultimate coming together of a man and a woman that was as old as time itself.

When Zack eased between her thighs and as she felt the hardness of his arousal touch her then enter her, Danielle felt a knife-edged rush of pleasure overcome her in short, convulsive spasms. She heard a low murmur of triumph burst from Zack, and smiled.

Making love with Zack had always been incredible, Danielle thought—as much as she could think with her body floating between one climactic release after another. But this time seemed extra-special.

Their bodies fell into a rhythm dominated by their individual needs; one moment frantic, as if exorcising demons, while the next found their movements slow. In turn, each withheld pleasure till the other took control and demanded satisfaction. Their roles switched back and forth—back and forth. One leading, the other following—one following, the other leading. On and on they went, till the roles became so intertwined, so inseparable they became one.

They soothed each other with kisses, with whispered endearments, with rough and gentle caresses. They continued the journey, holding each other in their arms and riding the crest of that final outpouring of their passion as it spiraled into an ever-tightening circle that finally exploded in their heads and in their hearts and in their sweat-sleek bodies.

"I should have been with you," Zack told Danielle. With their passion temporarily sated, they were sitting in bed, eating the meal Zack had ordered from a local restaurant.

He pierced a pink, plump shrimp with his fork, then offered it to Danielle, who was sitting beside him, wearing one of his pajama tops. Zack had on the bottoms—only because he'd answered the door when their food arrived.

She took the tempting morsel into her mouth. "Mmm," she murmured, briefly closing her eyes in appreciation. "Delicious. And no," she said, "you should not have been with me. I needed that time alone with Elizabeth. She probably would have panicked if you'd shown up."

"Would you mind telling me exactly what she said to you?"

At first Danielle was reluctant to do so. It had been a very painful experience for her, one she knew she would never forget.

"Talk it out, Dani," Zack told her. "I know you too well, honey. You'll let it eat away at you till it consumes you." He looked down at her, smiling, but serious as well. "I'm not about to let that happen, you know."

"You do realize we've slowly fallen into a very definite pattern, don't you?" she asked.

Zack frowned as he tried to follow her thinking. "How?"

"Little by little you've insinuated yourself into my life. You and Harvey Graham have helped with my in-laws and the potential custody suit. You've helped with Elizabeth—first, by suggesting that I let Harvey find her, then by being there for me today when I was falling apart." She reached out and placed her fingers against his lips when she saw that he was about to speak. "I'm not through. There are a number of other little ways you've helped. But today you literally picked me up and put me back together again."

"Are you complaining?" he asked, his lips moving against her flesh. He almost wiped all thought from her mind then by taking the tips of her fingers into his mouth, sheathing them with his tongue and sucking on them.

"N-no," she stammered, jerking her hand away from him before she became a blathering idiot. "But neither do I want you to think it's necessary for you to always be around to pick me up when I fall, Zack. I'm different from the Danielle you were once married to."

"And how," he agreed. "You're one hell of a woman, honey. But even the strongest person occasionally needs help from someone. You've had some rather unusual things happen to you in the last year. Some really rotten things, if you ask me."

"But that still doesn't mean you have to devote all of your waking hours to playing nursemaid to me." She was beginning to see glimpses of that old jealous Zack, and it bothered her.

That remark brought a frown from Zack, his mouth bracketed with displeasure. "All right, already. I'll present you with a damned gold plaque stating how independent you are. Will that please you?" he snapped. He jabbed at another shrimp and popped it into his mouth.

Danielle couldn't help but laugh at the picture of outrage he presented. He was so transparent. He cared for her, and his actions were simply an extension of that caring. "A plaque will do nicely, thank you," she said pertly.

Zack glared at her for a moment from beneath dark brows. "Tell me about Elizabeth."

Danielle did, leaving nothing out. When she finished, silence hung between them.

"Coming to new Orleans as often as you do, you're aware, aren't you, that you could run into her in the future?" Zack finally asked.

"Yes." Danielle nodded.

"Will it bother you?"

"I don't think so. Right now, I'm hurting, naturally. I've suffered the biggest rejection of my life. My natural mother told me she doesn't care to have me in her life. But...in time the hurt will pass, and I'll cope with Elizabeth's rejection the same way I'm learning to cope with Theo's death."

Zack caught her hand and squeezed it. "I know what you were hoping Harvey would tell you about the crash. I was hoping just as hard as you were that the authorities had found some mechanical malfunction. If I could take those two heartaches away for you, I would. You do know that, don't you?"

"Of course. But you can't. I have to deal with those things in my own fashion. And I will." A mischievous grin played at the edges of her lips. "Add that to your plaque, Zachary."

Without saying a word, and with an economy of movement, Zack removed all dishes from the bed. Before Danielle knew what he was about, she found herself on her back with Zack sprawled on top of her, his elbows supporting the weight of his upper body, his dark gaze studying her.

"I wish I could see into the future."

"But you can't," she murmured, "and neither can I."

"We're both still leery of commitment, aren't we?"

"Yes," she answered honestly.

Zack was quiet for a minute, then he laughed. "I think I'll also add that you're a sexy broad, that you have lovely breasts, that you—"

Danielle slapped a hand over his mouth, her eyes dancing with laughter. "I've changed my mind," she said, knowing he was just as apt as not to do the crazy thing he was teasing her about. "No plaque."

"I'm crushed." He grinned down at her. "I was thinking up all sorts of things I could compliment you on."

"I just bet you were."

He shifted position so that he had a free hand to unbutton the pajama top. The edges of the material fell back, revealing rose-crested nipples that puckered tightly, tempting Zack as he stared at them. "Incredible," he mused. "A touch, a look...we do that to each other, don't we?"

"Oh, yes." And he was doing that to her then, Danielle admitted, closing her eyes, giving over to his hands and the flames he was awakening.

Zack touched her face, his thumbs lightly brushing her bottom lip. "Open your eyes and look at me." When she did, he said, "Today, when you were so upset, you wanted me to make love to you. I couldn't do that...to you or to me. Any time we make love, it's special. It always will be. And don't ever again doubt that you're loved. You are. By Trish, by Chalie, by Birdie. Isn't that enough?"

There were tears in Danielle's eyes. Somehow she'd wanted to hear him say she was loved by him as well, but he hadn't...he hadn't. "It's enough," she whispered. "It's enough." She raised her head till her mouth touched his, then willingly gave control to him, knowing full well the kiss was just the beginning. Their bodies were still hungry, and they were both more than willing to assuage that need.

THE DAYS FOLLOWING her last visit to New Orleans saw Danielle going through some very difficult times as she tried to accept Elizabeth's decision. Zack did his best to help her by keeping her and Trish busy.

One sunny afternoon, the three of them went to New Orleans to the zoo. At one point during their outing they were watching the monkeys play, and Zack was holding Trish in his arms so she could see better.

"Is that big one the daddy?" she piped up as they watched the antics of three monkeys, two large ones and a baby.

"I imagine so," Zack said, nodding. "The other one is probably the mother and the little one the baby."

"Like me and Mommy and Daddy used to be," Trish told him.

"That's right, princess," Zack agreed. "Like you and your mommy and daddy."

"But now I don't have a daddy," Trish said sadly. She put her little hands against Zack's face and looked at him. "I told Mommy that I wanted you for my daddy. I even told God."

"Look, Trish honey," Danielle spoke up, hoping to distract the child from her favorite subject of late. "Look at the pretty yellow bird over there on the fence." With Trish's attention momentarily diverted, Danielle glanced at Zack. "I'm sorry," she murmured.

Zack shook his dark head, then found her hand and squeezed it reassuringly. "Don't let it bother you," he said quietly, then wondered why he wasn't taking his own advice.

He remembered Danielle saying how she felt pressured by Trish, because the child seemed so unhappy without a father. Zack also had to wonder—in the event he and Danielle ever got together again—whether or not he could be a good father to a child Trish's age. Had he been a bachelor too long? Was he too set in his ways?

After that particular trip, Danielle detected a subtle change in Zack. He seemed more preoccupied...quieter when they were together. And though he'd always dropped in at Oaklaine at random, he now began phoning to see if it was convenient. Something else Danielle noticed was the way she sometimes caught him watching Trish. It was as if he was struggling with something.

But Danielle, still hurt by Elizabeth's rejection, didn't dwell too much on Zack's peculiar behavior. She spent countless hours going back over and over each of her conversations with Elizabeth, wondering whether, if she'd handled the situation differently, they might have had a future.

The final outcome certainly wasn't what she'd pictured when she found the diary, she told herself repeatedly as she went about the normal course of her day-to-day life, but—it hadn't been her decision alone to make.

"So try to put it out of your mind," she lectured herself aloud one morning as she returned from a shopping trip. Halloween was only a week away, and Trish was asking for a witch's costume. Danielle had debated trying to make one, but after considering the idea briefly while sewing on a button, she'd gladly joined the crowd of mothers paying enormous prices for goblins, witches and every other conceivable costume.

As she walked across the kitchen and got down a mug and took out the instant coffee, she heard the sound of a car door being closed. By the time she'd measured the coffee and water, then placed the mug in the microwave, the doorbell was ringing.

Danielle was humming under her breath as she walked through the dining room, casting a pleased look at the fresh paint and paper that provided a much softer background for the antique table and chairs and the other pieces in the dining room. When she stepped into the entrance hall, she could see the figure of a man through the narrow leaded panels of glass that graced both sides of the front entrance.

Who could it be?

She opened the door, still not recognizing the man, but not having the slightest difficulty figuring out the uniform. And if that wasn't enough, she thought grimly, the lights on top of the car parked at her gate, the official lettering on the side and the badge he was wearing, let her know that her guest was a deputy sheriff.

The man removed his khaki-colored visored cap and nodded. "Ma'am. I'm looking for a Mrs. Danielle Kendricks."

"I'm Danielle Kendricks. What can I do for you?"

"I believe this is for you, Mrs. Kendricks," he told her, then handed her a folded legal document. "This is a copy of the bill of complaint. You have thirty days within which to answer." He stepped back and murmured, "Thank you, Mrs. Kendricks," then turned and walked to his car.

Even before unfolding the legal-size sheet of paper, Danielle knew its contents. When she saw the actual wording, however, she felt a moment of panic.

Without thinking, she hurried to the telephone and dialed Zack's office in New Orleans. The moment she heard his voice, a sense of relief settled over her.

"What's wrong?" he demanded as soon as he heard her speak. "You sound odd."

"Thanks," she remarked, trying not to let on how upset she was. "I just received a summons," she told him.

"Lenore and Simon?"

"Just as they threatened."

"Now listen to me, Danielle. Don't let that bother you for a single minute. Understand?"

Danielle smiled then. She couldn't help it. That was Zack. If he said smile, then the whole damned world had better hop to it. "Aye, aye, sir," she replied.

There was a pause, then the sound of a rough sigh. "Okay, I get the message. So I come on a little heavy once in a while. The point I'm trying to make is, Harvey will deal with the Kendrickses, honey. You don't have to do a thing. If they call, refer them to Harvey. Okay?"

"Okay. I suppose I panicked when I saw this thing," she told him, staring at the paper she was holding. "It's not really that much of a shock once I stop and think about it, but I'd been concentrating so much on Elizabeth, I'd kind of put the custody suit out of my mind. Which just goes to show that one should never underestimate a woman like Lenore."

"You think she's the one who's pushing it, hmm?"

"Oh, yes. She worshipped Theo. In her heart she's convinced I was the cause of his downfall."

"How do you think she'll react to the evidence Harvey has collected?"

"That," Danielle said thoughtfully, "will be interesting. I'm sure she has no idea we know anything about Theo's problems."

"But," Zack continued, "now that we do know, and when old Harv threatens to bring all that out in his defense of you, then I'd bet my last dollar Lenore will back down."

"I hope so. At any rate, I'll call Harvey and get this to him first thing in the morning."

"Go ahead and call him, if you want to, but don't worry about getting those papers to him," Zack said. "I'm meeting a man at Rosewynn later this afternoon about buying a bull. I'll be busy here in New Orleans again tomorrow, so I can see that Harvey gets the summons in the morning."

"You're going back to the office in the morning?" she asked curiously.

"Afraid so, honey. I have a seven-thirty appointment with a party from Mexico City."

"Oh?"

"There are still a number of buildings standing that were heavily damaged in the earthquake. At first it was thought they could be salvaged, but further study has vetoed that idea. Now the ones that need to come down pose a hazard to the homeless who insist on sleeping in them. As soon as we can get together on a price and contract, I'll be leaving for Mexico."

"Several buildings. If you take the job, that means you'll be gone for quite a while, doesn't it?" She didn't want to think of the days ahead without Zack. Though she knew he would be back when the job was completed, even that was too long.

"Is that a note of wistfulness I'm hearing in your voice?" he asked huskily.

"Yes."

"Which means?"

"I'll miss you. I've gotten used to you telling me what to do," she said pertly, trying to inject a light note into the conversation.

"I've gotten used to certain things, too," Zack answered. "Let's be sure and continue this conversation at dinner this evening. I have to go now, honey, I have a long-distance call on another line."

"I'm sorry," Danielle said briskly, just a tad put out that there were other things taking up his time and attention. Which was perfectly ridiculous, she told herself. Zack was a businessman. Why should she expect him to devote all his time to her? She shouldn't have bothered him at the office in the first place.

"We'll discuss your being sorry this evening, along with how much you'll miss me, honey. Take care."

Danielle replaced the receiver, her mind more at ease where the summons was concerned, but—as usual—up in the air over where her relationship with Zack was headed.

Common sense told her a showdown was inevitable. And in one way she welcomed it. Their previous track record where relationships were concerned—especially hers—left her troubled.

Hadn't she had similar feelings once before with Zack? And hadn't those feelings resulted in disaster?

CHAPTER FOURTEEN

"YOU'VE BEEN AWFULLY QUIET this evening," Zack remarked. They'd eaten and were just returning to Oaklaine. "Are you worried about the custody suit?"

"Not really," Danielle said as they approached the back entrance. She handed him the key. "I really do think Harvey has the right idea. There's no way Lenore will allow Theo's name to be bandied about."

Zack opened the door, then stepped aside for her to enter, just as Rosie Warren, the housekeeper at Rosewynn, came into the kitchen from the hallway.

"Is Trish asleep?" Danielle asked the short, portly woman.

"Like a lamb," Rosie told her. "I don't think she's moved a muscle since I put her to bed. She's a doll to look after."

"What did you do, Rosie, tie the poor kid in her bed?" Zack asked innocently.

The housekeeper puffed up like a small gray hen. "You know I wouldn't do anything like that."

"Of course you wouldn't, Rosie," Danielle said, patting the older woman's shoulder and looking at Zack sternly. "Ignore him. He's been in a teasing mood all evening."

"He does like his teasing," Rosie murmured, though there was little condemnation in her words. Zack was her favorite, and in her eyes he could do no wrong. She shrugged into the sweater she was carrying on her arm. "I'll be getting along now. Call me anytime you need a sitter, Danielle."

"I sure will. But wait, Zack will run you home."

"Nonsense," Rosie said, waving away the offer. "I'll be to Rosewynn before we can get out to the car. See you later," she called over her shoulder and then was gone.

Danielle turned to Zack, who was standing just behind her. "How about a cup of coffee? Bourbon and water? Scotch?" He was so close she could see the tiny flecks in his eyes.

Zack slipped his arms around her and drew her to him, clasping his hands behind her back, bringing their bodies together close, intimately. "I'd rather get into some heavy necking with a certain pretty blonde I know."

"Is that right?" Danielle asked, grinning up at him. "I've heard about you, buster. Heavy necking with you always seems to lead to something else."

"Mmm." He smirked comically. "I'm really good too, huh?"

Danielle just looked at him, amusement lurking in her blue eyes. The conceited, lovable jerk. "Pretty good, yes."

"And you love me. Right?"

"And I lo..." she halted abruptly. Danielle had admitted that she cared for him days ago. But to come right out and say she loved him? She did love him, but was she ready to share that truth with him?

"Say it."

"Why?"

"Because it's important to me. Do you love me?"

"Yes."

"Then say it. Say you love me." The teasing tone was gone from Zack's voice, and in its stead was a graveness that tore at her heart. It was hard to believe that a man as big as a mountain could be even the slightest bit insecure, but he was, and Danielle was touched by the vulnerability she saw in his features.

"I love you, Zack Carlsley."

He continued to stare down at her. And suddenly he knew. The realization washed over him like a brilliant ray of sunshine after the cleansing powers of a spring rain.

He was no longer afraid to trust her.

He loved her.

He loved Danielle. She loved him. He wanted to spend the rest of his life with her. "In a few days I'll be leaving for Mexico City. I want you to come with me."

To anyone else the invitation would have been exactly what it sounded like—a wonderful chance to spend some time in Mexico City. But Danielle knew there was more behind the invitation than just a few days of her company. Zack was asking for a commitment.

"Do I have to give you my answer tonight?"

"No," he said, gruffly, reaching out and brushing back a strand of hair from her forehead. "I don't want you to feel pressured in any way. Not by me, not by Trish or the fact that our families have been friends since Noah built the ark. Take all the time you need...make your decision. I'll even keep my distance—sort of."

"You're being very generous," Danielle said, teasingly.

"There's a lot at stake."

"I know," she murmured, becoming as serious as he was. "It's frightening. What if it's another mistake?"

"Our being together is no mistake. Us loving each other is no mistake. Me loving Trish is no mistake. Let fate work *for* us for a change, honey."

"You make it sound so easy."

Zack chuckled. "It's not easy...ever. Listen, I've fought this particular minute harder than anything I've ever come up against in my life. But I've finally decided it's something we both might as well accept. We married, divorced and went our separate ways. You remarried and you were miserable. I stayed single and I was miserable. Only when we're together do we feel complete. Need I say more?"

"I'd say you've covered it pretty well," Danielle told him. She stood on tiptoe then and kissed him, tracing the fullness of his bottom lip before allowing her tongue to become intertwined with his in an erotic ritual that sent libidos soaring and accelerated heartbeats.

With a superhuman effort, Zack stepped back. He continued to hold her—though at arm's length—his head turned slightly to one side, his gaze narrowed against the desire running rampant throughout his body.

"I'm not sure why I'm doing this," he told her, frowning. "But for some damned crazy reason something tells me that I shouldn't crowd you...that you need space. Does that sound absolutely corny as hell to you?"

Danielle laughed, a special lightheartedness taking hold of her. She couldn't explain it, especially in light of the summons regarding the custody hearing she'd received earlier in the afternoon, but it was there nevertheless, and she wasn't about to start asking why.

"Corny, no. Extremely thoughtful, yes."

"Will being extremely thoughtful keep me from having to take a cold shower when I get home?" Zack asked in a thoroughly aggrieved tone. He began walking toward the door, pulling Danielle along with him.

"Poor baby," she murmured, patting his arm sympathetically.

At the door Zack turned. He framed her face with his hands and kissed her hard and deep. "I'm a masochist," he muttered. "That's the only reason I can think of for me to be going home this early."

Danielle laughed and pushed him out the door. "Stop complaining. Go home before both of us forget our good intentions."

She closed the door on his dark mutterings, laughing as she turned off the lights, then went to check on Trish.

As she stood by the bed and watched her daughter sleep, Danielle couldn't help but think of the future.

Was she going to say yes? Would that future include Zack?

He'd make a terrific father for Trish, she quietly mused. And he'd make a terrific husband for her.

Those two very impressive facts went on the positive side of the ledger. The negative ones were pushed aside for the moment as she smothered a yawn and turned toward her room and her bed. There would be plenty of time to try and sort out the ghosties trying to take away her chance for happiness. Yes, indeed...there would be plenty of time.

WHILE DANIELLE WAS DREAMING of being in Zack's arms, Chalie was awakened by a telephone call from the hospital, telling her that Dane Ewing had been in a serious accident and was asking for her.

The first thing Chalie did after the call was to rush to Zack's room. In minutes they were in the car and on their way.

"I know it's pointless to tell you this, but try not to worry," Zack told her. He reached over with his free hand and patted his sister's shoulder. "If he's asking for you, then he's not in too bad shape."

Chalie only nodded. Her throat was frozen closed with fear. If Dane died, she wanted to die also.

Upon reaching the hospital, they went straight to emergency.

"Chalie!" A nurse rushed toward her, a harried expression on her face. "Thank heavens you're here. Dane is being impossible. Follow me. Hello, Zack."

"Sandra," Zack murmured, keeping a steady arm around Chalie. "How is Dane?"

"We know he has a broken leg, we think there are some broken ribs, and he's suffered multiple cuts and bruises." Sandra Thomas was a couple of years older than Chalie, and she was an acquaintance of the Carlsleys and Dane. "So far, he's refused all medication because he's afraid we'll give him something to knock him out, and he wants to see you first. He's right in here," the nurse told them.

Going into the emergency room Chalie took one look at Dane and was positive she was going to faint!

Parts of Dane's face reminded her of a piece of meat that had been pounded. One of his eyes was swollen shut, and his nose had a decided curve to it that hadn't been there before. He looked absolutely dreadful.

She swayed, and Zack's arm at her waist tightened.

"Hang in there, Chalie. Besides," he told her, smiling down at her, "if you faint no one will have time to take care of you. This place is a madhouse."

"Oh, Zack," she cried. "He looks awful."

"Chalie?" Though Dane's speech was slightly slurred, it was strong enough. "Chalie? Is that you?"

"I'm here, Dane," she replied, breaking away from Zack, who left them alone. She hurried to the side of the gurney and reached for his hand. It was resting on the sheet and she took it up, holding it between both of hers, her heart breaking as she saw the pain he was in. His poor face was contorted and he was biting his bottom lip so hard, she was afraid it was going to bleed. "Oh, my darling," she said softly, tears blurring her vision as she stared down at the bruised and battered features. "I'm so sorry this had to happen to you. So sorry."

"I want you to know that I love you," Dane told her, determinedly holding her gaze.

"I love you too, Dane. Please promise me you'll get well. I don't think I could live if something happened to you."

"Do you mean that?" he murmured so low she could barely hear him.

"Oh, yes, I mean it. All I want is you."

"What about children? Is that still a problem for you?"

"Whatever you say," she whispered, wiping away the tears with the back of her hand. "We'll adopt, we'll do without ... I don't care, just as long as we're together. When I heard you were hurt, I realized just how stupid I've been. What I want most is you."

"Are you by any chance proposing to me?" he said teasingly, trying to smile but not quite able to manage it.

"I most certainly am. Are you going to accept?"

"Of course."

"Good. Now please let them take care of you," Chalie said gently, smoothing the hair from his forehead. The top of his head looked to be about the only spot on him that wasn't bruised or bleeding or broken. "Will you do that for me? I'll be right here when you get back. I promise."

Dane nodded, his good eye fluttering for a moment, then closing. Chalie looked questioningly at the nurse who had appeared, instead of Sandra. She waited while the woman checked Dane's vital signs.

"He's all right. Why don't you go down to the waiting room now? Or," she amended, "you might even want to go back home. He's going to be in surgery for quite a while."

"No, I'll stay here till he's out of surgery," Chalie said, choosing her words carefully, her tone of voice decisive. Dane needed her . . . he wanted her, and nothing on God's green earth was going to move her from the hospital until she knew he was all right. She walked out into the corridor, and straight to the bank of phones she saw a few feet away.

"Hello?" Danielle muttered sleepily.

"Dani?"

"Chalie? What's wrong?" she asked, coming to full wakefulness with a jolt. It sounded as if Chalie was crying, and Danielle immediately thought of Zack. "What's wrong?" she repeated. "Is it Zack?"

"Zack's fine. It's Dane. He's been in a terrible wreck. I'm at the hospital."

"Oh, Chalie! Give me time to make arrangements for Trish, and I'll be there."

"No," Chalie said hurriedly. "Don't do that. I appreciate the offer, but there's not a single thing you can do. I'll need you more tomorrow and during the days ahead. Zack's here with me now." There was a moment or two of low-voiced conversation, then Chalie continued. "He said for you to stay put."

"Are you sure?" Danielle asked worriedly.

"Positive."

"Please, tell me about Dane."

"He looks terrible, but part of that's due to the blood. They're cleaning him up right now and trying to find exactly what is and isn't broken. Poor baby, he's such a mess."

"Is he conscious?"

"Conscious but very much in pain. In fact, it looked to me as if he's floating in and out of consciousness. At any rate, he refused to let them touch him till I arrived."

"Well, at least you two are talking now," Danielle said gently.

"Yes, we are, we even—I'm sorry, Dani, I've got to go. The nurse wants to see me."

Before Danielle could say a word, the line went dead. She replaced the receiver, then dropped back against the pillow, her thoughts with Dane and Chalie. Considerable time passed before she finally went back to sleep.

Early the next morning, Danielle was awakened again. This time, however, it was because of a steady tapping against the window beside her bed. As she rose to a sitting position, she peered at the clock and saw that it was only five-thirty.

"What the devil?" she murmured, frowning when she heard the noise again. There was no mistaking it.

With anger replacing her better judgment, she grasped the heavy curtains and jerked them back to reveal the head and shoulders of Zack, who had one hand braced on either side of the window.

She quickly raised the window, her anger evaporating as thoughts of Dane came to mind. "How's Dane?"

"Resting."

"Chalie?"

"At Rosewynn . . . sleeping for an hour or two."

Relief flooded her. "You really know how to wake up a gal," Danielle said and smiled at him. She leaned her elbows on the window ledge, her chin resting on her palms. Now that she knew Dane and Chalie were okay, she could enjoy the anticipation of being in Zack's arms.

Zack, on the other hand, was taking air into his lungs with deep, burning breaths, his eyes narrowing in on creamy breasts partially visible above the low, lacy cut of a beige nightgown. Rosy nipples, swollen and tight, teased him through the sheer material. His eyes moved upward, past smooth shoulders and the graceful curve of neck to meet sparkling blue eyes.

"Does this damned screen open?"

"'Fraid not, Carlsley," Danielle told him, then giggled at the thunderous expression on his face. "This is the only goof-up Mr. Smith made. When he was repairing the screens, he bought the wrong kind of latches. He had to nail them in. If throwing a leg over ladies' window ledges is your game, then come back in about week. My new latches should be in by then. And I promise you, I'll definitely let you in."

"I suppose it's just as well." Zack sighed.

"Thanks."

He grinned at her frowning face. "Anyway, this visit has nothing to do with lovemaking, honey. I just wanted to give you an update on Dane. I was afraid that if I called or banged on the door, I'd wake up Trish.

282   SECOND TIME LUCKY

Besides, I had the strangest urge to see you just as you
are right now.''

The words were like smooth silk caressing her body,
but thoughts of Dane took precedence. She wondered
what Chalie must be going through. "Exactly how se-
vere were his injuries?"

"He had a broken leg, multiple cuts and bruises and
some cracked ribs. One rib nicked his left lung, and
fortunately it didn't penetrate. Funniest damned
thing...he roused up just after he was brought to the
hospital and started raising hell for Chalie. They
couldn't do anything with him till she got there."

"Good for him. How is Chalie?"

"That's another story," Zack said, his voice grim.
"She's a basket case. I've been with her all night. She's
posed just about every hypothetical reason for the accident one can imagine. Actually, she's pathetic. Ironic
as it may seem, I don't think she cares at this point if
they ever have a child...adopted or otherwise."

"Did she say that?"

Zack nodded, a soft smile pulling at his sensuous lips.
"About a hundred times."

"I'll go to her just as soon as I can," Danielle told
him. "But what about you? Are you still going to your
office or to bed?"

"I'm afraid I'll have to go to New Orleans. I do need
to get that summons from you, though. I'll have it delivered to Harvey first thing. Besides Dane and Chalie
and any other reason for this meeting you might come
up with, I do want to kiss you."

"In that case," Danielle said pertly, "meet me at the
back door."

She closed the window, grabbed the summons from
the dresser, then hurried across the bedroom, down the

hall and through the kitchen. She was unlocking the dead bolt and both chains when she heard Zack's heavy step on the porch. Danielle hesitated for just a second to make sure he was in place, then threw open the door and took two steps straight into his arms.

Zack caught her high against his chest, high enough that her face was level with his. Danielle gently cradled his head with her hands, her fingers lovingly buried in his thick, dark hair. Their mouths came together, their bodies blending and shaping into one single unit.

Danielle forgot everything, save the sensations swamping her. She was in Zack's arms and nothing else mattered.

Zack felt his body surging with desire, felt the tightening core of his arousal throbbing against the smooth stomach pressing against him. He tore his mouth away from hers, and buried his neck in the creamy skin of her neck, groaning with the pain stabbing at his loins.

Danielle nuzzled her face against his hair, taking in the scent of him, glorying in the pure male feel of him. She wanted him, needed him inside her and all around her.

Zack lifted his head, his passion-dulled gaze meeting her tortured one. "I want an answer soon," he said hoarsely.

"You'll get it."

For the second time in less than twenty-four hours, Zack set her on her feet, his hands becoming locked into tight fists. There was a harshness to his features and his lips were rigid with control.

"When you get ready, why don't you take Trish over to stay with Rosie, then do what you can for Chalie. She's taking a shower and is supposed to sleep for a couple of hours. Don't forget about her."

Danielle swallowed against the thickness of her throat and nodded. She leaned against the door frame, needing the support for her trembling body. "I—I won't."

"Bye," he whispered. He touched her then, his fingers lightly stroking the lips he'd just kissed—lips that were soft and sweet and still moist from his kiss. "I love you." The words were spoken as he turned and closed the door.

"I love you, Zack," Danielle whispered, watching through the window as he got in his car and drove away.

Did she really need any more time? Was there any point in worrying and wondering if she was doing the right thing? Weren't there some things in life that had to be chanced? Wasn't it possible that her future with Zack fell into that category?

She thought so. Danielle nodded to herself as she pushed away from the wall and wandered into the kitchen. With slow, precise movements, she fixed herself a cup of coffee, then carried it to her bedroom, where she began to dress.

A short while later, as she was making up her bed, it occurred to her that, in spite of the Kendrickses and Elizabeth, her life was beginning to take shape—and that, in a large part, Zack was responsible.

Would the accident bring Dane and Chalie together as well?

Zack hadn't been exaggerating when he'd said his sister was beside herself. Chalie was an absolute bundle of nerves, Danielle thought as she listened to her friend. They were in the cafeteria at the hospital and Chalie was talking nonstop.

"He looks so bad. Don't you think he looks terrible?" she asked Danielle.

"Sure he does, but he was in a very serious accident, honey. The doctors say he'll be fine, though."

"I know," Chalie said quickly—too quickly. "I know. Oh, Lord! If anything happens to him, Dani, I don't think I can bear it."

"Chalie," Danielle said firmly. "Nothing is going to happen to Dane. You've got to get hold of yourself."

"I know," she agreed though she looked doubtful.

"You're sitting there, working yourself into one huge panic," Danielle told her. "Dane is fine, and the doctors say his prognosis is super. Believe them."

"What you're too kind to say is that I'm acting like an idiot, isn't it?"

"Yes," Danielle said. "Frankly, you are. I understand, but enough is enough. Dane isn't going to die and you're going to relax, because I'm tired of seeing you cry. Be happy. The man you love is going to get well."

A ghost of a smile flickered across Chalie's face. "Why is it that you always manage to calm me down when nobody else can?"

"Because I tell you the truth about yourself." Danielle grinned. "Just as you've done for me in the past. Why don't you tell me how the accident happened?"

That topic of conversation occupied the conversation until the two women returned to Dane's room. After checking on him and being assured by a nurse that he was going to continue sleeping for quite a while, they walked two doors down to a small waiting room.

During the day, several potted plants were delivered to his room, and several friends dropped by, most of them in the legal profession. Dane didn't have any close family, which worried Chalie.

"I don't care what he says, when he's ready to be discharged, I'm taking him to Rosewynn." She looked sheepish. "I guess you can tell that we're together again."

"I kind of got that idea," Danielle told her. "What about children? Did you come to some sort of agreement?"

Chalie got up and walked over to stare out the window at the wooded area behind the hospital. "Last night I told Dane we'd adopt or do without. I didn't care which. You'd be surprised how your own problems helped me see the mistakes I'd been making."

"Such as?" Danielle asked curiously.

"I've seen Zack with Trish," Chalie said, turning and facing Danielle. "They adore each other. One day when she was at Rosewynn, I spent a great deal of time watching them, and it occurred to me that Dane would be the same way with a child, any child, and I was denying him that privilege by refusing to budge from what I *thought* was best for us both. And then, when you had such a terrible experience with Elizabeth, well . . ." She shook her head. "Being a biological mother doesn't necessarily mean there's love between a mother and child, does it?"

"No, it certainly doesn't. I'm happy for you."

"Last night when he made the hospital call me . . . all those decisions just snapped into place. I knew then that he still loved me, Dani. Later he told me so, just before they took him to surgery. And just in case he's forgotten what we talked about, when he's fully himself, I'm going to remind him that I proposed and he accepted."

"You did?" Danielle asked, surprised.

"Yes," Chalie said firmly. "I made such a horrible mistake last time, I was afraid to wait."

"I think that's fantastic. Whisper that news in Dane's ear and you might witness a record recovery."

"I'll do that."

They talked a while. longer, then Danielle left. She stopped by Rosewynn to pick up Trish and to tell Birdie how Dane was doing. Birdie was having one of her better days and had been baking cookies with Trish.

"I'm so glad," the older woman said, drawing a huge breath of relief. "Maybe this will bring Dane and Chalie closer together."

"I think it already has, Birdie," Danielle told her godmother as she leaned against the counter and munched on a cookie. Trish was over in the corner playing with the kittens. "In fact, you just might be getting the front parlor ready for a wedding between now and Christmas."

Tears of happiness gathered in Birdie's eyes. "Wouldn't that be wonderful? They've been at cross-purposes for so long. Now if only you and Zack could work something out."

"Give us time, Birdie, we may get there yet."

"Really?" Birdie looked at her sharply. "Are you serious?"

"Yes . . . really," Danielle said, chuckling at her god-mother's expression of disbelief. "I'm quite serious."

"Thank heaven," Birdie said fervently. "It's about time something started working out for you, honey." They both knew she was referring to Elizabeth, but neither pursued the subject. It was past and done with.

"This may be your best Christmas yet, Birdie," Danielle told her. Then she began gathering up Trish's things. "Tell Chalie to call me when she gets home," she reminded Birdie.

Danielle and Trish stopped at the grocery store, and it was almost seven o'clock when they got home. Danielle fixed a quick supper of soup and sandwiches, while Trish had a bath. Sitting at the hospital almost the entire day had exhausted her, and Trish didn't seem to be much better off. In fact, the child almost fell asleep at the table.

"Did you have fun today with Birdie?" Danielle asked as she watched her daughter try to stifle a face-splitting yawn.

"Yes. I played with Dolly and the kittens. I like to go to Rosewynn. But I like it better when Uncle Zack is there."

So do I, Danielle mused, *so do I.*

Later, after she was in bed, Danielle wondered just where "Uncle Zack" was. That morning, when he'd come by to tell her about Dane and to pick up the summons to take to Harvey, he'd given every indication of seeing her in the evening. Or had he?

A disappointed Danielle turned and looked at the luminous dial of the clock next to the telephone on the bedside table.

Eleven-thirty.

She drew a disappointed breath, then bunched one corner of the pillow beneath her cheek and closed her eyes. Contrary to her belief that she would toss and turn all night, she fell asleep immediately.

The next morning Danielle dropped Trish off at Chalie's kindergarten, then stopped by the hospital and checked on Dane, delighted to find him awake.

"I feel fine," he told Danielle, grinning despite the awful bruises on his face.

"That's nice to hear, because you look terrible," she said, and they both laughed.

"Have you talked with Chalie?" Dane asked.

"Oh, yes. I was here most of the day yesterday, but you were sleeping. She called me last night and again this morning. Why?"

"It looks like things are finally going to work out for us," a beaming Dane told her. "Chalie's done a complete turnaround. I don't know what's happened, and I don't care."

His enthusiasm was infectious, Danielle thought later as she left the hospital. She took care of some errands and returned to Oaklaine. As she reached into her purse for her key, the back door swung open.

A startled Danielle stepped back, then stared, disbelieving, into a face she never thought she'd see again.

"Precious Love!" Danielle exclaimed, then rushed into the outstretched arms of the gray-haired woman. "I don't believe this," Danielle kept repeating over and over as they both laughed and talked at the same time.

"Neither could I when Zack called me," said Precious Love, wiping at her eyes with one of the many lace-edged handkerchiefs in her possession.

"Zack called you?"

"He sure did."

"How long can you stay?" Danielle asked, placing her purse and the items she'd bought on the table.

"How long do you want me to stay?"

"Forever—you know that! Seriously, how long will you be here?"

There was a long pause while Precious Love looked around the kitchen, noting the freshly painted trim, the new curtains at the windows and the new floor covering. "I'm tired of traveling. I'm tired of people staring at me like I'm crazy when I tell them my name is Esmeralda Phinney." She turned to Danielle. "You know,

I lived here for twenty-one years. A person gets used to a place in that length of time."

"Are you trying to say what I think you are?" Danielle asked, hoping against hope that what she was hearing was true. Precious Love at Oaklaine was something she hadn't counted on. And it was happening because of Zack.

"Can you use a housekeeper?"

"If it's you, then I most certainly can."

"That's good," Precious Love said, chuckling, "because I've already unpacked half my things."

"Why on earth didn't you say something in your letters?" Danielle asked as she began fixing coffee for them. "Each time I heard from you, you were always off on some trip with your sister or involved in some project or other. I thought you were happy."

Soon they were sitting at the table, bringing each other up-to-date on the different things that had happened in their lives, sharing the happier moments and the heartaches. They were so engrossed in their conversation that they didn't hear Zack until he opened the door and walked inside.

"You are a regular sneaky Pete," Danielle told him a few minutes later when Precious Love had left them to finish unpacking. Danielle was standing in the circle of his arms, drowning in the love she saw in his eyes.

"I wanted it to be a surprise," Zack told her, his lips dropping light, teasing kisses on her face.

"That better be why I didn't see you last night."

"Miss me?" he asked, smiling down at her.

"Yes. Where were you?"

"Sitting on my behind at the airport. Precious Love's plane was due in at ten-thirty. It was almost an hour late." He brushed his lips against hers. "Forgive me?"

"Yes."

"Going to marry me?"

"Yes."

"Soon?"

"Of course." In her mind Danielle envisioned a Christmas wedding, with the smell of pine and cedar and cinnamon filling the air.

"Good. I do like a woman who can get things done in a hurry."

"Hurry? How much of a hurry?"

"A week," Zack said, then burst out laughing at her shocked expression. "You have six days, sweetheart. And not a minute longer."

CHAPTER FIFTEEN

"WHAT'S MY SURPRISE, Uncle Zack?" Trish asked for at least the tenth time in the past half hour. They were having dinner in her favorite restaurant, the fast-food one, and she was sitting beside Zack, while Danielle smiled at them from across the table.

"What surprise?" he asked, teasingly. "I don't know anything about a surprise." He looked innocently at Danielle. "Do you?"

Danielle shook her head, but was unable to keep from laughing at the look of disappointment on Trish's face. "Well, maybe I remember something about it," she replied.

"You really think we should tell her?"

"I think so."

"Okay then," Zack said, nodding. He looked at the squirming Trish. "I've decided I want a little girl. I want one with blond hair and blue eyes. Do you have any idea where I can find one?"

Trish's eyes were bright as she eagerly nodded her head, her ponytail bobbing up and down like a yo-yo. "Of course. I'll be your little girl. Then you can be my daddy. That's what I asked God for."

Zack was quiet for a moment, his rough-hewn features smoothing into an expression of tenderness as he watched the child. Finally he lifted her in his arms and caught her to him. "I think you're the perfect one to be my little girl, princess, and I know I'm definitely going to be your daddy. Okay?''

"Okay," Trish said brightly, her arms going around his neck and hugging him.

"Well, then," Zack said, allowing her to move out of his arms and back to her seat, "let's get to eating these hamburgers and fries."

Danielle, who had remained relatively silent during the conversation, had seen the shimmery brightness in Zack's eyes, and she had her own problem of dealing with a lump in her throat. She met his steady gaze across the table and smiled tremulously. "I love you," she mouthed.

Zack reached across and caught her hand, then raised it to his lips. Though no actual words passed between them, she knew the look in his eyes. She was certain that he was sending her a message of love, and that later he would put unspoken words into action.

Trish, too excited to be still or quiet, began asking question after question. Danielle and Zack told her about the wedding plans, and how, if she wanted to, she could be the flower girl.

Later that evening, after Trish was in bed and as Zack was leaving, Danielle thanked him for being so understanding with her daughter.

"It's easy, honey," he said huskily. His hands were molding her soft, pliant body to his with long, sure strokes that were meting out more punishment than pleasure to both of them. "When I look at Trish, I see you all over again. I love you and I love her."

"And I love you, Zack Carlsley. With all my heart. I do have one question, though."

Zack's hands linked behind her back, allowing her upper body to ease back just a bit. "Let's hear it."

"I think we understand each other, but I have to be sure. When we were married before, you tried to isolate us from our friends, and—"

"And you're wondering if I've learned to control my jealousy. Right?"

"Frankly...yes," Danielle said, relieved that he wasn't annoyed. It was a sensitive topic, and she really had no desire to hurt him. Yet she knew it was something that had to be discussed before they went further.

"Let me put it this way, honey. I doubt there'll ever be a time when I'm not jealous of you. But where I once thought I could lock you away from the world, I now realize that would be the quickest way to lose you again. I've learned to love deeply and freely again, and with that love comes trust."

"That's beautiful, Zack," Danielle said softly.

"Of course, Dani," he murmured, teasingly, bending his head and letting his lips wander in an excited path over her face. "Haven't you been listening to your daughter sing my praises? Don't you know Trish considers everything I do to be perfect?"

FOUR DAYS LATER, late on a typical fall afternoon, Elizabeth Harrison, dressed in beige and black, was moving with ease among the guests assembled in the Harrison's elegant apartment.

She was hosting a party made up of influential individuals she was hoping would support her husband's bid for a political career. Except for one no-show, the evening could certainly be deemed a success, the hostess decided.

"That Harvey Graham you asked me to invite is the only one who hasn't shown up," she told Nathan as he appeared at her side. "Though I've never met the man, he certainly seems to be lacking in manners. A simple telephone call wouldn't have hurt him.''

"He did call you," Nathan told her, his shrewd gaze scanning the group and liking what he saw. "I talked with him yesterday. I simply forgot to tell you. He was driving up to Natchez to be best man in a wedding.''

"Oh? Is someone in his family getting married?" But even before Nathan spoke again, Elizabeth had a horrible feeling she knew exactly what he was going to say.

"A friend, actually. Zack Carlsley. I've met him a time or two...really a nice man. Seems Carlsley and his wife, who were divorced from each other a few years ago, are remarrying. We'll probably be seeing something of them in the future. I'd like to get to know Carlsley better.''

"Is there any other connection between Harvey Graham and Zack Carlsley?" Elizabeth asked, almost dizzy with the fear that was sweeping over her.

"Harvey is Carlsley's attorney.''

And being in that position, Elizabeth knew in her heart that Harvey Graham was the lawyer Danielle mentioned as having helped her locate her birth mother.

THE AIR WAS BRISK. The sky was overcast. Leaves of all shades of gold and brown and yellow fell at random. It was a typical autumn afternoon that made one long for a warm fire, a good book and a broad shoulder to lean on.

Danielle, dressed in ivory lace, and holding a bouquet of pale pink rosebuds, stood staring out the window of her bedroom, her heart filled to overflowing with happiness.

It was her wedding day.

In less than an hour she would be Mrs. Zachary Carlsley. She'd worn that name once before but, God willing, she would cherish it and guard it more carefully this second time around.

"Well, I suppose that's everything," Precious Love said softly as she closed the last of the suitcases. She looked at Danielle and smiled. "You look so beautiful."

"Thank you, Precious Love. And thank you for coming back."

The housekeeper walked over to Danielle and kissed her on the cheek. "Be happy, honey," she whispered, then left the room.

Only one or two regrets were keeping her world from being perfect on this day, Danielle told herself as she turned back to the window.

One of the things on her mind was that in the years ahead, when it came time to explain about Theo's death to Trish, she hoped her daughter would judge her gently.

And in the immediate days ahead, Danielle prayed she would be able to put Elizabeth out of her mind. She knew it had been a mistake to find her natural mother. But she had, and nothing could undo what was done. Hopefully, time would heal the hurt. She didn't hate Elizabeth. She felt sorry for her. Sorry that she was so wrapped up in her own fears of losing the way of life she'd come to know that she couldn't allow Trish and Danielle even a tiny part of herself.

Yet, Danielle mused, she didn't want to judge the woman too harshly. And she certainly didn't hate Elizabeth. Hopefully, in time, she'd be able to look back on the experience and find some good that had come from it.

SECOND TIME LUCKY   297

Even the Kendrickses had cooperated on this day, though Danielle knew for certain they hadn't done so intentionally. Harvey, who was to be Zack's best man, had stopped at Oaklaine earlier in the day to tell her that the custody suit had been dropped. Danielle couldn't think of any nicer beginning for her new life.

A smile curved her lips. Knowing Precious Love would be looking after Trish while she and Zack honeymooned in Mexico added the perfect touch.

In the distance she could hear Cathleen Summers playing the piano. Soon the notes she would be hearing would be the "Wedding March." And in a few minutes there would be a knock on the door.

She would leave the bedroom, walk down the length of the hall to the wide foyer. There she would be met by Zack.

They would enter the front parlor and join Chalie and Trish and Harvey Graham, waiting with the minister and their guests before twin candelabras holding white candles, intermingled with tall white baskets of pink rosebuds and the delicate beauty of Queen Anne's lace.

They would kneel on a satin-covered prie-dieu that had been used in all Carlsley weddings for generations. Precious Love and Birdie would be quietly sobbing. There would be tears in the other women's eyes and the men would be clearing their throats.

Danielle smiled to herself. That's the way it always was at weddings. A quiet knock sounded at the door. "Danielle?" Chalie's voice called out, interrupting the gentle litany of thoughts.

The door opened and a smiling face peeped around the edge. "It's time," Chalie told her.

Danielle turned to her maid of honor, who was gorgeous in pale pink and glowing with happiness. "So it is. I'm so happy, Chalie, I feel guilty. Can you believe that?''

"Yes," Chalie answered, nodding thoughtfully. "I suppose that's not so unusual, considering the circumstances. You and Zack have been this way once before and I'm sure—knowing you as I do—that you've probably come up with all sorts of ideas or reasons why it might not work this time, haven't you?''

Danielle looked down at the bouquet she was holding. "You're right. For a while I almost drove myself crazy doing that very thing. I finally made myself stop worrying and started enjoying. But," she said, smiling, "as I said, every once in a while I feel guilty as sin. Everyone should be so happy.''

"I honestly think what you're suffering from is an affliction quite common to females," Chalie replied, laughingly. "For some weird reason we seem to enjoy punishing ourselves.''

"You know, in a few weeks we'll be doing this again for you and Dane. It's a shame he can't see you right now.''

"He will, just as soon as I see to it that you and Zack are truly hitched.''

"Afraid one of us will run out?" Danielle asked, trying to laugh, but finding her face so stiff it felt like it would break with the effort. "I'm petrified. Are you sure I look all right? Are you sure the dress is right?''

"For the tenth time, you look like a dream. The dress is perfect. Now let's get this show on the road before Zack thinks you've left him at the altar.''

They smiled and left the room, Chalie hurrying ahead. Looking for all the world like a real princess, Trish scattered rose petals happily before them as they walked down the aisle.

Minutes later Danielle joined Zack, who had watched her coming to him, the glow in his dark eyes bathing her in its warmth.

She placed her hand on his arm. He smiled down at her, reading the panic in her eyes. He winked reassuringly and murmured, "I love you, sweetheart."

Tears came to Danielle's eyes. Her throat was full.

She was happy. She was sad...a happy sad. Was that possible, she wondered fleetingly as they walked toward the diamond-crested flames of the candles that cast a golden glow over the room in the quiet twilight.

She smiled down at a beaming Trish, who was standing beside Chalie.

"Dearly beloved, we are gathered together," the minister began.

Danielle was fully aware that she got though the ceremony only because of Zack's strong support. When she stumbled, he was there to keep her from embarrassing herself by falling flat on her face. When she faltered in repeating the vows, he supplied the words. When she was so nervous she couldn't even get the ring on his finger, he smiled at her, then calmly put the ring on his own finger.

Zack helping her. He was her mainstay, her future.

His solid support during the ceremony was simply the beginning of how her life with him was going to be, Danielle thought. She cherished the notion at odd moments during the reception at Rosewynn, and as the goodbyes were made and while she and Zack drove to New Orleans.

At the apartment, supper was waiting for them. Danielle peeked under the domed covers and found each dish to be something that was a favorite of hers.

She looked at her husband and shook her head. "You're incredible."

"I disagree," he said in a husky voice that made her know the food would be enjoyed later...much later. He slowly closed the space separating them, his head inclined slightly to one side, his dark gaze narrowed against the love he held in his heart for the woman facing him.

When the tips of her breasts pressed against his chest, he stopped. His wide hands went to her waist and held her against his body. "I promise to cherish you till the day I die. Standing here with you...knowing you're my wife again is overwhelming. I keep thinking it's all a dream."

Slowly, and with infinite care, Danielle took his hands in her own small grasp. "Come with me, Zachary," she told him, looking up at him as she began walking toward the master bedroom. "We're going to make those dreams a reality. Believe me, when I'm through with you, you'll never wonder again."

Zack stopped her at the door of the bedroom, then reached down and swept her up into his arms. "Are you as happy as I am?" There were tears in his eyes, tears that bespoke the pain he'd suffered and overcome when she'd left him, of the happiness that had been given back to him, and of the future he was walking into with his heart whole again.

Danielle leaned forward and gently licked the wetness from the corners of his eyes, loving him for his gentleness as well as his strength. "More than you'll ever know. I want to be your lover, your wife and your best friend. With you and Trish, my life is complete."

"Always?"

"Always, my darling, Zack. Always."

♦ *Harlequin Superromance*

COMING NEXT MONTH

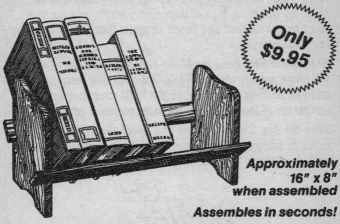